INTENTIONAL

INTENTIONAL

A SEAN WYNN THRILLER

KEITH J. WEBER

ISBN (ebook): 979-8-9898229-2-8

ISBN (print): 979-8-9898229-3-5

Cover design by GetCovers.com

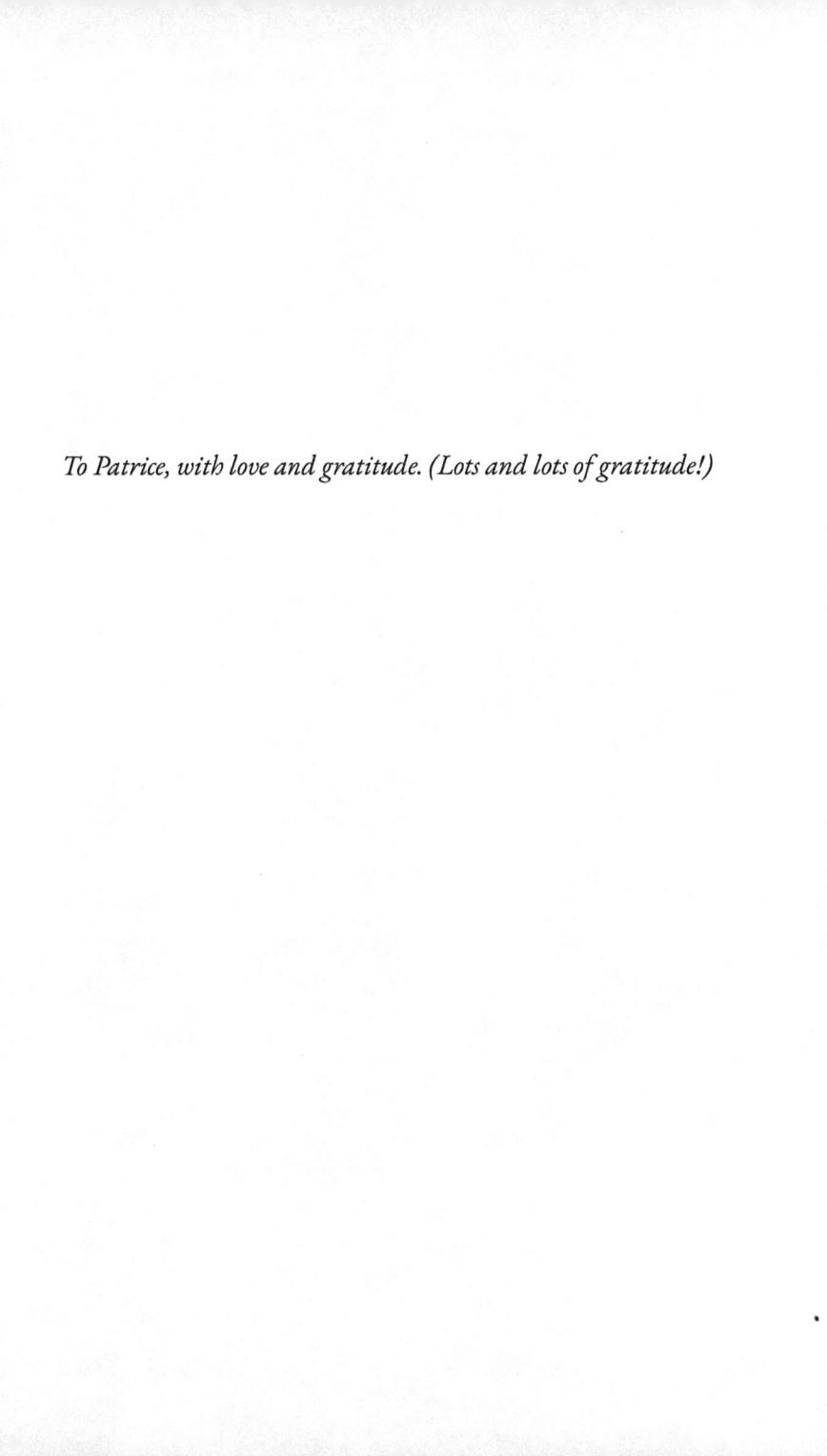

To Patrice, with love and gratitude. (Lots and lots of gratitude!)

For more Sean Wynn thrillers, including a free short story, visit
www.keithjweber.com

PROLOGUE

Three years ago

TWO LITTLE DIGITS.

Put one before the other and millions of dollars are lost. Reverse the order, and billions could be made.

And how much difference is there, Neil Carson thought, *between 97.8 and 98.7? It's so close! A different test group, different subjects, it could have easily been the 98 needed to pass.*

Carson's toe nudged the body under the desk. He hated doing it, but she wouldn't listen. The real trick had been getting her to keep her mouth shut for the afternoon, then agree to meet him after everyone else had gone home. He thought he'd be able to convince her, but she wouldn't budge.

Stubborn bitch.

He tensed as footsteps echoed from the tiled hallway. They stopped outside the lab door, followed by a gentle rap on the glass.

"Mr. Carson?" The voice was smooth and silky. Male.

Carson swallowed to find his voice. "Yes?"

"Mr. Jameson sent me."

Carson released the breath he'd been holding, then rushed to open the door. A thin, bald man with a gray goatee and wearing a nondescript delivery uniform stood in the hall. He pushed a hand-dolly carrying a large, brown box into the lab while Carson closed and locked the door.

"It's about damn time. You came in the southeast entrance, right?"

The deliveryman gave him an annoyed look, his sharp features accentuating his disapproval. He turned away and scanned the room. "Where is it?"

"Under the desk."

The deliveryman wheeled the box behind the desk, where he unfolded the top flaps to reveal a fifty-five-gallon barrel. He removed the lid and laid the box, with the drum still inside, next to the body, then pulled a pair of surgical gloves from his pocket and methodically put them on. Dropping to one knee, he unwrapped the electrical cord from the woman's neck and handed it to Carson. "Wipe it with a disinfectant, then get rid of it. Somewhere far away."

He slid the body into the drum, righted it, then put the lid on the barrel. After folding the flaps closed on the box, he used a roll of clear packing tape to secure everything in place.

"What are you going to do with her?" Carson asked.

The deliveryman gave him another annoyed look. "Just make sure those cameras stay off. Have a good night, Mr. Carson."

CHAPTER 1

Today

SEAN WYNN CLUTCHED the granite kitchen countertop with one hand while sinking hard onto a barstool, blinking feverishly to refocus. The sound of the television faded into the background. His entire world narrowed to the three handwritten words in black ink on white paper.

It wasn't stray.

The letter had come from the California state prison in Corcoran, where Wynn had only one connection. Jamaal Johnson, JJ as his grandmother called him, or Jay-squared as he was known on the street, was serving fifteen years to life for the random shooting death of Wynn's wife, Nicole. It happened more than two years ago, but the images were seared into Wynn's brain, haunting his dreams. He squeezed his eyes closed as the memories flooded back, playing like a movie through his mind...

———

Sean hustled up the sidewalk, past the bright glass storefronts. Viacci's was Nicole's new favorite restaurant, along with everybody else's, so reservations were in high demand. Anything more than a few minutes late meant your table was going to someone else.

In addition to its food and wine list, both among the best in town, Viacci's benefitted from its location on the outskirts of Ventura's newest, and most expensive retail shopping complex. Covering six city blocks, shoppers could spend hours in the likes of Nordstrom's, Neiman Marcus, Saks Fifth Avenue, and Bloomingdale's. Sean didn't understand the appeal of overpriced, ripped-up blue jeans, but they sold a lot of them.

Unfortunately, with the good also came the bad. Or more accurately, with the money came the crime. Rival gangs, who couldn't have cared less about those six city blocks before they were redeveloped, now fought almost weekly to claim the surrounding neighborhoods and the mall within. Which made Sean nervous when Nicole told him to meet her there at seven o'clock. He didn't like the idea of her going there alone.

He breathed a quiet sigh of relief, and felt the familiar rush of dopamine when he spotted her standing among a small crowd outside the restaurant. She still had that effect on him.

Nicole's eyes brightened as he approached. "You made it," she said as she rose onto her tiptoes for a kiss.

"Of course," he replied. "Am I late?"

"Right on time."

Taking his hand, Nicole led him to the host station outside the front door.

"Reservation for two. For Wynn," she said to the young woman behind the podium.

"Wynn. Ah, yes." The hostess smiled warmly, her white teeth luminous against her dark skin. "Our anniversary couple."

Nicole smiled brightly as she squeezed Sean's arm.

"Right this way." The hostess led them through the restaurant to an elevated outdoor patio overlooking an expansive courtyard. A massive rock waterfall with palm trees and greenery occupied the center of the courtyard. Tendrils of clear-running streams created an oasis within the jungle of glass and concrete. Cars cruised slowly by on the street beyond. A knee-high wall next to a sparkling brook separated their elevated table from the throngs of shoppers bustling through the complex.

When they were settled, Sean scanned the courtyard. It was a habit left over from his days in the Marines, an ingrained behavior whenever he was in a large crowd. Countless missions in Afghanistan will do that.

Nicole gave a small wave to a woman seated along the outer railing a few tables away.

"I didn't realize Janelle was going to be here," Sean said. "Do you want to go somewhere else?"

"Not at all. For a boss, she's pretty cool. I think they're celebrating their anniversary, too."

"I just thought you might want to get away from work."

"I am. Relax, this place is great." Nicole smiled wide and took his hand in hers. "Can you believe it's been four years already?"

"Best of my life." He surveyed the surroundings again. While most everyone looked like typical shoppers, three young guys loitered around the waterfall. Their baggy jerseys seemed out of place on this warm, summer night.

"Sean? Hello? Is everything okay?"

"Hmm?" He brought his attention back to Nicole. "Yeah. It's fine. What were you saying?"

"I was asking, how was your day?"

"Oh. Good. The trap we set for those hackers worked. Traced them to a small town outside Vienna. Interpol's got it now, but I don't think they'll be bothering anyone else for a while. At least not any of our clients. Yours?"

"Ugh. Spent the whole day trying to make sense of trial data. But I do have exciting news." She raised one eyebrow.

"Really? What's up?"

"I have something to show you."

"Here? I thought that'd wait until we got home." He smiled mischievously.

"Don't worry, big guy. I've got something for you there, too." She dug into her purse and pulled out a small, rectangular package. It was wrapped in dark brown metallic paper with a gold foil bow.

A pen set? For our anniversary? He suddenly felt very good about the topaz earrings he had waiting for her at home.

"Go ahead. Open it," she urged.

Three girls had joined the guys loitering near the waterfall. The group made their way closer and stood just opposite the stream from where Wynn and Nicole sat. A black Lexus sedan approached from the street on the other side of the courtyard.

Wynn pulled on the bow and unwrapped the box. Nicole's eyes beamed. Her lips were drawn in a tight smile with her hands clenched in front as she leaned forward.

This is either the world's greatest pen or....

He flipped open the box to see a small, white plastic stick. There was sudden movement on the periphery of his vision.

"I'm pregnant!" Nicole squealed, no longer able to contain her joy.

Shots exploded to Wynn's right, the sound unmistakable. He dove across the table, grabbing Nicole by the shoulders and pushing her to the floor beneath him as chaos erupted all around. Shoppers screamed as a new volley of gunfire flared closer, louder. Dishes shattered as he glanced through the courtyard to see the black Lexus accelerate swiftly, its engine roaring, tires shrieking on the pavement.

And then, as quickly as it started, a shocked silence fell over the scene. The sounds of the engine, the screams, and the patter of running feet all faded away.

Wynn pushed off the floor, his hand slipping on the warm, wet pool of blood seeping from beneath Nicole.

"Nicky!"

Her frightened eyes fluttered back and forth, searching for the source of his voice, finally finding him and locking onto his.

"Hang on, Nicky, help is coming."

"I... I'm pregnant," she whispered, then stared frozen into space.

Johnson, part of a street gang known as the Acid Dawn, had been arrested a week later following an anonymous tip. At first, he played the typical card: knew nothing about anything. After nine hours of interrogation, however, the detectives wore him down, finally getting him to admit he was in the car, eventually to even pulling the trigger.

His tough-guy facade changed once he got a lawyer. Going for leniency, Johnson expressed tremendous remorse, saying he had no intention of killing Nicole. Rather, he'd been aiming at the rival gang members in the courtyard. It didn't matter. His reckless disregard for human life led to a charge of second-degree murder, which resulted in a sentence of fifteen years to life. Now, barely over two years in, he had sent Wynn this note.

What the hell? It wasn't stray? Does that mean it was intentional? Was Nicole a target? Why?

It made no sense. Nicole was only twenty-nine years old, working a boring nine-to-five job. She had no association with gangs. Why would they target her?

Wynn sat down at his computer and pulled up Johnson's case file. He'd kept everything the prosecutor had given him or that he could find online in a single file. A quick scan provided the number as he picked up his phone.

The call was answered on the third ring by a friendly female voice. "McDermott and Schmidt. How can I help you?

"May I speak to Linda Trilby?"

"Let me see if she's available. Can I tell her who's calling?"

"Sean Wynn."

"Thank you, Mr. Wynn. Hold one minute, please."

After a few moments, the call was picked up by a different voice. "Linda Trilby."

"Ms. Trilby, this is Sean Wynn. I need to see one of your clients."

"Hello, Mr. Wynn. I had a feeling you might call. I assume you're referring to Jamaal Johnson?"

"That's right. Why?"

"Mr. Johnson reached out to us saying he has information he wants to trade for a commuted sentence. As you know, we were assigned his case by the court, so technically, after the plea deal was reached, he was no longer a client. But we were curious, and since this sprang from the original case, we decided to take it on. I went up to Corcoran and spoke to him about two weeks ago."

"What did he say?"

"You know I can't answer that, but let me ask, what prompted your call?"

"He sent me a note," Wynn replied. "At least I assume it was him. The envelope came from the pen in Corcoran. Inside was a single piece of paper with three words, 'It wasn't stray.'"

Trilby sighed before continuing. "Mr. Wynn, you have to understand. These guys will say anything in hopes of getting out. They'll make up any story, make it sound very believable. But they're all lies. Attorney-client privilege prevents me from telling you what he said, but I can tell you we did not find it credible."

Wynn paused as he considered that for a moment. "I understand," he finally said. "But I'd still like to talk to him."

"I have to advise against it. It'll only open old wounds."

Wynn laughed softly to himself. *No chance of that. They've never healed.*

CHAPTER 2

FIVE DAYS LATER, Wynn savored the steady, boiling rhythm of his red and black Harley-Davidson Custom Sportster as he cruised north on Highway 33, out of Ventura toward the state penitentiary in Corcoran. He'd left his other bike, a Harley Street Glide, at home, instead opting for the smaller, more nimble Sportster as he wound through low forests of pinyon, conifer, and oak along the winding roadway. The morning's bright blue skies belied the fact that the mid-October air was cooler than average, requiring him to suit up with his black leather jacket and tinted full-face helmet.

He wasn't sure what to expect from his meeting with Johnson, or if there would even be one. Trilby had helped Wynn with the necessary paperwork and arranged the interview, but warned that inmates sometimes ignored scheduled visits. Whether it be to exert their limited power or simply mess with the minds of those who made the three-hour drive north of Los Angeles was anyone's guess.

If it was the latter, Wynn had to admit, Johnson had already won.

Since receiving the letter, he'd thought of little else. His mind was in a constant battle, wanting to believe Nicole's death wasn't as simple as random bad luck. But logic told him Trilby was most likely right, that Johnson was lying to try to negotiate himself out of prison. During the day, consciously, logic won. But at night, subconsciously, when his mind was free to wander, the nightmares took hold.

Two-and-a-half years ago, Nicole worked as a research analyst for pharmaceutical developer Mynogen. But she wasn't a player. She wasn't in charge of any units, departments, or special projects. She was a worker bee. Like thousands of others. Doing the methodic and painfully slow research that would hopefully, eventually, bring new medicines to market. It's not like she controlled multi-million-dollar budgets. From a professional perspective, there was no reason for someone to target her.

Other than that, who was she? John and Elaine Riedman's daughter. Sister to Bret and Julia. Was something going on with one of them that got her killed? Not likely.

But she was also Wynn's wife. There were lots of folks in the Middle East who would love to get their hands on him, but they knew him only by reputation, not by name or sight. He'd made plenty of enemies during his eight years as an operative in the Marine Forces Special Operations Command, but MARSOC kept a tight lid on their operatives and assignments. He was anonymous. Safe. And besides, he'd been out for ten years. Forgotten. If someone wanted to get to him, wouldn't they have made contact by now?

Which made Johnson's note all the more confusing.

Wynn pulled into the parking lot of the sprawling penitentiary complex about twenty minutes before his scheduled noon meeting, the sun already baking the dirt lot. Double rows of concertina-topped chain-link fencing enclosed an area roughly a mile square, while thirty-foot tall watchtowers punctuated the perimeter every few hundred yards. He hung his helmet on the handlebars and stuffed his jacket, along with everything else he wasn't allowed to take inside, into the saddlebags.

Following the sidewalk to the visitor's entrance, he signed in, passed through a metal detector, endured a wanding and pat down, and was escorted out the back door into a mantrap. When the door closed behind him, he felt a tiny shot of adrenaline as he found himself in a small, outdoor, six-by-eight-foot chain-link cage.

Damn. He was suddenly aware that his biker appearance—six-one, one hundred ninety pounds, long hair, and a goatee—made him look as much like a potential inmate as a visitor. *At least I shaved the beard.*

An electric motor hummed as the wire panel in front of him slid to the side, allowing him to pass through the first line of fencing. Once through, the panel slid back into place, capturing him between the two rows. Thirty seconds later, a second panel also slid away, clearing the way into the prison.

The mantrap opened into a wide, visitor's courtyard, enclosed on either end by more chain-link and concertina, while a sidewalk led to a two-story concrete building directly ahead. Inside, Wynn was greeted by another round of metal detectors, wands, and pat-downs, then was told to take a seat in the waiting area while they brought Johnson to a room.

As he sat, Wynn became keenly aware this would be his first time seeing Johnson since the sentencing hearing. Back then, Johnson had tried to act remorseful. Tried to play on the judge's sympathy in hopes of a lighter sentence. But Wynn saw through it. Johnson was a punk kid that didn't give a shit about anyone but himself. Didn't care that his actions robbed the world of a beautiful, young, and promising life. And Wynn of his future.

He'd hoped the judge would also see through it. Hoped Johnson would receive the maximum sentence.

He did. But it didn't change a thing.

Nicole was still gone, their dream of a happy family shattered, leaving Wynn empty, alone, and sending him on a two-year spiral of aimless wandering, cruising the country on his Harley, searching for answers that were hidden either somewhere along the roadway or deep at the bottom of a bottle.

Good thing we'll be separated. I'd kill the little shit if given the chance.

Considering where he was sitting, Wynn smiled grimly at the thought. While civilian lawyers might consider an act of vengeance against Johnson to be murder, eight years in the Marines and a life-time of watching decisions made by the U.S. Air Force via his lieu-tenant colonel dad, taught him that killing and murder were two very different things. In his mind, some people, by their own actions against innocent others, forfeited the protection of the law, forfeited the right to have their killing called murder. Johnson was one of them.

Eventually, Wynn was escorted to a small visitation room where a plexiglass wall divided the space into two mirror images. On either side, a chair sat in front of a desk-high counter that butted against the clear partition. Two phones hung on the walls on either side of the glass.

Wynn paused, startled when he saw Johnson slouched low in the chair on the other side. At five-eleven and well over two hundred pounds when Wynn last saw him, Johnson now looked small. He'd lost weight. A lot of weight. He wore blue jeans and a light blue prison smock, with a long-sleeved white t-shirt underneath, all hanging loose on his lanky frame. His black hair was shaved to a quarter-inch, and new tattoos crept out from beneath his collar and up his neck.

Taking a deep breath to calm himself, Wynn pulled out the chair and sat down while the guard closed the door, leaving him alone. He looked at Johnson, but the killer refused to meet his eye. The cocki-ness Wynn sensed outside the courtroom was gone, replaced by something akin to fear. Wynn knew that life inside a prison has its own ecosystem, with predators and prey. Johnson, it would appear, had become the latter.

They sat for a full minute, Wynn watching, Johnson looking down. Finally, Wynn picked up the phone and used it to tap the glass. When Johnson picked up, Wynn said, "You sent me a note."

Johnson finally met Wynn's eyes. "Yeah. So?"

"What's it mean?"

"It means I know things."

"What things?"

"Things to help catch your wife's real killer."

"We've already done that."

"No, man. It was a setup. A hit."

"Why?"

"Uh-uh. In here, everything's a deal," Johnson said. "You help me get out of here, I'll tell you everything."

Wynn stood, hung up the phone, and turned to leave. He was about to press the call button for the guard when he heard an insistent pounding behind him. Turning back, Johnson was now standing, leaning forward with his hands on the plexiglass, pleading silently. Wynn came back and sat down, then picked up the phone. "I'm listening."

"We were paid."

"By who?"

"I don't know, man. It was Devon," Johnson said, referring to Devon Harris, leader of the Acid Dawn. "He said some suit approached him and offered us a hundred large if we'd off some bitch."

Wynn's eyes narrowed.

"Sorry, man," Johnson said quickly. "His words, not mine."

"Why?" Wynn asked again.

"Man, I don't know. Some dude offers you a hundred G's to do a job, you don't ask why. You just do the job."

"Assuming I believe you, how'd you do it?"

"Shit, man, you know how! We drove by." Johnson's voice rose, imploring Wynn to believe him.

"Not what I mean, asshole. How'd you know where she'd be, sitting right there, at that table?"

"I don't know, but Devon knew. We scoped it ahead of time. He pointed out exactly which table she'd be at."

"How about the Vipers?" Wynn asked, referring to the three guys he'd seen loitering in the courtyard, the rival gang members Johnson was supposedly shooting at. "How'd you know they'd be there?"

"Those dudes weren't no Vipers. They were just dudes, man. We put 'em there."

"How?"

"We used the bitches. Had Lashika and a couple of her hoes arrange to meet 'em. Made 'em think they were gonna get lucky. Ain't no dude able to resist that fine ass."

That got Wynn thinking. Even after bringing in almost every known member of the Vipers, the cops never did find those three guys.

"Who's Lashika?" Wynn asked.

"Lashika Collins. Devon's girlfriend at the time. Now she's dumped his ass."

"And you told her to meet those guys?"

"Devon did."

Wynn sighed heavily. "Your story has a major problem, Johnson. According to you, Devon Harris is the only one who actually knows anything, so unless he's willing to talk, you've got nothing. Why would he corroborate what you're saying?"

"Jewel, man."

"What's that?"

"Greatest thing since ecstasy. The Dawn is dealing it."

"I'm not DEA," Wynn said.

"Yeah, but maybe if you brought him in on that, he'd tell you about the suit."

"I'm also not a cop. Unless you've got something else, we're done here."

Johnson paused, his eyes darting down in a desperate attempt to come up with something more. "Bills, man. I got bills. Two G's a month, showing up like clockwork at my Gran-maw's door. That's why I confessed. Devon said I was toast anyway. If I kept my mouth shut, he'd make sure my maw was taken care of. But she died last month, man. Now I'm stuck in here with nothing to show for it, and the dudes who set it up are running free. It ain't right."

Wynn shook his head. "No, Johnson. What isn't right is your story. I'm not buying it."

He hung up the phone and walked back to the door. Pressed the call button. Looking back, Johnson was still sitting at the counter, still had the phone to his ear.

A tear had run down his cheek.

CHAPTER 3

WYNN HAD A lot to consider as he rode past manicured fields of alfalfa and cotton along the highway back to Ventura. He'd always had trouble accepting that Nicole's death was simply random bad luck, but the idea that she was targeted seemed even more unlikely. And while he could see why Trilby had dismissed Johnson's story, there were a few leads that could be followed up. Four, to be precise.

First, there was Devon Harris, leader of Johnson's street gang, the Acid Dawn. Wynn had seen him hanging around the courthouse during Johnson's sentencing hearing. If there was any truth to this story, Harris would be the one to know it. But Wynn couldn't imagine this guy would tell him anything voluntarily. Maybe the idea of bringing him in on a drug charge wasn't so bad after all.

Second, was Johnson's assertion that the three guys in the court-yard weren't Vipers, but regular guys lured there by Lashika Collins and her friends. But as with Harris, the chances of her corroborating Johnson's story were slim.

Third, was Viacci's, and more specifically, the hostess who directed them to their table that night. Johnson's story hinged on this point. Eight years in the Marines taught Wynn that for a hit to work, you had to know when and where your target was going to be.

Viacci's had over fifty tables, only sixteen of which were on the patio outside, eight that lined the outer railing and allowed an unobstructed view from the street. For Johnson's story to be legitimate, the hostess had to have intentionally sat Wynn and Nicole at that specific table.

Finally, there was Johnson's grandmother. Even though she'd passed, there were still banking records, utility bills, and mortgage or rent payments. If her sources of income didn't match up with her monthly expenses, that might help support Johnson's story. It was the least conclusive piece of evidence, but the only one that didn't rely on someone telling the truth.

Assuming Devon Harris or Lashika Collins weren't likely to be overly cooperative, Viacci's became his first stop. It was a long shot that the same hostess would still work there, but he might get lucky. If not, maybe someone knew how to reach her.

He pulled off the freeway and onto the side streets bordering the mall complex, eventually rumbling past glass storefronts opposite the parking lot. Several people sitting on benches outside the stores paused their phone conversations and gave him an annoyed look as he thundered by. He parked the bike and for the first time in two years made his way up the same sidewalks he had walked that fateful night.

As he approached the restaurant, his mind produced an image of Nicole standing out front. It happened a lot, especially when he was someplace they'd visited together. Five-foot-seven, slender, dirty blonde hair, sparkling blue eyes. And the tight blue jeans she liked to wear didn't hurt. She wasn't the kind of beauty that stopped men in their tracks but had more of that girl-next-door look. To Wynn, she was the most beautiful, sexy woman he'd ever seen.

Her image faded as he crossed the street and glanced toward the patio next to the courtyard. The same small stream bubbled next to the knee-high wall as shoppers bustled past. An older couple sat at the table where it happened.

I wonder if they know.

A young woman with pale skin, offset by jet-black hair shaved close on one side of her head, long on the other, stood at the hostess station outside the door. It was still early, a little after four o'clock, so the dinner rush hadn't yet begun.

"Welcome to Viacci's," she said as he approached. "Will you be dining with us this evening?"

"No, thank you. Is there an owner, or general manager available?"

"Is there something wrong?"

"No, nothing's wrong." He wondered how much he should go into with this girl. "I'm trying to track down a woman who worked here a couple of years ago. The night of the, uh..." he nodded his head toward the patio.

The girl stared at him, blankly.

"How long have you worked here?" he asked.

"Six months."

"Is there anyone who's been here more than a couple of years?"

"Let me get Luke," she said, then turned and went inside.

Wynn waited as people came and went around the courtyard. He looked at the spot where he had first seen the three gang members. It was empty now, but again, his mind produced their images, taking him back in time.

"Can I help you?"

Wynn turned and saw a tall, thin man, with short dark hair looking at him expectantly.

"Hi. I'm trying to track down an employee you had here a couple of years ago. I don't know her name, but she was the hostess who sat my wife and me at a table on the patio." He paused. "The night of the shooting."

The thin man creased his eyebrows. "And why would you want to speak with her?"

Wynn knew this would be coming. If he told the guy he suspected she might be involved in a hit by knowingly placing the target in a particular location, he'd shut down in fear of lawsuits.

"The woman that was killed was my wife. I found a note on her phone calendar that she was going to call your hostess an hour before our reservation. It was our anniversary. I'd always assumed she was calling to confirm the reservation, but I was told recently by a friend that she had something special planned. Obviously, we never got around to it. I'm wondering what it was, trying to find closure."

"And you think our hostess would know?"

"According to this friend, yes, it's a distinct possibility."

The man's eyes turned from suspicion to sympathy. "What did you say your name was?"

"Sean Wynn."

"Come on back, Mr. Wynn. Let's see what we can find."

The man led Wynn through the restaurant, introducing himself along the way as Luke Creviston, the manager of Viacci's since it opened. They went through the kitchen to a small office where a middle-aged woman sat behind a desk.

"Mr. Wynn, this is Reyna Wu. She's our HR Director and might be able to help. Reyna," he said, turning to the woman, "this is Sean Wynn. He's the husband of the woman who was killed in that drive-by shooting two years ago. He's looking for one of our employees from that night."

"Which one?" Reyna asked.

"The hostess," Wynn replied. "A pretty Black girl. Five-six, maybe five-seven." He knew it wasn't much, but it was all he remembered.

"Diana," Reyna replied. "Diana Williams."

"You know her?"

"Of course, but I should say I did. I'm sorry to tell you she died shortly after your wife passed."

Wynn hadn't been expecting that. "How?"

Reyna looked hesitant. "That's not really for me to say. Maybe you should take your questions to the police."

"The police? Why? What happened?"

"I'm sorry, Mr. Wynn, but my hands are tied. You'll have to ask the police."

Wynn bit his lip in frustration. "But you're sure it was her? Can you at least tell me that?"

"You said a Black girl, right? Definitely a hostess, not a waitress?"

"Yeah."

"Diana's the only one who fits that description."

Wynn wasn't ready to go to the police. He didn't have enough information. They'd blow him off without even looking into it. "Did she have any family? Anyone I could contact?"

"Even if she did, I can't give you that."

"What about friends? Was she close to anyone here?"

Reyna looked up at Creviston, who still stood in the doorway. "Can I talk to you outside for a second?"

"Sure. Mr. Wynn, would you mind waiting here?" Creviston said.

"No problem."

Reyna got up from her desk and went out the door, closing it behind her and leaving Wynn alone. A large, four-drawer file cabinet sat in the corner. If he was more desperate, he might consider rifling through it, but figured anything useful was probably in the computer on her desk.

Reyna returned several minutes later. "I've got something that might help. We have someone who's friends with Diana's old roommate. This is obviously a sensitive situation, so we have to be extra careful about the information we give out, and quite frankly, in this case, we just can't. But if you want to leave your name and number, I'll pass it on to our staffer, who can then pass it on to the roommate. If she wants to reach out to you, that'll be up to her."

Wynn let out a long breath through gritted teeth. He understood, but it wasn't in his DNA to wait around for other people to call him. While his first instinct was to push harder to get the information, he'd learned long ago that you needed to befriend the locals if you had any hope of getting valuable intel later on. He wrote his name and number on a sheet of paper, thanked them for their help, and then walked out through the kitchen. A tired-looking blonde waitress made eye contact with him as he left.

She didn't smile.

———

Eighty miles to the southeast, inside a warehouse about halfway between the Los Angeles International Airport and Long Beach Harbor, Ishan Chan patiently waited while one of his men knelt at his feet, ensuring there was no trace of blood on either his Giorgio Armani suit, or his Christian Louboutin shoes. Chan was in his late fifties, thin, and stood ramrod straight. When his man finished, Chan stepped off the plastic sheeting so it could be used to wrap the still-warm body that lay sprawled on the floor.

Li, a young lieutenant whose boyish features made him appear considerably less than his twenty-eight years, strode over to where the cloudy plastic hung from a large carpet-like roll overhead. The sheeting had been spooled down from the top of an industrial shelving unit stacked with crates, and then stretched across the floor. He found the single hole about waist high, where the bullet, after exiting the dead man's head, had passed through the plastic. He stretched up with a nine-inch knife, and began cutting the plastic sheet away from the roll.

When the sheeting fell away, Li took a cordless screwdriver from a shelf, and removed the screws from the wooden side panel on the crate behind where the hole in the plastic had been. As he worked, Li counted the bullet holes in the crate and was bothered for a moment that he couldn't recall the men for whom each had been made. Was it because there were too many, or the fact that he truly didn't care?

When the panel was finally removed, Li shone a flashlight into the clear ballistic gel inside the crate until he found the bullet buried a mere twelve inches in. Pulling a rubber surgical glove up to his elbow, he reached into the solid, gooey mess and pulled it out. The bullet wore traces of blood and was slightly misshapen, but overall, still in good shape. He slipped it into a plastic bag, removed the glove, and stepped over to Chan.

"Is there any truth to his claim?" Chan asked.

"Some," Li admitted, his voice high, matching his youthful appearance. "The shipment was sixteen hours late."

"But it didn't affect the others?"

"Minimally."

"Good," Chan said, straightening his already perfect tie. "This should serve as a reminder to the others that the numbers must be hit, regardless."

"Agreed. But now that they've moved the production lab to Palm Springs, these interruptions have become longer and more frequent. What if the next one is more than a day?"

"Then we'll invite Mr. Carson to the warehouse."

CHAPTER 4

TAKING A CORONA from the fridge, Wynn grabbed his laptop and the letter from Johnson, then stepped out to the patio. He lived in a two-story, 2,400-square-foot home on Beachmont Street, backing up to Ventura Harbor. It was more space than he needed, but it had a two-car garage large enough for his Lexus RX and his two Harleys, as well as access to the water, via a private boat dock.

His boat, which was a source of endless ribbing from his friends, was little more than a dinghy used to tool around the harbor. It was especially embarrassing when his neighbor docked his thirty-two-foot cabin cruiser next door.

He'd bought the property primarily for the patio overlooking the bay. Late in the afternoon, as it was now, the cool ocean breezes wafted the scent of saltwater throughout the neighborhood, while the sun slowly finished its work for the day. Regardless of the time of year, temperatures seldom deviated more than twenty degrees between high and low, making it the perfect place to do his work outside.

He set the beer and laptop on the table and sank into a chair, then once again opened the letter from Johnson. He rubbed the paper between his index finger and thumb, feeling the texture of the linen paper that gave weight and substance to the three simple words, almost as if making their message real.

After leaving the Marines, Wynn had studied computer systems at the University of Southern California. That's where he'd met Nicole, who was getting her master's in biochemical engineering. Upon graduation, they both found jobs in Ventura County, and moved out of Los Angeles to what they thought was a sleepy little suburb.

Wynn took a job with a private computer security company. He left after a year to start his own firm, one dedicated to securing the technology infrastructure of small defense contractors and other firms doing business in hostile territories.

The idea came to him when he was still in the Marines. He'd been on a mission to rescue an American businessman who had been kidnapped after his computer was hacked. The Taliban had gained access to his calendar and therefore knew when and where to intercept him. Unfortunately, it did not end well for the businessman. But it did serve as a valuable lesson to Wynn's potential clients. With first-hand knowledge of how the Taliban treated American prisoners, Wynn was able to graphically illustrate the risk, to both the firm's intellectual capital as well as to the executive's physical well-being, of doing business in the Middle East. As such, it didn't take long for his services to be in extremely high demand.

After Nicole's murder, he sold the company and retained a minority stake along with the title of "Strategic Consultant." He'd pocketed enough to buy the house and the Harleys, and still make the need for future employment optional.

He took a draw from the Corona, watching the sky transition from bright orange on the horizon to a pale blue above. The spider-sense that often told him when he was on to something started tingling when he'd learned of Diana Williams' death. It pulsed through his veins now. Afraid his emotions were getting in the way, he forced it down, willed himself to think logically. It would be too easy to let himself believe Johnson's story, that Nicole's death wasn't random, that there really was someone to blame. He hated to think what he might do if he ever found a focused target for his pain and anger.

Tapping his credentials into the computer, he brought up Nicole's case files, this time searching for Johnson's grandmother's name and address. Eunice Johnson lived at the same address as Jamaal, in Oxnard, directly south of Ventura. A quick check of public records confirmed that Ms. Johnson did indeed own the home she lived in, but he couldn't determine if there was a mortgage against the property. He made note of the address and moved on.

Next up was the Acid Dawn, sometimes referred to as the ADs, and specifically, their leader, Devon Harris. The ADs first emerged onto the Ventura scene about fifteen years ago around the same time as their rival gang, the Vipers. While the ADs were exclusively young Black men, the Vipers were exclusively Hispanic. When prepping Johnson's case, Wynn had asked the prosecutor how the rivalry had started in the first place. *Someone slept with someone else's girlfriend*, had been the answer. Wynn didn't know if that was true, but nations had gone to war over less.

Since that time, the city of Ventura had basically been divided; the ADs controlled the area south of the 126, the Vipers claimed the north. And while skirmishes had flared up from time to time, both sides had, for the most part, settled into a fragile truce, allowing the law-abiding citizens to essentially ignore them.

Until the mall was built right in the center.

In the year before Nicole's shooting, there had been a half-dozen other incidents within a mile of the mall. Although a few residents' homes had been hit by gunfire, thankfully no bystanders were hurt, the only victims being the gang members themselves.

But Nicole's murder changed all that. Since then, the police had cracked down, forcing the gangs to go underground. They now settled their disputes privately, and as a result, there was little recent news coverage about either the ADs or Devon Harris. There were no social media accounts, no emails, and no phone numbers to be found for any of the known members. He did find an address for Harris, but a further search showed the property was owned by a Charles Harris, likely Devon's father.

And unlikely that Devon still lived there. Which meant Wynn would have to go searching for him in person. *That should be fun.*

The next lead to follow up on was Lashika Collins, one of the three AD girlfriends who lured the three Hispanic guys into the courtyard. A quick Google search revealed pages on both Facebook and Instagram. Clicking on the Facebook link, he found two helpful pieces of information.

First, it looked like Lashika was a new mother. There were pictures of her and a baby girl all over the page. Looking through the comments, he found the baby's name was Ayel, but there was nothing about the father. That could mean a couple of things. Either he was completely gone from the picture, or maybe for privacy reasons, didn't want to be a part of the picture. *Have to be careful until I know more.*

Second, he saw that Lashika worked at a small costume jewelry store called Yvonne's. He pulled up the store's website, found their phone number, and called it. A quick conversation with the woman who picked up revealed that Lashika still worked there and would be in from noon to six tomorrow.

Need to pay her a little visit.

By the time he hung up, the sky had darkened and the breeze stilled, creating a quiet calm across the water. Wynn loved this kind of night. Tiny lights on top of the sailboat masts sprinkled throughout the harbor reminded him of stars in the night sky, but closer, reachable, as if he might lose himself among them.

He drained the last of his beer and sat for a few minutes, allowing his mind to wander, wondering what it would have been like to share this place with Nicole. How she would have loved it, how they would have sat right here on warm evenings with a baby monitor and a glass of wine. How their children would have played on the patio and the dock, and how, as they got older, they'd have insisted he get a real boat. He smiled at the thought. *Children I don't even have giving me a hard time.*

He swallowed to clear the lump in his throat. His mind came back to reality and the question at hand. He was not at all convinced that Johnson's story was true, but there was no way he wasn't going to follow up on each lead. The ghosts of his non-existent children deserved nothing less. Needing to stretch his legs, he went inside to grab another beer and a sandwich before continuing his research.

The next order of business was to find out more about Diana Williams' death. He was surprised he didn't remember hearing about her passing at the time, considering the proximity in both time and relevance to Nicole's murder. But maybe that was why. He didn't remember much of anything around that time.

The search results showed multiple Facebook pages for Diana Williams, but he quickly eliminated several based on the most recent posts. Eventually, he was able to find the right one, a photo and the word 'Remembering' prominently displayed beneath her name. Looking at the photo, he recalled her bright smile and sparkling eyes. He replayed the brief interaction in his mind, trying to remember if there was any tell, any hesitation that might have indicated she knew what was to come. *Our anniversary couple,* she had said. Or was he imagining that? It was hard to distinguish what was truly a memory versus what his mind was simply filling in.

The timeline contained several posts from friends and family expressing shock and sadness at her passing. Many were of the *I can't believe you're gone* variety, while others shared fond memories of good times. An obituary was pinned to the top of the page.

A beloved daughter and cherished friend, Diana Marie Williams left this world unexpectedly on August 16th, at the age of 23. Born in Los Angeles to John and Michelle Williams, Diana grew up in Santa Clarita, where she attended Peach-land Elementary and Hart High School. She was currently taking classes at Ventura College where she was studying Child

Development and Elementary Education in hopes of becoming an elementary school teacher.

Diana loved children, the arts, and music. She enjoyed playing the guitar and piano, as well as singing in the church choir. She was funny, outgoing, and vivacious, always able to brighten someone's day. We will always remember her infectious smile, piercing bright eyes, and caring personality. Her presence in our lives will be sorely missed.

The rest of the obituary listed grandparents who had preceded her in death, and details of a memorial service. There was no mention of the cause of death.

Wynn spent ten minutes going through the remembrance posts before moving on to Williams' actual timeline. This gave him a better feel for who she was in life, not just of how she was remembered in death.

Williams had been fairly active on Facebook, which always surprised Wynn. *Don't people realize how dangerous that is?* Posting information about friends, family, where you hung out, or where you were at any given time could make you an easy target for stalkers or thieves. But at least outwardly, according to these posts, Williams had none of those problems. Her timeline was filled with posts about parties and friends, days at the beach, schoolwork, and her favorite musicians. She gave shoutouts to friends on their birthdays—*I love you, Jenna!*—which were returned in kind.

Moving on, Wynn scanned through dozens of photos that showed much the same. One girl in particular seemed to show up in a lot of pictures. Hovering over the girl's face, he eventually found her name, tagged on one of the photos.

Vanessa Carow appeared to be about the same age as Williams, maybe a little shorter, a little thinner, but with the same infectious smile and bright eyes. Several photos showed them with their arms around each other, clearly the best of friends. More importantly, several of the photos appeared to be selfies taken inside an apartment, at a kitchen table, or reclining on a couch.

Like roommates.

Wynn went back to the timeline and searched for posts containing Vanessa's name. It took a few minutes, but eventually, he found what he was looking for. From Vanessa to Diana, a birthday greeting. *Happy birthday to the best roomie ever! Love you!*

Take that, Creviston, Wynn thought. *Found the roommate without your help.*

Wynn pulled up Vanessa's profile page and clicked on the messaging app. He debated what to say for a few minutes and finally started typing: *Hi Vanessa. My name's Sean Wynn. My wife was an acquaintance of your roommate Diana's and passed about the same time. Trying to find closure, hoping you can help. Can we talk?*

He put his phone number on the message, re-read it to make sure it sounded innocent enough, then hit send.

Feeling good about the intel he'd gathered so far, he finally turned his efforts to John and Michelle Williams, Diana's parents. Unlike their daughter, the Williamses didn't have Facebook accounts or any kind of online presence. Santa Clarita, however, seemed a good place to start. It was clear from the obituary that's where Diana had grown up before moving to Ventura, and likely her parents still lived there. A search of their names and the city, however, produced another disappointing surprise. John's obituary. He had passed about a year after Diana. A tough year for Michelle.

Focusing his search now solely on Diana's mom, he eventually found an address on the south side of Santa Clarita, near Newhall, that he was able to confirm via county property records. There was also a phone number.

It was a little after eight o'clock, he hoped not too late to call. He sat back, gathered his thoughts, then dialed the number. It was picked up on the third ring.

"Hello?" said a woman's voice.

"Hi. Is this Michelle Williams?" Wynn asked.

"Who's calling?"

"Mrs. Williams, my name's Sean Wynn. I'm sorry to disturb you this evening, but my wife was an acquaintance of your daughter. She also passed away about the same time as Diana, and I know I'm hitting you out of the blue with this, but I was wondering if I could ask you a few questions about your daughter that might help me find closure with my own wife's passing."

There was silence on the other end of the line. Wynn let it stretch until it became uncomfortable. "Mrs. Williams?"

"What did you say your name was?"

"Sean Wynn."

"And your wife?"

"Her name was Nicole. Nicole Wynn."

"She was the one shot at the restaurant where Diana worked." It was said as a statement, not a question.

"That's right."

"And you have some questions for me?"

"Yes. If that's alright."

"Can you come over tomorrow? I have some questions for you, too."

CHAPTER 5

THE NEXT MORNING, Wynn checked his Facebook account to see if Vanessa Carow, Diana Williams' old roommate, had responded to his message. It might be helpful if he could get more information before he spoke to Diana's mom, but his message box was empty.

By nine a.m., he was cruising the Sportster east along Highway 126, following the Santa Clara River from Ventura to Santa Clarita. This time of year, the riverbed was mostly dry as it wound between low mountain ranges; fields of avocado, lemons, and oranges filled the rich soil in the base of the valley. The air was cool as he leaned into the turns and rumbled east.

A little more than an hour later, he pulled up in front of a small, cream-colored ranch-style home.

The door opened as he came up the walk, revealing a middle-aged woman standing inside, undoubtedly having heard his Harley as he arrived. She was of average height, trim, and probably at one time considered extremely attractive. He could see where Diana had gotten her looks. But now, even from ten feet away, an overwhelming sense of sadness seemed to envelop her. Her eyes were dull, and creases had formed at the corners of her mouth, exaggerating a permanent frown. Her shoulders slumped slightly, and her right hand held the door, her left hand grasping her right elbow across her stomach as if to ward off any further pain. Wynn felt a pang of guilt, knowing that was exactly what he was about to bring her.

"Mrs. Williams?" He removed his sunglasses as he approached the door. "I'm Sean Wynn. It's nice to meet you."

She looked toward his bike, then back at him. Riding up on a Harley with long hair and a black leather jacket, he was probably not what she expected when she'd invited him to her home.

"It's nice to meet you, too. Please, come in."

He followed her into the house, the front door opening into a nicely furnished and mostly well-kept living room. Straight ahead was a dining table with four chairs, and to the right of that, behind the living room, was the kitchen. A hallway led off to the left between the living and dining rooms.

Wynn paused to examine a cluster of pictures hanging on the wall. They showed Mrs. Williams and a man, presumably Mr. Williams, along with Diana at various stages of her life. The tops of the picture frames were coated with a heavy layer of dust.

Can't bear to look at them but can't bring herself to take them down.

"Would you like something to drink?" Mrs. Williams asked.

"Coffee would be great."

"Do you take cream or sugar?"

"No, thank you. Black will be fine."

She moved further into the house, motioning to the dining table as she made her way to the kitchen. "Please, have a seat."

Wynn pulled out a chair and sat down as Mrs. Williams went into the kitchen, took two ceramic mugs from the cupboard, and poured the coffee. Bringing both cups to the table, she set one in front of Wynn, then eased herself into a seat across from him.

"Thank you for coming. I hope it wasn't too inconvenient," she said as she settled in.

"No trouble at all. I appreciate you seeing me."

"So, tell me, why did you call?"

Wynn had rehearsed this part on the ride over. He needed to be vague so as not to be caught in a lie. "First, please accept my condolences. I know what I'm going through, and that's been hard enough. I can't imagine what the last couple of years have been like for you."

"Thank you. Yes, it's been challenging. But you didn't ride all this way just to offer sympathy. What can I really do for you, Mr. Wynn?"

Get to it, Sean. "A friend of Nicole's told me she had something special planned for that night at the restaurant, but she never got around to it. The friend said Nicole had coordinated with the hostess who was working that night. At first, I was hoping Diana might be able to tell me what that was, but when I learned she'd passed, I thought maybe you or one of her friends might know what they had planned. I've already asked the manager at Viacci's, but he didn't know anything."

"No, that man surely doesn't know a thing." Her voice was bitter.

"What do you mean?"

"After Diana passed, we asked around. That man, her friends, coworkers, roommate. She'd never been into that stuff before. We wanted to know where she got it. Thought maybe it was from work."

"I'm sorry, Mrs. Williams. I'm confused. Where she got what?"

She paused for a moment and looked him in the eye. "Are you a truthful man, Mr. Wynn?"

"I like to think so."

"So if an old woman asks you a question about her dead daughter, you'll tell her the truth?"

"You have my word." A twinge of guilt flared in the pit of his stomach.

"What did your wife do, Mr. Wynn?"

"She was a research analyst."

"Who'd she work for?"

"Mynogen."

"The drug company?"

"Yes..."

"Did your wife get my baby into that?"

"I'm still confused," he said, trying to follow her logic. "Into what?"

"The drugs," she said, her voice rising. "Did your wife get Diana into drugs?"

"What? No. Are you saying Diana died of a drug overdose?"

"You didn't know?" The words began to spill like water. "The doctor said it was a lethal dose, enough to kill an elephant. My baby never did drugs. Wanted to be a schoolteacher, help the kids, then she experiments one time, and...." She paused, trying to catch her breath. "I want to know where she got it and who got her into it. The police have closed the book on Diana and nobody seems to know anything. I'd read in the paper your wife worked at Mynogen, so when you said they knew each other, I thought maybe your wife was Diana's dealer. Maybe that's why she was shot?"

"Mrs. Williams, Nicole was a research analyst. She looked at numbers and analyzed trial data all day. She never had access to the actual drugs. And even if she did, she knew the dangers. Never touched the stuff. Even made me stop smoking weed."

"Your wife didn't deal drugs?" Her voice deflating.

"She wouldn't have known where to start," he said softly.

"Damn," she muttered under her breath. "Whoever it was killed my baby. I'm sorry, Mr. Wynn. It's been over two years, cost John his life. I'm trying to make sense of it."

"I understand. I'm doing the same thing. What do you mean it cost John his life?"

"He was heartbroken. We both were. He came down with cancer eight months later and simply lost his will to fight it. Lost his will to live."

"I'm so sorry. I can't imagine." Wynn sat back, processing this new information. "What kind of drug was it?"

"Something called Jewel. Some kind of opioid. The doctor said it's in the heroin family."

Wynn's pulse quickened. "Jewel?"

"I think that's what they called it."

"You say Diana had never done drugs before?"

"Never."

"How can you be sure?" he asked, leaning forward. "Teenagers do a lot of things their parents never know about."

"We were close with Diana. Her friends, too. We knew who she was hanging out with, who she was dating. Like I said, we asked around. None of them were into it."

"Did you ask her roommate?"

"Vanessa? Sure. They were besties. She didn't know anything, but it was something she said, or rather something she gave us, that got us thinking. Wondering if maybe Diana *was* doing something we wouldn't approve of."

"What'd she give you?"

"About three weeks after the funeral, we were cleaning out Diana's apartment. As we're finishing up, Vanessa hands us an envelope with four thousand dollars in it. Four thousand dollars! She said it was from tips at the restaurant, but we knew that was a lie. Diana was a hostess, not a waitress. They shared tips once in a while, but never close to that much. And besides, the bills were all nice and neat, as if they'd come from the same stack. That doesn't happen. I know, I waited tables when I was younger. You get stray bills here and there. Never a neat stack. There's no way that money came from tips."

"But that's what Vanessa told you?"

"That's what she said."

"Why'd she give it to you? I mean, you didn't know about it and that's a lot of money to a college kid. She could've easily kept it for herself."

"We wondered the same thing. Vanessa was like a second daughter to us but still, we would've never known. I think she felt guilty, but John thought maybe the money was dirty, came from something illegal."

"Did you tell the cops about it?"

She lowered her head and squeezed her eyes shut as her shoulders trembled. After a few moments, she took a deep breath and looked up. "No. We were afraid. And ashamed. We didn't want to ruin Diana's memory or get Vanessa into trouble."

"I understand. What did you do with it?"

"Hold on." She got up and walked down the hallway to the left. A door opened, then silence. She returned a few moments later.

"We kept it," she said, holding a thick white envelope in her hand. "I spent half of it on John's wake, but the rest is still there. I don't want it anymore. Feels like this money is cursed. Maybe you can do something good with it."

Wynn had no need for the money, but wanted the envelope. Under the right conditions, fingerprints had been known to last as long as two years. That time had passed, but it might be worth a shot. He asked Mrs. Williams—*Call me Michelle, please*—to place the envelope on the table, and then had her get a plastic baggie to place it in. Using a spoon, he slid the envelope into the bag. Only then did he gently open the envelope, touching it through the plastic to briefly examine the bills inside. She was right. Neatly stacked. He'd bet the serial numbers were sequential as well, but didn't want to handle it that much to look.

Of course, his gentle treatment of the envelope immediately raised her suspicions. "What do you think is going on, Mr. Wynn?"

"Call me Sean, and I honestly don't know. But I agree, this is suspicious. Did Diana seem stressed or worried around the time this all went down?"

"Not beforehand. But after, well, yes. She was very upset about the shooting. About what happened to your wife."

"More than normal?"

"That's hard to say. I mean, what's normal? I only talked to her on the phone. We didn't see her in the days between."

"Who did?"

"I suppose that would be Vanessa. They lived together, went to school together. I assume she would've spent the most time around her."

"Do you happen to have her address or phone number?"

"I've got her phone number, but she moved shortly after Diana died. Didn't want to live in that same apartment, I guess. I don't know her new address. It's like we lost them both."

Wynn paused, letting her gather herself. "A phone number would be great." While she clicked through her phone, looking for the number, Wynn asked, "Did Diana have any other friends she was close to at the time? Maybe a boyfriend?"

"She had lots of friends but wasn't dating anyone special. Vanessa was her closest friend. Here's the number." She forwarded the contact information to Wynn's phone.

"Is Vanessa still in Ventura?" he asked.

"I believe she's teaching in Oxnard."

Practically next door.

Unable to think of anything else to ask, Wynn thanked Mrs. Williams for her time and got up to leave, taking the clear plastic bag with the envelope and money inside with him.

"You will let me know if something comes of all this, won't you?" she asked.

He turned as he opened the door. "Of course. Don't get your hopes up, but if something does come about, I'll be sure to let you know."

With that, he walked out into the clear, southern California sunshine, wondering about the odds of hearing about Jewel twice in two days, and how an envelope full of money found its way into the hands of a restaurant hostess.

CHAPTER 6

Wynn eased the Sportster into a small park and pulled out his phone to call Vanessa Carow. He hadn't wanted to make the call in front of Mrs. Williams' house, thereby revealing the urgency he was feeling. But he also didn't want to wait until he got back to Ventura. He tapped his clenched fist against the gas tank as the call went straight to voicemail.

"Hi, Vanessa. This is Sean Wynn. I sent you a Facebook message last night. I got your number from Diana's mom. She told me about the four thousand dollars, and I would really like to talk to you. Please give me a call as soon as you get this."

He left his number and disconnected, hoping she would call when school let out. Diana's death, and now the mysterious money, had ratcheted his spider sense to another level. He still wasn't convinced, still wouldn't allow himself to fully believe Johnson's story. But each new piece of information, no matter how obscure, seemed to support, rather than disprove what Johnson had said.

The clock on his phone read a little after eleven, meaning Lashika Collins should be at work by the time he got there. With one stop to make first, he fired up the Sportster and pushed west, his pipes thundering as he leaned into the curves of the Santa Clara River valley, this time paying no attention at all to the fruit fields on either side of the road.

————

The town of Oxnard lay directly south of Ventura, on the other side of the river's wash basin. Home to the Navy's Port Hueneme, the city had a strong military influence, very similar to Wynn's hometown of Colorado Springs. Which also meant it had neighborhoods full of 1940s-era tract housing, originally built to accommodate the families of sailors who moved in to staff the then-new base, but had now fallen into disrepair. It was in one of those neighborhoods that Wynn found the home of Jamaal Johnson's recently deceased grandmother, Eunice Johnson.

Wynn rolled to a stop in front of a small, single-story home with faded tan stucco and a dilapidated asphalt shingle roof. A thin sidewalk split the burnt-grass front yard and led from the street to two chipped-concrete steps leading to the front door. An infant's walker and several other toys lay scattered about the yard.

There was no garage, but a long cement drive extended along the right side of the house, all the way back to a fence at the rear of the property. A group of teenage guys was playing basketball in the back. An old, tan Toyota Corolla sat parked at the curb out front.

The Sportster's rumbling died away when he killed the engine, immediately drawing the attention of the guys playing ball. Wynn took off his helmet as one of the guys stepped away from the game and approached.

"What you want?"

Wynn looked the guy over. Sixteen, maybe seventeen. Shirtless and thin, but muscular, the way young guys are when their bodies are maturing faster than they can consume calories. His jeans were belted tight around his hips, his white boxers showing above.

"Is this Eunice Johnson's place?" Wynn asked.

"Who wants to know?"

"A potential buyer. I heard she passed. Wondering if the family or whoever got it might want to sell."

"Ain't nobody selling shit around here."

"Are you the owner?"

The guy stared back at him, silent and menacing. Another of the ball players, a kid of maybe thirteen or fourteen, slipped away from the group and went inside.

"I'll take that as a no," Wynn said.

The guy continued to stare when a young woman with a toddler on her hip appeared in the doorway behind him. Wynn got off the bike and brushed past the guy, then moved up the narrow sidewalk.

The girl was a study in contrasts. On the one hand, she appeared no more than eighteen years old. But on the other, her face wore the exhausted look of someone who had seen far more than their share of pain and disappointment.

Wynn took a guess at her name. "Miss Johnson?"

"Yeah?"

"I'm sorry to come by unannounced. I know your family's been going through a difficult time lately, but as I told the young man out front, I heard the previous owner, Eunice Johnson, passed away recently. Was that your grandmother?"

"Uh-huh."

"I'm very sorry for your loss. Did your parents, or maybe an aunt or uncle, inherit this place?"

"I did. My parents are gone."

"I see. I was wondering, what are your plans for the home?"

"What do you mean?"

"Well, I know it's sometimes hard to keep up on the mortgage payments on a place like this. I'd hate to see you lose it to the bank. When they come in, it's typically at a very lowball price, practically stealing the house from you. But if you wanted to sell, I'm sure you could get a very fair price for it."

"We're not selling," she said firmly. The ball players had abandoned their game and gathered in a loose circle.

"That's fine, that's fine," Wynn reassured her as he glanced around the group of young men. "You're able to make the payments?"

"There are no payments. Grands owned it free and clear."

"That's great. And the taxes and insurance? You've got all that handled?"

The kid who had gone inside now slid around from behind the girl and down the two steps until he stood in front of Wynn. "You're the one going to be needing insurance if you don't get your ass out of here."

"Shut up, Jer," the girl said. Then to Wynn, "It's handled. We're not selling, so you can go on and get back on that bike and get out of here."

A small chorus of voices mumbled in agreement.

"Alright," Wynn said. "Glad to hear it. If I may, can I get your full name? I'll pass the word that the lady of the house isn't selling and hopefully no one else will come around to bother you."

Her eyes darted over Wynn's shoulder before coming back and settling on his. "Trish Johnson."

"It's nice to meet you, Trish." Wynn reached into his jacket and pulled out a business card. "I'm Sean. If you change your mind, feel free to give me a call."

"Keep it. I won't be changing my mind."

"Well, okay then." He turned and looked at the gauntlet of young men that now stood between him and his bike. "You have a good day now."

Wynn stepped off the sidewalk and wove his way through the young bodies. He could feel their eyes on him as he brushed past. He half expected the guy who'd first approached to challenge him, but he just stood back and stared angrily. Wynn slowly put on his helmet, then swung a leg over the seat. He fired up the engine, nodded toward Trish, and rumbled away.

Grands is gone less than two months, and it's already turned into a gang house.

———

Wynn took the side streets as he rode north back to Ventura. The store Lashika Collins worked at was in the same complex as Viacci's, but a couple of blocks away, near the opposite end. Wynn parked where he had in the past, near the restaurant, then strolled up the sidewalk, willing himself to maintain a casual pace.

He spotted the store, Yvonne's, a block away across the street. Its name was spelled out in fanciful script above the doors, which were propped open with two tables set outside to lure shoppers. Wynn stayed on the opposite side of the street and walked past, looking for any sign of gang presence, inside or out. Not seeing anything on his first pass, he continued to the end of the block, crossed the street, and came back toward the store.

As he approached, he paused at one of the displays, pretending to be interested in the trinkets and baubles that littered the table. After a few moments, he went inside. He stopped at the first rack and circled around until he had a good view of the rest of the store.

A handful of shoppers were scattered throughout, as well as two girls helping customers at the cash registers. Neither was Lashika. He made his way further into the store and finally found her, arranging new merchandise near the back. He watched for a few moments, his eyes hidden behind dark sunglasses, until he was sure she was alone, then approached.

"Lashika Collins?"

The girl stopped what she was doing and turned warily toward him. "Can I help you?"

"I hope so. Do you know Jamaal Johnson?"

"Who's asking?"

"I'm an investigator, Ms. Collins. Do you know Jamaal Johnson?"

"Are you a cop?"

"No, Ms. Collins. I'm conducting a private investigation. Mr.

Johnson said you might have information about what happened the night that ended up putting him in prison."

She turned back to her work. "I don't know nothing 'bout that."

"Are you sure?"

"I'm sure."

Wynn leaned in close and whispered, "Who's going to take care of Ayel when you're in prison, Ms. Collins?"

She froze.

He continued, his voice barely a whisper. "You can either talk to me or the cops. Now me, I'm a nobody. I know whatever role you played was minor. You probably didn't even know the big picture. Just did what you were told. If so, I take that information and move on, maybe even forget where I heard it. But the cops," Wynn paused and exhaled heavily for effect, "they like to bring in everybody, make lots of arrests. Makes them look good. Maybe helps them get a raise or promotion. They don't care what it means to you or your baby, but I'd hate to see a mother and daughter get separated. Now, Jamaal tells me you invited three guys to meet you and your friends in the courtyard that night. I want to know why."

She stood frozen, staring straight past him. "I don't know nothing 'bout that." Her voice was monotone, as if repeating a well-rehearsed lie.

"Okay. I get it. But here's my number." He placed a business card in her hand. "In case you decide to remember. But don't wait too long. I've got at least five other people I'm going to ask, and I only need one to talk to me. The rest are talking to the cops. You sure you have nothing to say?"

She gave a small shake of her head.

"Call me when you do."

With that, he slipped away through the racks and out onto the sidewalk.

Wynn felt about two inches tall as he walked down the street. He hated being a bully but knew a gentler approach would yield him nothing. She had no reason to talk to him, so he had to invent one. He hoped it would work.

————

A hundred and seventy-five miles east, just off the Sonny Bono Memorial Freeway north of Palm Springs, Neil Carson and his two top chemists watched as the last of the pallets was loaded onto the truck. Each contained sixteen four-foot-tall canisters, each slightly less than a foot in diameter. The pallets were covered in white plastic shrink-wrap and labeled as liquid nitrogen, but Carson knew that was bullshit.

"We're still one short," one of the chemists said. Rick was tall, athletic, and good-looking, almost the direct opposite of his shorter, heavier, co-worker.

"It's either that or be a day late," Carson replied. "And you know how Chan feels about that. We can send the rest tomorrow." Carson turned toward Rick's co-worker, a paunchy, middle-aged guy with a receding hairline. "It will be ready tomorrow, won't it, Howard?"

"Uh, yeah...absolutely." Howard fidgeted nervously.

Looking at the two of them, Carson was reminded of the old comedy duo Abbott and Costello, but figured Rick and Howard probably wouldn't even know who they were. *Maybe Channing Tatum and Jonah Hill? Still outdated.*

"Good," Carson said. "We're going to have to work round the clock for the next week to catch up. I'll take eight to two. Rick," he said, grateful he didn't slip and call the guy Channing, "gets two to eleven, and Howard will take eleven to eight."

"Those aren't eight-hour shifts," Rick said.

"Yeah." Carson turned and walked away. "But I didn't fuck up and get us off schedule in the first place."

CHAPTER 7

WYNN STROLLED A couple of blocks up the street through the center of the mall, eventually stopping to grab coffee at a small shop. Sitting at a table outside, he reviewed what he knew, which in reality was next to nothing. Johnson's grandmother had paid off her house in full, which may have been done recently or years ago. From that info alone there was no way to tell if she'd been receiving payments as Johnson alleged. Lashika Collins, as expected, hadn't given him a thing, except for maybe acting a little more guilty than he would have thought if she truly didn't know anything.

Which left Diana Williams. Both the circumstances of her death and the mysterious envelope with four thousand dollars in it were puzzling. Could the money have been a tip or a payoff to make sure Wynn and Nicole were seated at that particular table? And if so, who paid her? Could her death have been a murder disguised as an overdose? If the ADs were dealing Jewel, could they have been the ones to supply it? Could they have had a hand in it? Very likely those answers died with Diana, but he still wanted to talk to Vanessa. Maybe Diana had let something slip. One little bit of info that could crack this thing wide open.

Or maybe Johnson was full of shit.

He'd never know without some help.

Pulling out his phone, Wynn scrolled through the contacts until he found the number for Ty "Lenny" Lenihan. He'd been the second detective on Nicole's case two years ago and was about Wynn's age, so they'd struck up a loose friendship, but hadn't talked in a couple of months. Wynn tapped the number and waited for Ty to pick up.

"Lenihan," he said by way of greeting.

"Lenny..." Wynn drew the name out.

"Wynn? What the hell, man? To what do I owe the pleasure? Heard you've become a big federal operative. Bustin' up bad guys and saving damsels in distress."

Ty must've heard about Wynn's role in bringing down a sex-trafficking ring in Wyoming a couple of months earlier. "Don't believe everything you hear. I saw a couple of things and reported them. What you'd hope anyone would do."

"Yeah, well, that's the shit urban legends are made of, and you, my friend, are becoming a legend. What can I do for you?

"I know this is gonna sound crazy, but I spoke to Jamaal Johnson the other day, and—"

"Shit, dude. Bad move. Nothing good can come of that."

"I know, I know. But listen, he gave me a story about Nicole's murder that I've been trying to check out. The reality is I'm barely scratching the surface. Nothing solid so far, but a couple of vague pieces might fit. I want to come by and lay out the details for you. There are a couple of leads I can't do anything with, but maybe with your badge, you could dig a little. Any one of these might prove his story is bullshit, and then we're done. But I've got to at least look into it."

"You really think there's something here?"

"Not really, no. But humor me. It'll eat me up if I ignore it."

They arranged a time for Wynn to come into the station the next day and then disconnected. It was now past four o'clock, so he pulled up his Facebook message app.

There was one new message. From Vanessa Carow.

Mr. Wynn, I promise I don't know anything. Please don't contact me again.

What the hell? His jaws clenched. It was short and sweet and completely unhelpful. *Why doesn't she want to talk to me?*

The phrasing was odd. *I promise I don't know anything.* What did that mean? He took a few deep breaths while deciding if or how to respond. He had hoped to keep the relationship friendly, but the message was clear she wanted no relationship at all.

It was also pretty clear a phone call wasn't going to happen. Maybe a face-to-face conversation would be best, but he didn't want her to feel stalked or intimidated. He still didn't feel good about what he'd said to Lashika Collins, and didn't want to go down that path here. He'd have to think carefully about the best way to approach her.

Setting thoughts of Vanessa Carow aside, he focused instead on the last big lead, Devon Harris, the leader of the Acid Dawn, and the link back to whoever supposedly ordered the hit. He looked up at the sky, still bright and sunny in the late afternoon. Too early to go searching. The ADs were night crawlers. He'd wait a few hours and then go out.

———

Around ten o'clock, Wynn fired up the Sportster, sure he was pissing off the neighbors, then rumbled into the night. Some things couldn't be helped.

After leaving the mall, he'd gone home, fixed dinner, and spent the next couple of hours doing research online. Jewel was a synthetic opioid that first appeared in L.A. about six years ago. Its street price had skyrocketed due to the unique, blissful high it produced, along with its relatively low supply. More recently, its price had come down, as it seemed to be more available. Still, it seemed a stretch for a struggling college student like Diana Williams to get her hands on enough "to kill an elephant," as her mother had said.

He then spent a little time studying a map of the southern part of Ventura, assumed home turf of the ADs. He also checked the various social media sites for information about Devon Harris. The fact that he couldn't find anything told him Harris was smarter than most. After an hour of mostly fruitless searching, he gave up and printed out a sheet of business cards, blank except for his phone number.

Before leaving, he climbed the stairs to his bedroom and grabbed his Glock 19. He checked the magazine and chamber, then slipped it into a holster he'd slid onto his belt. It allowed him to carry the Glock on his hip, perhaps not as hidden as inside his jacket, but more accessible. He wasn't expecting trouble, but better to be prepared.

Wynn figured the most likely place to find the ADs would be in an area north of the 101 Freeway, but south of Highway 126. Because the 101 angled to the northwest, it created a triangular area roughly two miles long on all three sides. Most of the region was filled with neighborhoods of single-family homes, but there were also apartment buildings, gas stations, grocery stores, strip malls, and shopping centers. Everything a thriving community needed.

At this time of night, most of the neighborhoods were quiet. He cruised through slowly, hoping not to wake the folks who needed to get to work in the morning, but loud enough to ensure those who were on the street knew he was there.

As he pulled into a 24-hour convenience store, he noticed a couple of young guys hanging around outside. He stopped next to a gas pump, removed his helmet, and began to fill his tank. Stealing quick glances, he could tell the two guys were watching him.

When the tank was full, he casually replaced the nozzle and the cap, then ambled over to where the two guys stood outside the store's entrance. He made eye contact with one of them and nodded. "Evening, guys."

There was no response.

"Maybe you can help me. I need to talk to Devon Harris. Wondering if you know where I can find him?"

Still nothing.

"Maybe you would know where I can score some Jewel?"

The two guys exchanged a look but remained silent.

"Tell you what," Wynn reached into his pocket and pulled out one of the cards with his phone number. "If you see him, give him my number. Have him call me."

Wynn held out the card but neither guy made any effort to take it.

"That's okay." Wynn turned and placed the card on top of a trash can next to the door. "I'll leave it here. Maybe someone else will know." Turning back to them, he said, "You guys be careful. I hear there can be some bad dudes prowling around this time of night. I'd hate for something to happen to you."

He smiled and walked back to his bike, fired it up, and rumbled away.

Over the course of the next hour, he spotted two more groups of guys and stopped both times, giving basically the same pitch and receiving basically the same response.

He was fishing, and he knew it. *But that's what fishing is. Bait some hooks, throw in a couple of lines, and hope something bites.*

A little before one in the morning, Wynn pulled into an all-night diner sitting across a parking lot from a strip mall. Lucky's. Bright light spilled from the hip-to-ceiling glass windows illuminating a row of booths just inside. Further back, two men sat at a counter while a waitress busied herself behind it, as if Edward Hopper's painting *Nighthawks* had come to life.

Perfect.

Wynn strolled inside and slid into a booth next to the window, making himself as conspicuous as possible. The Sportster was parked immediately outside the front doors, also highly visible in the wash of light.

The waitress came over with a carafe and flipped over a cup that was already on the table. "Coffee?"

"Yes, please."

"What can I get you?" she asked as she poured.

He ordered his standard breakfast—eggs over easy, bacon, and pancakes—then sat back to wait. Looking outside, it was hard to see much beyond the immediate sidewalk, the light from inside turning the glass into a mirror.

A few minutes later, the two guys at the counter looked up when three young Black men came in. The first guy strolled down the aisle and sat in the booth behind Wynn, the second took a seat at the counter opposite Wynn, and the third took a seat in the booth in front of him. Wynn looked at the two guys at the counter and slowly raised his hand from the table, nodding in a calming, *it's okay* kind of way.

The cook, a big, burly guy in a greasy white t-shirt and apron, came out from the back and stepped up to the register, his hands out of sight below the counter.

"It's okay," Wynn said to the cook. "They're friends."

As he spoke, a fourth guy came through the front door and slid into the booth across the table from Wynn. "You're looking for Hitter."

"Hitter?" Wynn asked.

"D.H."

Oh. Wynn finally got it. *D.H., as in Devon Harris. Also as in Designated Hitter, as in the designated hitman. Aren't these guys clever...* "Yeah, I am."

"Why?"

"Your boy up in the pen is telling stories. I want to know if there's any truth to 'em."

"Which boy?"

"Jamaal Johnson. Aka Jay-squared."

The guy paused, then nodded. "What kind of stories?"

"Really good ones. About murder for hire, payoffs, drugs, that sort of thing."

"What's it to you?"

Wynn shrugged. "I love a good story."

The guy smiled. "You hear that, Mikey? He likes stories."

The guy sitting at the counter across the aisle nodded.

"The problem with stories is that the good guy always wins. But that ain't real life. Especially where Hitter's concerned. He's one bad dude, and he ain't lost yet. You get messed up in one of his stories, you ain't gonna like the ending. Especially if he tells 'em to you personally."

Actually, that's exactly what I want. Wynn nodded. "Understood. I'd still love to hear them."

The guy's eyes narrowed. "Who are you?"

"Not important," Wynn said. "What is important is that if what Johnson says is true, I don't care about you or Harris or the ADs. I want to know who put you up to it. That's it. But that's me. If the cops get wind of this, which they will, they love uncovering a good conspiracy. Makes them look smart. So I'll tell you what, as an act of good faith, I'll tell you my name is Sean. You've got nothing to worry about from me, *if*," and he emphasized the word, "Harris tells me who hired you. I'll make sure the cops leave you alone. Otherwise, you can expect a lot more visits."

The guy sat silently, looking at Wynn.

"What's your name?" Wynn asked.

"Fuck off."

Wynn sighed. "You see that camera behind the register? It recorded you and your boys the moment you came in. And if you haven't heard, the state is now using facial recognition software. If you've got even a driver's license anywhere in the state in the last few years, they've got your picture, which means I can get your name with little more than a phone call. But once again, the cops are going to want to know why I'm asking, so why don't you save us both some trouble and just tell me."

The guy paused, then said, "DeAndre Renker. They call me Doc."

D.R. as in Doctor. Same format. Maybe these guys aren't so clever.

"It's a pleasure to meet you, Doc." He turned his head to the guy sitting at the counter. "And you?"

The guy looked at Doc, who nodded. "Mikey. Martin."

"Let me guess. M 'n M?"

The guy looked at Wynn blankly.

Definitely not clever. "Nice to meet you, Mikey." Turning back to Doc, Wynn said, "Tell Harris if Johnson's story is true, I've got no beef with him or the ADs or whatever else you're into. I only want the name of whoever hired you. Give me that and you won't hear from me again."

Doc sat staring at Wynn for another few moments without speaking. Finally, he pushed up off the table and said, "I'll let him know."

"I'd appreciate it."

With that, Doc turned and walked out, his companions falling in step behind. The diner turned silent as the door closed behind them.

"Mister," the cook said from behind the register, exhaling loudly, "You've got strange friends."

———

Devon Harris felt his stomach tighten as he listened to Doc and Mikey, his finger sliding idly around the edges of Wynn's card. *Fucking Jay-squared needs to keep his mouth shut.* It'd been a good deal, and Harris had delivered what he promised. Jay-squared needed to man up and hold up his end.

But that wasn't happening. Jay-squared spilled it. Everything. This biker asshole had shown up at Trish's house earlier today and now was cruising around AD turf. The only saving grace was that the biker didn't realize how much he already knew. He didn't believe Jay-squared's story.

When they finished, Harris asked, "Anything else?"

"He mentioned drugs. Seemed to know we were into it," Doc said.

"Did he say it by name?"

"Nah. Just drugs. Generically."

"He's fishing. Doesn't know shit. Give me a minute." Harris nodded toward the door.

After Doc and Mikey left, Harris pulled out his phone and dialed a number he tried calling as little as possible. He hated doing it now, especially at two in the morning. It rang several times before finally being picked up.

"We have a problem."

CHAPTER 8

ALEXANDER JAMESON PARKED his Tesla Model S in the reserved spot right outside the front doors of his two-story office building in Thousand Oaks. Early morning sunlight glinted off the dew on the charging station in front of him. He glanced at his finely manicured nails, frowned, then got out and went inside to a large, open lobby.

"Good morning, Ralph," he said to the security guard behind the counter.

"Good morning, Mr. Jameson."

"Hey, Ralph, when it dries up outside, would you plug in my car?"

"Of course, Mr. Jameson."

"Thanks." He pressed his keycard against a pad next to a door on the right side of the lobby, heard the click and went in. While the building itself contained over eighty thousand square feet of Class A office space, J&L Enterprises occupied only about ten percent, the rest rented out to a data processing company. Which was fine by him. Most of his business was run out of a small lab in Palm Springs and a warehouse down by the harbor.

The suite was dark as he strode down the hallway to his corner office. He was used to being the first one in. It gave him time to take care of matters the rest of his employees didn't need to know about.

He stepped into his office and flipped on the light.

"Good morning, Alex."

Jameson startled but recovered quickly. Stuart Legrea, a thin, wiry man, bald except for a gray goatee set against a sharp nose and chiseled cheek bones, lay on a couch in the sitting area, looking out the window.

"Your sunrises here really are quite beautiful," Stuart said, his voice silky smooth.

"Yes, they are, Stuart." Jameson stepped behind his desk. "What are you doing here?"

"A situation has arisen. Two, actually."

Jameson took off his suit jacket and put it on a hanger, then hung it on a coat tree in the corner. "What is it?"

Stuart swung his feet off the couch and moved to a chair in front of Jameson's desk. "Jay-squared is talking."

"Who?"

Stuart sighed. "Jamaal Johnson? Remember that gangbanger from two years ago? The one who's sitting up in Corcoran for the hit at the restaurant? He contacted the woman's husband and told him the whole story. Now this guy, Sean Wynn, is trying to find out if there's any truth to it. Went looking for Harris last night."

"Did he find him?" Jameson sat and leaned back in his chair, steepling his fingers in front of his chin.

"No. Harris sent one of his boys to talk to him. Wynn told the guy, the guy told Harris, Harris told me."

"Sounds like junior high."

Stuart smirked. "Better than a direct line to us."

"How much does Wynn know?" Jameson asked.

"From the point we brought in the ADs, almost all of it. Harris says he doesn't believe it. Thinks Johnson's making it up to try to bargain his way out. Wynn's looking for verification."

"Will he find it?"

Stuart crossed his legs as he adjusted his seat in the chair. He sighed heavily. "Hard to say. Pieces of it, maybe. But Harris is the only one of the ADs I've ever interacted with and even he doesn't know my real name. The dumb shit calls me Mr. S. Doesn't even know you exist."

"So if we get rid of Harris, there's no way to connect us."

Stuart exhaled slowly. "Agreed," he admitted.

"Why the hesitation?"

"Harris and his boys have been... useful. He's provided an outlet on the streets and protection to some of our shipments."

Jameson raised his eyebrows. "I thought distribution was Chan's job?"

"It is, but Harris allows us to go a little wider."

"Does Chan know?"

"He doesn't have to know everything."

"Be careful," Jameson warned. "He'll take out your eyes if he learns you're going around him. At best."

"I'm well aware of Chan's methods."

Jameson tapped his steepled fingers against his chin. "If we don't take out Harris, what are our other options?"

"I still think it's important to lay low until this HCM thing wraps up. We could keep an eye on Wynn. If he's like most people, he'll give up in a couple of days. If he doesn't, we can take him out. Poetic tragedy."

"And you like that better than taking out Harris?"

"For the time being."

"Who do we have that can provide surveillance?"

"I'm sure Chan's got guys who can do it."

"Okay, set it up. Let's see where it goes." Jameson paused. "You said there were two things?"

"Carson. Ever since we moved the lab to Palm Springs, production's been slipping. He was sixteen hours late the other day."

"Sixteen hours?"

"May not seem like much, but Chan was pissed."

"Does that have anything to do with the move?"

"That's Carson's excuse. Says the materials don't arrive on time and that's what makes him late."

"Bullshit." Jameson leaned forward and tapped the keyboard on his desk. "Talk to him. Get him back on schedule."

"How? You know we've got limited leverage with him."

"Tell him Chan will pay him a visit. That'll light a fire."

Stuart raised his eyebrows as if to say *Maybe* but didn't say anything.

Jameson nodded. "Anything else?"

"That's it."

"What about Johnson?"

"I thought that was assumed."

———

By mid-morning, Wynn pulled into the parking lot of a broad, single-story brick building barely a mile from the diner where he'd met the ADs just nine hours ago. Metal letters attached individually to the wall outside read, "City of San Buenaventura Police and Fire Headquarters." When the railroad arrived over a hundred and twenty years ago, they shortened the name to Ventura to better fit on the print schedule, but apparently, sign makers were still paid by the letter.

Taking the concrete steps two at a time, he pulled open the tinted glass door. Inside, a woman in civilian clothes looked up from a large, round reception desk. "Can I help you?"

"Sean Wynn. Here to see Detective Lenihan."

"I'll let him know."

Wynn waited less than a minute before Ty came out from a hallway. "Sean," he said with a wide grin, "it's good to see you!"

"You too, Lenny." Wynn grabbed Ty by the palm and drew him into a quick bro-hug.

Despite the fact they hadn't met until after Nicole's death,

Wynn and Ty had the kind of relationship that felt like it'd been there forever. Ty had grown up in southern California, the son of an L.A. policeman, grounded in the same sense of discipline and duty that pervaded Wynn's upbringing. Which meant, despite Ty's sometimes laid-back, surf-bum attitude, they viewed the world very similarly.

It also meant that Ty's wife, after what she viewed as an acceptable mourning period, had been trying her damnedest to set Wynn up with some of her single friends.

"You're looking good," Ty said. "You still doing that sissy kata stuff?"

He was referring to Wynn's morning workout routine, a combination of martial arts and yoga he'd been doing since his days in the service. Wynn shrugged. "It keeps my mind clear so I can deal with idiots like you."

"Yeah, we're the worst. Come on back."

Ty led Wynn down a hallway into a small conference room that held a table and six faux-leather chairs. "You want something to drink? Coffee, water?"

"No, I'm good, thanks." Wynn settled into a chair. "How are Stacey and the kids?"

"They're good. Brie just started third grade, and Matty's in first. Growing like weeds but no drama so far. How about you? You know Stacey's going to ask if you're seeing anyone."

Wynn smiled. He thought about Samantha Miller, a deputy sheriff he'd gotten to know while attending the Sturgis motorcycle rally a couple of months ago. They'd talked on the phone once or twice since he'd been back, the last time more than a month ago. They were friends, but it would never be anything more.

"Tell her yes," he lied, "but it's too soon to be thinking double dates. We're taking it slow."

"Fuck the double date, man. I'm looking for a sitter so I can take Stacey to a hotel."

Wynn laughed. "I'm available any time."

"Nah, I'm looking for a hot, young babe. Someone who'll make her jealous."

"Maybe she's thinking the same thing."

"Well, then it's not you."

Wynn laughed. It felt good, shooting the shit with someone. It's what made their friendship special. They fell into a comfortable silence. Time to get down to business.

"So, you talked to Johnson, huh?" Ty asked.

"Yeah."

"Why?"

Wynn pulled the letter from his inside jacket pocket and handed it across the table. "He sent me this."

Ty unfolded the paper and looked at the three words. "Asshole. What'd he say?"

"He said it was a hit. Some guy offered them a hundred grand to shoot Nicole and make it look like a random gang thing. Said they knew exactly where we'd be sitting, and the Vipers were planted. It was all a setup."

"Do you believe him?"

"Not really, but like I said on the phone, I have to check it out."

"What have you done?"

"For this thing to work as he said, they had to know where Nicky and I would be sitting, and it couldn't be random. We had to have been placed there. So I went back to Viacci's to see if the hostess who showed us to our table that night might still work there."

"That's a long shot. I'm surprised you remember her."

She's part of that damn dream almost every night. "Yeah. Well, that's all anyone can do. She's dead. Died of a drug overdose about a week after Nicky was killed. And there are two strange things about that. First, her mother swears she never did drugs—"

"All moms say that."

"Agreed, but her mom says she died of a Jewel overdose. Johnson says the ADs deal it."

"Jewel, huh? I thought all that was coming out of L.A., but still, could be a dozen explanations. What else?"

"This." Wynn pulled the plastic baggie containing the envelope and the money he'd gotten from Diana Williams' mom from his pocket. "Her roommate gave this to her mom when they were cleaning out her apartment. It started as four thousand dollars, but the mom used some. The roommate claims it came from tips, but the mom doesn't believe it. She was a hostess, not a waitress, so she didn't make a lot of tips. Also, by the look of it, I'm betting those bills are sequential."

"Meaning she got it all at one time. Like maybe she was the one dealing."

"Exactly."

Ty made a note on a yellow pad in front of him, then took the bag and looked at the contents. "That would make this thing close to two years old, right?"

"Yeah."

"Tough to get prints off anything that old."

"What about opioid residue?"

"Same. Has it been sealed in this bag the whole time?"

"No. I just put it in there yesterday when I got it."

"Not likely, then. We can test it, but even if we find something, it still doesn't tie it back to Nicole."

"No, it doesn't. We need the ADs to do that."

Ty's voice took on a cautious, accusing tone. "What'd you do?"

"Last night I found a couple of them. Johnson told me their leader, a guy named Devon Harris, was approached by some guy who made the offer, and even told him exactly where we'd be sitting. So I went out looking for Harris. Didn't find him, but I spoke to one of his troops. A guy named DeAndre Renker. Goes by Doc. Told him Johnson was telling stories, and I wanted to know if they were true. Left him my number, hoping he'll call."

"But he knows you're looking, and he knows why."

"Yeah."

"Shit, Sean. In police work, we usually try *not* to tell the bad guys we're coming after them."

Wynn smiled wryly. "Sorry."

"Don't worry about it. Anything else?"

Wynn told him about his conversation with Trish Johnson. "It's no Taj Mahal, but this girl couldn't have been more than twenty. And based on what I saw, I can't imagine there being a legitimate source of income. I was wondering if we could request some of the grandma's bank and utility records to compare her income and expenses. Maybe see something that doesn't fit."

Ty made another note on the yellow pad. "Okay. Is that it?"

"One more. A girl by the name of Lashika Collins. According to Johnson, she's the one who helped lure the fake Vipers to the court-yard outside Viacci's that night. She clammed up tight when I spoke to her yesterday."

"Damn, Wynn. How many people have you talked to?"

"That's it. I swear."

Ty shook his head. "Talking to the ADs and their girlfriends, that'll make you real popular."

"Let 'em bring it."

"Oh, there it is." Ty tossed his pen down, laughing. "That Marine machismo. You're still the baddest ass around, right?"

Wynn smiled and shrugged.

"Okay. For a minute, let's assume this is all true. In Detective one-oh-one, they teach us to ask a question that is a glaring hole in this case. Why? What's the motive? Why would someone target Nicole?"

Wynn shook his head. "I have no idea."

"You guys didn't owe anyone money?"

"No."

"Is it possible she kept something like that from you?"

"No way."

"Alright. I apologize but you know I have to ask: is it possible she was having an affair? Maybe with someone higher up at work?

Someone to whom a hundred grand was a lot cheaper than fifty percent of his assets if they were found out?"

Wynn had to admit he'd never considered it. The thought hadn't even crossed his mind. He loved her so much he knew he'd never cheat, and he thought she felt the same, but who knows? "She'd never given me any reason to doubt her, so no, I can't believe that's it, but I suppose anything is possible."

"But you've got no doubts?"

"No. None."

"Then don't let this asshole plant any. Don't let him stain her memory."

Wynn nodded.

"So to summarize, we've got no motive, but we do have a two year old overdose that might've been a murder, an envelope of money from the dead girl that we don't know where it came from, a dead grandma who might've had more money than she should have, and a gangbanger who might be a dealer and his girlfriend. Is that about right?

Wynn sighed. He knew it sounded crazy. "Yeah."

"If you weren't my brother-from-another-mother, I'd throw your ass out of here, you know that, don't you?"

"Yeah, but I am your brother," Wynn coaxed.

"Shit... I'm making no promises. I'll dig around a little. See what I can find."

"Great. I appreciate it. Thanks."

"In the meantime, you lay low. Don't go talking to anyone or stirring this thing up. More than likely it's all bullshit, but let's not cloud the waters, okay?"

Wynn raised his palms reluctantly. "I'll stand down. For now."

Ty laughed and shook his head. "You sure you don't want to tell me about this girl you're seeing?"

"Nope."

"Is she hot?"

"My lips are sealed."

"It's her lips I'm wondering about."

Wynn laughed. "Go home to your wife."

They said their goodbyes, and Wynn walked out to his bike. While patience was not in his nature, he'd learned that sometimes it was needed, so he did what Ty asked. He went home, parked the Sportster in the driveway, then pulled out a bucket, a hose, and some rags, and went to work washing the few days' dirt off the bike. He'd been warned when he bought it that there was something about Harleys. Where most people didn't care about a little dirt, something about a Harley made you want to keep it clean, keep the dust off the chrome. He finished up the Sportster, and decided to wash the Lexus also, and then, for the hell of it, the Street Glide.

When he was finally finished, and the afternoon sun had begun its downward arc toward the horizon, Wynn put everything away and closed the garage door. He went through the house and out the back, down the dock, then hopped into his dinghy and sailed across the harbor in search of a quiet place for a drink and a mid-afternoon lunch.

CHAPTER 9

L I S A T I N his car a block away from Wynn's house, examining the bullet slug he had taken from the warehouse two days earlier. *Stupid son-of-a-bitch. He should have known not to try to blame Carson. Even when it is someone else's fault, Chan expects all his people to take personal responsibility.* The slug made a dull tinkling sound when it dropped into the baggie with more than a dozen others, each representing a lesson Mr. Chan was attempting to teach.

In the rearview mirror, an elderly couple approached from behind. Li made sure his AirPods were visible, then started singing, hoping to appear like any normal teenager. Which was odd, considering he was closer to thirty than twenty. For whatever reason, puberty just hadn't had that much effect on him. And while there weren't many advantages to being a man trapped in a teenager's body, it did allow him to sing along with Journey's Steve Perry in perfect pitch.

His phone rang, interrupting his private concert. "Yeah?"

His partner Xiang's voice came through the earbuds. "He's gone."

"I didn't see him leave."

"He came out the back door a few minutes ago. Got into a tin can of a boat and cruised away. He's gone."

"You're sure?" Li pulled the handle and climbed out of the car.

"Definitely. I can still see his wake. Doesn't mean there isn't someone else home."

"Stuart says he lives alone. Keep an eye out and let me know if he comes back."

"How long is this gonna take?"

"Ten minutes, if it works."

Li walked up Wynn's driveway and dug around in the bushes next to the concrete, eventually pulling out the small black box he'd hidden there earlier.

"You want to explain to me exactly how you're getting in, again?" Xiang asked.

"It's called a RollJam. Most garage door openers use rolling codes these days, right? To prevent people from stealing the signals. My magic box here gets around that. When he came home, he pressed the button on his remote to open the garage door. But he probably didn't realize he had to hit it twice. The first time, this thing jammed the receiver and stole the code. Now, when I press the button, the opener should recognize it as legit."

"You're lucky he carries a remote on his bike."

"A guy like that? No doubt about it. Now let's see if this thing works." Li pressed a button on the device and the garage door rolled up. "Boo-yah."

"Aren't you clever..."

"More like brilliant, my man."

"Where do you learn this shit?"

"It's called the internet. Maybe if you used it for something besides porn, you'd learn something."

"Your girlfriend likes what I've learned."

"You wish." Li went inside, opened the Lexus' door, and found the garage remote. He pressed the button and a little green LED flashed on his device. *Might need this later.* He pressed the button again, and the garage door closed.

"Why are we watching this guy, anyway?" Xiang asked.

"Stuart said to keep an eye on him."

"Yeah, but what's Stuart's interest?"

"Don't know, don't care. But it must be important. Stuart went straight to Mr. Chan with this one, and Chan said do it, so here we are."

Li got down on his knees and crawled under the Lexus, placing a magnetic GPS tracker on the towing frame underneath. He then took a screwdriver from the workbench and removed the seat from the Sportster and wired another tracker directly to the motorcycle's battery, hiding it in the small space beneath the seat. Five minutes later, the Street Glide had one also.

Li opened the app on his phone and saw three red dots on a map, exactly where they were supposed to be, in Wynn's garage next to the water.

"You there?" Li asked.

"Yeah."

"Check the app. Make sure you can see them."

There was a slight delay, then Xiang said, "Looks good. You done?"

"Hold on. I want to check this place out." Li pulled a Ruger from the back of his jeans and checked the door leading from the garage into the house. Locked. *Gotta be an entrance out back.* He stepped over to a door leading to the side yard.

He made his way around the house to a large patio overlooking the harbor. He strolled across the terrace like he belonged there, until he came to a pair of sliding glass doors. Also locked. *Damn, this guy's careful.* He put his hands to the glass and peered inside but saw nothing unusual. He sighed and stepped away from the glass.

Glancing left, he spotted Xiang sitting on a bench under a tree across the water. "Glad to see you're working hard. Next time I get the park bench and you can sit in a hot car all afternoon."

"Wouldn't matter. I can't do what you do so you'd have to be there anyway."

Li looked to his right and noticed a large cabin cruiser tethered to the neighbor's dock. "What kind of boat did you say he left in?"

"A dinghy, man. Couldn't seat more than three people."

Li paused. "Why would a guy own a house on the water if he doesn't have a decent boat?"

"No idea."

"Do we need to put a tracker on it?"

"Nah. He can't go far in that thing."

Li took one last look at the neighbor's boat. *Gotta get me one of those.* He made his way around the side of the house to the garage, where he pressed the button on the wall and the garage door slid up. He stepped outside, hit the 'Enter' button on the keypad, and the door closed. "Then we're all done."

"Cool. Pick me up near the restrooms. I gotta take a leak."

———

It had taken Stuart Legrea over three hours to cross the northern edge of the Los Angeles basin from the J&L offices in Thousand Oaks to Palm Springs. Why Carson had insisted on relocating the lab out to this decaying, former playground-of-the-stars made no sense. Maybe it had something to do with Carson's new girlfriend. Mr. Jameson had told him she was a hot young thing, close to thirty years Carson's junior. With so many retirees moving here, maybe Carson wanted to look young by comparison. The fact that it was two hours further away from Chan was its only redeeming quality.

After stopping at the lab and being told that Carson had already left for the day, Stuart drove to his house and parked in the circular driveway of a white, Spanish-style, two-story with a red tile roof.

No wonder he's behind schedule. He's only working half days.

Stuart purposefully hadn't called to tell Carson he was on his way. Just as he'd done in Jameson's office this morning, he liked to show up unexpectedly. It kept people off balance, which could be useful. He followed a red brick walkway to the front and put his ear to the door. Hearing nothing, he used a key that Carson didn't know he had to unlock the deadbolt and let himself in.

Once inside, he quietly closed the door and paused to listen. Still hearing nothing, he made his way through the house to the kitchen, where a set of sliding glass doors led to a patio and pool outside.

Beyond the glass, beneath the shade of a large umbrella, Carson stood with his back to Stuart, his swim trunks bunched around his ankles, the bare feet of a young woman on either side of his legs as she knelt backward on a pool chair. Thankfully, the long tail of Carson's unbuttoned Hawaiian shirt covered his ass as it jerked back and forth. That was not something Stuart needed to see.

Stuart paused and shook his head, then opened the slider and stepped out. He cleared his throat loudly. "Neil?"

Carson leaped back as if the girl were suddenly electric. He frantically pulled up his trunks as he turned to see who was there. Stuart stifled a laugh as Carson stumbled about.

"Shit, Stuart! How about a little privacy?"

A curvaceous blonde, naked, stepped off the chair and nonchalantly reached for a cover-up.

Stuart shook his head. "You know, I told Mr. Jameson if he let you come out here, you'd spend all your time fucking around. Guess I was right."

"I'm on my own damn time in my own damn house, Stuart. I can do what I want. How'd you get in here?"

"The front door was unlocked. I thought maybe you were back here but couldn't hear me. Apparently, I was right about that, too."

The blonde slipped the cover-up on, but it was badly misnamed. It was sheer, white, and perfectly see-through. It didn't cover anything.

Stuart turned to the blonde. "Forgive me for interrupting, my dear, but since Neil seems to have forgotten his manners, let me introduce myself. I'm Stuart, one of Neil's co-workers." He held out his hand.

The blonde giggled and jiggled. "I'm Jasmine." She took his hand.

"Of course you are." Stuart covered her hand with his and smiled. "It's a pleasure to meet you."

"Jaz, go inside," Carson said.

"It's nice to meet you, too." Jasmine smiled as she withdrew her hand, turned around and bent to pick up her swimsuit, then went inside.

"What do you want, Stuart?"

"Just a friendly visit."

"We're not friends, Stuart. Co-workers with mutual interests at best."

"That hurts, Neil. After all I've done for you."

"I've done plenty for you, too."

"True, but I don't remember *you* ever dressing up like a deliveryman to get rid of a body." Stuart remembered the night clearly. Carson had been an arrogant prick then, and he wasn't any better now.

"That was three years ago," Carson said. "I've paid you back plenty since then."

"Regardless. You still have obligations. Like delivering your product on time."

"I have been. We sent a shipment yesterday."

"But you were a pallet short. And before that, you were sixteen hours late. Mr. Chan is not happy."

"Fuck him. He's getting what he needs."

"That's not a very team-oriented attitude, Neil. We all need to do our part. What would happen if all of a sudden Mr. Chan couldn't distribute all you produced? Or if Mr. Jameson couldn't secure the raw materials? This little gravy train would run right off the tracks."

"The only reason Chan's able to sell so much is because of the quality of the product *I* produce." Carson jabbed his finger down onto a table. "He, hell, all of you, would have nothing if it weren't for me."

Stuart smiled. "True. You are an artist, and we appreciate that. How are Rick and Howard coming along?"

"They're imbeciles."

"Then I guess we're lucky we have you."

"Don't forget it," Carson said.

"But we still have a problem with getting the product on time."

"He'll get it."

Stuart paused. "Maybe I should let you and Chan work it out directly."

Carson was silent. Chan's methods of dealing with problems were well known. After a long moment, Carson said, "We moved the lab out here to keep him away from me. I expect you to continue to do so. Next week he'll have the full order, on time."

"Perfect. Manufacturing and distribution, both working in perfect harmony. Mr. Jameson will be so pleased."

CHAPTER 10

ZANE SAT ON a steel bench, leaning against the chain-link fence, scanning his domain. The basketball game in front of him had been going for almost forty-five minutes, the mid-afternoon sun baking the court. The shirts had been getting their asses kicked by the skins, but were slowly coming back, making a game of it. The intensity of the match surprised him. A crowd of inmates had formed on either side of the court, cheering on their chosen side, making vulgar references about the wives and moms of those on the other.

He scanned the perimeter of the yard. The guards stood nonchalantly in pairs outside the fence, paying little attention. Next, he looked for the kid, finally spotting him hanging back, away from the court, like he always did. Zane glanced toward the game, caught a player's eye, and nodded. Moments later, the player drove to the hoop, then went down hard, grabbing his ankle and wheezing in pain.

One of his teammates, a guy covered in tattoos, knelt beside the injured player. "Can you go?"

"I don't think so."

"Then you're done," said a guy on the opposing team. "You forfeit. It's over."

"Fuck that. Where's Jay-squared? He's in."

A chorus of voices took up the call. "Jay-squared! Hey, Jay-squared! Get your ass in here. We need a sub."

The kid looked scared and confused as the crowd parted, creating a path straight from where he stood on the outskirts directly to the court.

One of the skins trotted over to him. "C'mon, man. I've seen you play. You got game. We need you."

Just as Zane had planned, with all eyes on him, the kid had no real choice. He took off his shirt and followed the other player onto the court. They allowed him a few moments to warm up, then the game resumed.

The skins took the ball at the top of the key and passed it around while the shirts left the kid wide open, virtually unguarded. When the kid finally got the ball, his teammates yelled, "Drive! Drive!" He dribbled the ball twice as he drove to the basket, where all five shirts converged, fists, knees, and elbows battering the kid brutally as he went up for the shot. The kid crumpled to the ground, his nose bleeding, his eye swelling.

"Welcome to the league, kid," one of the shirts said. "Now get your ass up."

The beating, disguised as a basketball game, continued for the next ten minutes, his teammates setting him up, the shirts delivering the blows. Elbows to the face. Knees to the groin. Fingers crushed under stomping feet. At one point he tried to crawl away, but the crowd forced him back to the court. He was bloody, bruised, and exhausted. And completely alone.

Zane didn't know much about the kid but wondered what he'd done to become a target. Not that it mattered. Word had come in with the first batch of visitors this morning, and when a job came up, you did it. Regardless of who it was. And the instructions had been clear: Get it done now.

He knew the kid worked in the laundry, but so many jobs had been done in there over the years that the guards now had cameras covering every inch of the place. Besides, over time he'd gotten bored with the quick hit. He'd developed. Evolved. Now he wanted to have fun with his targets. There was so little entertainment to be had on the inside. And when the fun was over, he wanted to finish the job with finesse and stealth. Ninja style.

The kid's shirt was pressed into Zane's hand, a nine-inch shiv wrapped inside. He hefted himself from the bench and slowly made his way courtside. He waited, making sure everyone knew he was there, then nodded.

The court erupted. Inmates from both sides swarmed forward, kicking and screaming, swinging their fists in a giant melee. Zane eased up next to the kid who was doubled over, held upright by two teammates. Surrounded by a frenzy of bodies, he jammed the shiv upward, straight into the center of the kid's chest, then twisted it like a joystick. The kid's shirt, still wrapped around the weapon, absorbed the small spray of blood. Eventually, he let go, dropping the shiv and the kid onto the court.

Zane slid away through the crowd before the guards even opened the gate. Within seconds the fighting ended, the combatants slipping away, disappearing inside. An eerie stillness settled over the yard, leaving Jay-squared lying dead beneath the hoop.

Alexander Jameson felt the phone vibrate in his pocket. It was approaching five o'clock.

About damn time.

He excused himself from the conference room meeting and stepped into the hallway. "Please hold." He strode to his office, closing the door behind him. "Status?"

"It's done," Stuart said.

"Which one?"

"Both. Carson and Wynn."

"Excellent. Did Carson make any more threats?"

"No." Stuart laughed slightly. "I caught him in a compromising situation. He was in no position to threaten."

"Good. And Chan's guys will keep track of Wynn?"

"Already doing it."

"Okay, good. I've been thinking. If one of Harris' guys is talking, how safe do we feel about the others?"

"Remember, the one that talked was in prison trying to negotiate his way out. The others have no reason to talk."

"Understood, but it wouldn't hurt to reiterate the importance of that to Harris."

"I'll take care of it. And by the way, Johnson is taken care of."

Jameson smiled. "As you said earlier, that was assumed."

———

Devon Harris's heart froze when he saw the number ringing on his phone. *The only thing worse than calling this guy is getting a call from him.*

"Hello?"

"Devonnnn..." In one word, the voice was smooth and silky and menacing. Harris couldn't believe a guy that skinny could have such an intimidating voice. "I assume you've heard?"

"Heard? No, sir. Heard what?"

"Your buddy. Jay-squared. He's got a new nickname. Now they call him Jay-six."

Harris was silent.

"As in six feet under, Devon."

A lump rose in Harris's throat. "Oh. Yeah."

"Now Devon," Stuart continued, "I seem to recall you assuring me that your crew wouldn't talk, but Jay-squared did, and that cost me a favor."

"I'm sorry, sir."

"Favors of this caliber are hard to come by, you know that, right?"

"Yes, sir."

"So I need you to do something for me, Devon. And this is very important so I'm going to lay it out in easy steps. Are you ready?"

"Yes, sir."

"First, I need you to go through your little list of accomplices there, and identify anyone who might know anything about what happened that night. Can you do that?"

"Yes, sir."

"Good. Second, I need you to talk to these people and make sure they keep their mouths shut. Because if they don't, Devon, not only are they going to get the same treatment as Jay-squared, but I'm going to hold you personally responsible. Understand?"

"Yes, sir."

"That's good. Now Devon, I don't want to put you in an uncomfortable position, so here's the third and final step. If you have any doubts about any of your people, you don't have to do a thing. You just give me their names, okay?"

"Yes, sir."

"Good. That's good. I'll expect to hear back from you tomorrow."

"Yes, sir." Devon stayed on the line until the other end disconnected. He exhaled loudly and set the phone down, then rubbed his hands across his face.

Besides Jay-squared, there were only three other people who knew anything at all about the AD's role in the hit two years ago. He could trust Doc, but who knows what Trish Johnson would do? She'd already asked Doc where last month's cash was.

And then there was Lashika. The bitch had broken up with him a month after the shooting and taken up with one of the dudes that was supposed to be a decoy.

Even had his kid.

Depending on how much Jay-squared said, she could be a problem.

CHAPTER 11

Wynn awoke early the next morning, scenes from the restaurant on his last night with Nicole haunted his sleep. But now there were new scenes. Flashes of images he'd never seen before. A frowning waitress. A foreboding face. In the past, the dreams had always been peaceful until the shooting started, but now, he was tense, anxious, suddenly aware of unseen dangers the moment they walked in.

He got up and went outside to his patio overlooking the harbor. He spent the next forty-five minutes going through his morning kata, the combination of martial arts and yoga that Ty had called sissy. Funny how he could always keep up with Ty's workouts, but Ty never wanted to try the kata. Some people just didn't get it.

Afterward, he showered, fixed breakfast, and was finishing the dishes when his phone rang. It was Ty.

"What's up? You got something for me?"

"There's been a development," Ty said.

"What happened?"

"Johnson. He was killed up in Corcoran yesterday."

"I'll be right there."

———

Thirty minutes later, Wynn was seated in the same small conference room as yesterday. They were joined by Ty's boss, Lieutenant Lou Akins, and another detective, Ian Gruebauer, from the Gang Crimes Unit. Wynn had met Akins before, but didn't know Gruebauer. Ty had been laying out the case, hoping to get Akins' permission to open an investigation.

"Johnson was pointing at Harris as the key to this thing," Ty said. "He's the obvious and most direct route to find out if there's any truth to this, assuming we can both find him and get him to talk."

Akins turned to Gruebauer. "What do you think?"

Gruebauer nodded toward Wynn. "Shouldn't we have this conversation in private?"

"Mr. Wynn is a known entity," Akins said. "For purposes of this conversation, he's clear. Go ahead."

"We've been watching Harris on and off for over eight years." Gruebauer laid out more than a dozen eight-by-ten photos on the table. "Back when he was a juvie. He was a suspect in a couple of murders, but we could never pin anything on him. He's dropped out of sight the last few years. It appears the ADs are taking their orders from the guy Mr. Wynn met the other night, DeAndre Renker, a.k.a. Doc. Honestly, we thought maybe Harris was one of the lucky ones who found a way out."

Wynn thumbed through the photos. Most of them were taken at a distance, at night. They showed Harris walking down the street or hanging around outside a convenience store with other ADs. One showed an apparent drug deal going down, while another showed him talking with some guy in a suit, probably another drug deal, but not as obvious. Only one photo zoomed in close enough to get a good look at his face.

"Johnson said the ADs were dealing Jewel," Wynn said, holding up one of the pictures. "Is that what this is?"

Gruebauer shrugged. "Could be."

"When were these taken?" Wynn asked.

"Various times. The oldest is probably five years ago, the newest maybe two. Like I said, he's been quiet lately."

"Since right about the time of Nicole's murder," Ty said.

"Doesn't mean it's connected," Akins said.

"Understood. And if it weren't for what happened to Johnson yesterday, I wouldn't even be bringing it to you. But what's the first rule you taught me?"

Akins sighed. He was older, mid-sixties, probably only a few years away from retirement. He had a fatherly, paternal air about him. Patient. Always teaching. Wynn could tell he hated having his own words thrown back at him. "There are no coincidences," he said.

"That's right," Ty said, pressing his point. "But it'll stay a coincidence until we can find some hard evidence. This thing is going to come down to money. It always does. Let me request a subpoena to get the grandma's bank and financial records. Let's find out how that house got paid off. If it's innocent, then we drop it, but if we find something, we might be able to use it as leverage to get Harris to talk."

Ty let that last idea hang in the air.

"That's assuming you can find him," Akins said. "Grueb?"

"If he's still in the area," Gruebauer said, "we'll find him. But we've got our eyes on this 'Doc' guy and the ADs for other things. I don't want to fuck that up chasing this bullshit."

"Then let's start with the grandma's bank records," Ty suggested.

Akins paused. "Alright," he finally agreed. "You can open it, but on a limited basis. Let's check out the grandmother's finances and see if there's anything there. But Mr. Wynn, I hope you'll understand. We'll look into it, but if there's nothing here, we can't go chasing ghosts."

Wynn nodded. "I understand."

"And further," Akins continued, "You are *not* an official part of this investigation. If you want to help Ty look through the lady's finances, that's fine. But otherwise, you need to stand down and let us handle it. Understood?"

Wynn nodded.

Addressing Ty, Akins said, "Then get to it."

Ty bolted from his chair and tapped Wynn on the shoulder, indicating he should follow. He strode out of the conference room and down a hallway to his small office.

"Close the door." Ty sat down at his desk.

Wynn did so, then pulled up a chair. "What are we doing?"

"I've got to open the investigation so we can get a case number. Only takes a minute." Ty tapped the keyboard for a few minutes, then wrote down a number on a piece of paper. "Alright. First thing is to search the county's probate records. I'm assuming Eunice Johnson didn't do a lot of estate planning, meaning there should be some info in the system about her assets, bank accounts, et cetera. Probate is a public process, so we don't even need a warrant."

"She just died last month. You think it's there already?"

"You said it yourself yesterday. The granddaughter has no visible means of support. If grandma died at ten, they were probably filing paperwork to get access to her bank accounts by eleven. I'm sure it took a few days, but I'll bet a file is open."

Ty worked the keyboard while Wynn sat in silence.

"Bingo."

"You found it?" Wynn asked.

"Yep." Ty paused as he scanned the screen. "She did her banking at First National, had the house and a few bills. Doesn't look like much else."

"Balances are helpful, but Johnson said they were paying her two grand a month. We're gonna need statements over time to try and spot either those deposits or some other trend."

"We'll want to go back several years before Nicole's murder. That'll allow us to establish a baseline and see if it changes after he took the plea."

"Sounds good," Wynn agreed.

"We'll need to get a subpoena. Judges are a lot more likely to grant one on a current case when someone's in imminent danger, rather than an old one. You think it's fair to assume the granddaughter, Trish, might be in danger?"

Wynn thought about it. Johnson was likely killed because he talked when there was no more money coming in. No reason to think Trish might not do the same. "If there's really something here, absolutely."

Wynn sat impatiently for the next twenty minutes, while Ty did the paperwork and made a couple of phone calls to request a meeting with a judge.

"Judge Thompson's pretty good," Ty said, hanging up the phone. "Usually friendly to what we need. Hopefully, we can get in this morning."

Five minutes later, the paperwork was printing out when Ty's phone buzzed. He hit a button to put it on speaker. "Yeah?"

A female voice filled the room. "Judge Thompson can see you at ten-fifty. He only has ten minutes, so you need to be quick."

"We will. Thanks, Jean." Ty disconnected and glanced at the time. He quickly reviewed the paperwork and put it into a manila file folder. Then he opened a drawer and pulled out the plastic baggie containing the envelope and money Wynn had gotten from Michelle Williams. "We've got about a half-hour. Come on."

Ty led Wynn down a hallway and into a large bullpen area. "This is our crime analysis unit." He weaved through rows of cubicles, finally stopping at a cube where a young, skinny, dark-haired guy sat. "Jason. Just the man I'm looking for."

Jason turned away from his computer screen. His face was pock-marked with acne scars. "Oh. Hey, Ty. What's up?"

"This," Ty said, holding up the baggie. "I've got a challenge for you."

"Oh, yay," Jason said with a sarcastic lack of enthusiasm. He took the bag. "What's the story?"

"I need you to look for three things. First, we're looking for some old fingerprints."

"How old?"

"More than two years."

"That's tough."

"I know, but there's more. You'll probably find at least three other prints..."

"Four," Wynn interjected. "Vanessa and all three Williamses. I'm sure John would have handled it before he passed."

"Right. Four other prints of people we know have handled that envelope that are newer, one of which is only a few days old. We'll leave you the names of these folks. We're looking for prints that don't belong to those four."

Ty picked up a small notepad sitting on Jason's desk and handed it to Wynn. "Write down the names for him." Turning back to Jason, he said, "Second, also check the bills and the envelope for any traces of opioids."

"Drug money?"

"Maybe."

"Okay. How was it stored?" Jason asked.

Ty looked at Wynn.

"I think it was stuffed in a drawer most of the time," Wynn said. "I know it had been handled about a year ago, but other than that I think it just sat."

"That helps, but I can't make any promises on something this old. You said there were three things?"

"Yeah. See if you can track down any of those bills, find out where they came from. They've been out of circulation about the same two years."

Jason shook his head. "Not asking for much, are you?"

"Work your magic," Ty said.

They walked back to Ty's office, picked up the subpoena paperwork, and headed out to Ty's car for the short drive over to the courthouse.

"When we get there," Ty said, "why don't you wait downstairs while I go see the judge. If you go, he'll ask what your involvement is, and it'll get complicated. Best to avoid that."

Wynn agreed, so when they got to the courthouse, Ty took the elevator to the judge's chambers on the third floor, while Wynn got coffee at a small cafeteria and settled in to wait. With time on his hands, he opened the Facebook app on his phone and pulled up Vanessa Carow's profile. Her public page didn't expressly indicate which school in Oxnard she worked at, but scrolling through her timeline he found several recent references to Christa McAuliffe Elementary. Odds were pretty good that was the place.

Fifteen minutes after Wynn sat down, Ty came striding back up the hallway.

"We got it. Let's go."

———

Three hours later, they were back in the small conference room, Eunice Johnson's bank records spread out on the wooden table. From the courthouse, they had taken the subpoena to the First National bank branch closest to Eunice's house. The branch manager was cooperative but insisted on getting his own compliance manager's approval before gathering the records, then needed time to collect everything they requested. Ninety minutes after arriving at the branch, they finally left with almost ten years' worth of Eunice's banking history.

"Let's start three years before Nicole's murder," Ty said as they spread the paperwork out. "If we need to go back further, we can, but that should be enough to establish some kind of pattern."

The story it told was sad. Eunice was seventy-one when she passed away, having retired four years earlier from a job with a local manufacturer. Her only sources of income were Social Security and withdrawals from a small IRA. She'd paid off the mortgage when she retired, but they were unable to verify the source of funds. Probably with money taken from a 401(k), but it didn't matter, as it was done well before Nicole's murder.

An hour after they'd begun, Ty had his head down, examining a pair of statements. "I think I've got something. Come look at this."

Wynn walked around the table and leaned over Ty's shoulder.

"These are her monthly checking account statements the year before Nicole's murder. Notice the total amount of withdrawals each month. Around two thousand dollars, give or take every month. See?"

Wynn looked through the statements. "Okay…"

"Now look at these, the year after the murder. It declines each month until it gets down to around eight hundred, then levels off."

Wynn saw it immediately. "So what isn't she buying anymore?"

Ty set two statements, one older and one newer, side-by-side on the table, and looked closer at each line item. "She stopped buying groceries, gas…"

"Things you can easily buy with cash."

"Looks like it."

Wynn glanced at the time, a little after three in the afternoon. "Listen. I think I found where Vanessa Carow works. At McAuliffe Elementary. I want to run over there and see if I can talk to her. Find out if Diana said anything about how she got that four grand."

"Alright. Let me put this stuff away."

"I got it. You stay here and keep digging."

"What part of 'not an official part of this investigation' is not clear to you?"

Wynn rolled his eyes. "I came to you to move this thing along faster."

"Fine. I'll get Jason to keep working on these while we go. Will that help?"

Wynn shook his head and sighed.

CHAPTER 12

T y d r o v e W y n n in his unmarked Ford south on Victoria Avenue to McAuliffe Elementary, rolling into a parking lot that was about half full. Assuming Vanessa Carow worked here, it looked like a fifty-fifty chance she would still be around. Several kids, sitting by themselves or in small groups on the grass in front of the school, watched as they walked by.

"Even the kids can tell you're a cop," Wynn said.

"Or that you're a douchebag," Ty shot back.

Wynn smiled and pulled open the door. Once inside, they stepped into an administrative office next to the entry. A middle-aged woman sat behind a desk.

"Can I help you?"

"We're looking for Vanessa Carow," Wynn said.

"Are you a parent?"

"No. Just an old friend."

"Okay. Let's have you sign in, and I'll call down to make sure she's available."

"That's alright," Wynn said while picking up a pen. "I'd kind of like to surprise her."

"I'm sorry, but with all that's happened over the years, we don't do surprises here. I'm sure you understand."

Ty stepped forward and flashed his badge. "Yes. We certainly do. I'm Detective Lenihan with the Ventura PD. We have a few questions we'd like to ask Miss Carow regarding a cold case we're working. It has nothing to do with your students or the school, and she's done nothing wrong. Just a few routine questions. If you could point us to where she is, we'd appreciate it."

The woman looked stunned for a moment, then said, "Room one-sixty-three. Across the commons, down the hall on the left."

They thanked her as they left, then followed the directions down the empty, carpeted hallway. Wynn stopped when they were two rooms away. "Listen, people tend to get weird around cops, filter what they say. She's already expressed some reluctance to talk to me, and I don't want her clamming up because there's a cop in the room. Let me go in and talk to her first and then I'll bring you in."

"Maybe she'd prefer to talk to a cop."

"Maybe, and we can go that way if she doesn't talk to me, but we can't go back if we play that card first."

Ty nodded. "Okay."

They proceeded down the hall and stopped outside the room. The door was propped open. Wynn paused for a moment and listened to make sure he wasn't interrupting anything. Hearing nothing, he rapped his knuckles on the door and stepped inside. "Vanessa Carow?"

A young woman looked up from her desk across the room, the expression on her dark complexion conveying both confusion and annoyance. She appeared to be grading papers, no doubt wanting to get it done so she could go home. "Yes?"

"Hi. I'm Sean Wynn." He extended his hand as he strode over.

The confusion turned to recognition as her eyes opened wide and she shrunk away. Wynn picked up on it and stopped short, retracting his hand and stuffing it into his pocket. "I'm sorry for barging in like this, but your message confused me. I was hoping we could talk for a minute."

She exhaled hesitantly and put her pen down, then pushed away from the desk and folded her arms. "About Diana?"

"Yeah. And the four grand you gave to her parents."

"I told you, I don't know anything about it."

"Her mom said you two were best friends. I thought she might've said something."

"Nope. Not a word."

Wynn was confused. He still couldn't understand her attitude. Concerned he might be intimidating her, he pulled out one of the child chairs and sat down, his knees rising to his chest. He felt silly. "If she didn't say anything, how'd you know she had it?"

"I found it. After she died."

"Uh-huh. Where?"

"In her room. That night... I couldn't believe she was gone. I went into her room to be around her things, tried to feel close to her. It was just sitting there, on her dresser."

Wynn squirmed in the small seat. "And she never mentioned it? Never told you where she got it?"

"Not a word."

"Didn't you wonder?"

Vanessa shrugged. "I figured it was tips from the restaurant."

"In a nice, neat stack like that?"

"Maybe she exchanged it at the bank."

"Or maybe she got it doing something else," Wynn suggested. "Something her parents, or maybe the cops, wouldn't approve of?"

"I wouldn't know." Vanessa tightened her grip on her crossed arms.

Wynn paused. "How long were you two roommates?"

"Three years."

"So you knew her pretty well?"

She shrugged. A tiny sheen of perspiration appeared on her forehead.

"C'mon. You had to have gone out together. Group dates? Parties?"

"Sometimes." Her eyes darted to the doorway.

Wynn turned and looked over his shoulder, expecting to see Ty. No one was there.

"Listen, Vanessa. I'm not here to hassle you or cause trouble. I'm just trying to find out what happened to my wife. I don't care if you and Diana were dealing drugs, or robbing banks, or turning tricks, I just need to know where she got the money."

"I told you I don't know! Now would you please leave."

Wynn sat, curious. Her reaction was way out of context for the situation. He leaned forward. "What are you afraid of?"

A tear leaked from her eye. "I swear. I don't know anything." She was trembling.

Wynn looked at her silently for a moment, then called over his shoulder, "Ty!"

Ty stepped through the doorway. Vanessa's eyes popped wide and her jaw dropped. She jumped out of her chair and stood behind it, then started crying. "Oh, no. No. I swear. I don't know anything. Don't hurt me."

Sitting cramped in the child's chair as he was, Wynn wasn't sure how he could hurt anyone.

"Whoa, whoa, whoa," Ty said as he reached into his pocket and pulled out his badge, "No one's going to hurt you." He shot Wynn a dark look. "I don't know what my friend here said, but I can assure you, no one's going to hurt you."

Vanessa saw the badge and relaxed a little. She sniffled. "You're a cop?"

"Detective Ty Lenihan. Ventura PD."

"How do I know that's real?"

"Look it up." Ty nodded toward her computer. "My picture's on our website."

Leaning over the back of the chair, she reached toward the desk and tapped the keyboard.

Ty caught Wynn's eye and silently mouthed, *What did you do?*

Wynn opened his eyes wide as he shrugged.

"What did you say your name was?" Vanessa asked.

"Ty Lenihan."

"Detective?"

"That's me."

She dropped her head to the desk, let out a deep breath and groaned. "I am so embarrassed."

Ty smiled. "We're good then?"

"Yeah. We're good."

Ty put his badge away and took a deep breath. "You want to tell me what this knucklehead said that got you so upset?"

Vanessa spun her chair around and sank into it, then pulled herself tight up to the desk and buried her face in her hands, elbows on the desk. She sat that way a long moment, until finally she looked up and stared straight at Wynn.

He could feel her eyes boring into him. Thinking. Considering.

After another long moment, she whispered, "It wasn't you?"

"Wasn't me, what?"

She turned toward Ty. "Diana told me the night before the shooting that some guy came in. He asked if she had a reservation for a couple celebrating their anniversary the next night, then gave her five thousand dollars to make sure they got that specific table. Said he wanted to make their night special. After the shooting, she thought it was crazy bad luck, but then she began to wonder if it'd been set up. She freaked out, thinking she'd helped get that poor lady killed."

Vanessa looked back at Wynn. "She thought you did it."

"What? That's insane. She saw me. She knew I wasn't the guy who gave her the money."

"She thought maybe he was a friend of yours. That you set it up."

Wynn couldn't stay folded in the little chair any longer. He squirmed his way out and began pacing. "And six days later she OD'd?"

Vanessa laughed. "Yeah, right."

He spun around to face her. "What's that mean?"

"Diana didn't do drugs. She never touched the stuff."

"What?" Wynn said quickly. It was beginning to overwhelm him. "So how'd she die?" He knew the answer, but needed to hear her say it.

"I thought you did it. You or one of your friends."

Ty jumped in. "You think she was murdered?"

"All I know is she didn't do drugs. I saw her smoke a little weed at a party one time but that was it. And that Jewel stuff or whatever? She didn't have a clue."

"And that's why you were afraid to talk to me?" Wynn asked.

"Well, yeah."

"Why didn't you come to the police?" Ty asked.

"I had no proof! They'd just killed my roommate. And his wife. No way I was talking to anyone. And besides, you got the guy a day later."

Johnson, yes, but not the guy who set it up. Wynn considered the position she'd been in. *Understandable, but damn! If she'd come forward, we might have been able to catch those bastards. Now they're gone.* He resumed his pacing around the room.

"Let's back up," Ty said. "How much money did the guy give Diana?"

"She told me five thousand."

"But there was only four thousand in the envelope you gave her parents. Where'd the other thousand go?"

"Diana wanted to make sure that table was available when you came in, so she hadn't sat anyone there for almost two hours. A waitress complained. No tips if it's sitting empty. Diana gave her a thousand so she wouldn't tell."

"Who was that?"

"I never knew. I mean, I knew a few of the waitresses over there but not everybody. I didn't take her that seriously at first, so I didn't bother asking. When she died, it was too late."

Wynn stopped pacing in front of a bulletin board, the ABCs in capital and small letters running across the top. Various art projects, mostly colorful finger paintings from children's small hands, were tacked to the board.

"What grade do you teach?" he asked.

"Second."

"What's that make them? Seven? Eight?"

"Mostly, yeah."

There were pictures of houses and cars, trees and birds, the sun and sky. Oceans. Families. Mommies and daddies and brothers and sisters and dogs and cats. All the things Nicole wanted. All the things she—he—would never have.

He wasn't sure how long he stood there, but eventually, he felt her hand on his back, bringing him back to the moment. He tasted salt in his mouth and realized his face was wet with tears he didn't remember crying.

"Are you okay?" Vanessa asked.

He shook his head and breathed deeply. "Yeah. I'm fine." He pulled his sunglasses from the top of his head and put them on. "All good."

"I'm sorry," she said. "I thought..."

"Yeah. No problem."

Wynn nodded, then walked out of the room.

———

"Detective?" Vanessa asked as Ty was about to follow Wynn out the door. "Can I ask you something?"

Ty waited.

"I feel really bad about not coming forward." She paused. "I... I don't know how to ask this, but how well do you know Mr. Wynn?"

Ty's eyebrows creased. "Pretty well. Why?"

"How do you know he didn't do it?"

Ty sighed. "Let's start with the facts. This case was closed. Done. But he went out and did some digging, then came to us with new information and asked us to re-open it. Why would he do that if he was involved? Second, we'd already cleared him. Whenever a woman is murdered, the first person we look at is the husband or boyfriend. We put that poor guy through the wringer, and he came out sparkling clean. Lastly, I've gotten to know him. That emotion you just saw. That was real. You and I can only hope that someday someone will love us as much as he loved his wife."

"So, there's no question?"

"None."

Vanessa felt a tug on her heart. *I'm such a sucker for vulnerability.* "Damn. I totally screwed up. How can I help?"

Ty handed her a business card. "Just call me if you remember anything more."

"I'll definitely do that," Vanessa said. "But I mean for Mr. Wynn." She paused. "I don't know. I feel like I owe him something... to make up for not coming forward. Is there anything I can do for him?"

"The best thing is if you can remember something that would help." Ty turned to leave. "Even if it doesn't seem important, you never know what missing piece might bring it all together."

"Okay. I will," Vanessa said. *But there's got to be something more.*

———

Devon Harris debated all day. Though he'd never admit it, Lashika had been his first love. He'd have done anything for her. But she dumped him right as he was making the biggest score of his life.

Which proved one thing.

She couldn't be trusted.

He picked up his phone, found the number, and dialed.

The silky-smooth voice came over the line. "Devonnnn."

He hated the way this guy said his name. "Hello, sir. Yesterday, you asked me to call?"

"Yes?"

"I have a name for you."

CHAPTER 13

A HEAVY FOG clouded Wynn's mind as they rode back to the police department. He followed Ty down the hall and eased into the conference room where Jason was still seated at the table.

"Let me grab you some water," Ty said.

Wynn slipped into a chair. Jason looked at Wynn, then buried his eyes in a statement until Ty returned.

"Jason," Ty said when he walked into the room and handed Wynn a bottle of water. "What have you got for us?"

"It's like you thought. Prior to Johnson's conviction, Eunice was taking withdrawals from her IRA to make ends meet. Social Security wasn't enough. But after, she stopped using her checking account as much. If she was buying groceries and gas and clothes, she was doing it with money from somewhere else. She wasn't running those transactions through her bank anymore. In fact, her balance started increasing, and she stopped taking withdrawals from her IRA."

"How much was she getting?" Ty asked.

"Impossible to tell, but it wouldn't take much. A couple of grand a month would do it."

Ty nodded. The room went silent.

"I've made notes and written up my findings. I'll email it to you," Jason said. "If there's nothing else..."

Ty nodded again, and Jason quickly got up and left the room.

Wynn and Ty sat in silence for several moments before Wynn finally said, "I've got to figure out who knew we were going to be there that night."

Ty sighed. "Agreed, that would be helpful, but that'll just give us a list of names. The more important question is why? That'll give us motive, and that's what'll narrow it down. Are you sure Nicole didn't have anything going on at work?"

"Not that I'm aware of."

"And sorry for being insensitive, but no boyfriend?"

Wynn shrugged.

"Akins is going to ask if we found anything."

"Tell him."

"You know the first person he'll assume, right?"

Wynn nodded. *Just like Vanessa. The husband. Me.*

"I can't have you help with this anymore," Ty said.

"I know."

"Why don't you go home. I'll fill in Akins, then give you a call when we know what he wants to do."

Wynn pushed up from the table.

"Sean," Ty said as Wynn stepped toward the door. "I'm sorry, man. I know you didn't do this. I promise, we'll find the people who did."

Wynn stared blankly back at him, then walked out the door.

———

Li used a six-inch hunting knife to cut through the plastic packaging of the new burner phone. He had a dozen of them in a drawer. He took a piece of white tape and wrote "S.L." on it and then stuck it to the backside of the phone. He plugged it in, and then pulled out his old burner and punched Stuart's number into the new keypad. After two rings, the line was picked up but remained silent.

"Stuart. It's Li. I've got a new number."

"Why?"

"Because I don't want to go to jail. You should switch more often yourself."

"Yeah, well, it's not so easy for me," Stuart said. "What's up?"

"Calling with an update."

"On Wynn?"

Li knew he had his attention now. "Yeah. As you know, at this point we're providing electronic surveillance only. Not actual eyes-on. We're keeping track of where he's going based on where the trackers go."

"Understood. Where's he been?"

"One of his bikes has been parked outside the Ventura PD all day."

"All day?"

"Since about ten this morning," Li said.

"Is he still there?"

"So far."

"Okay. Keep an eye on him. Call me if he goes anywhere besides home."

"Will do."

"And Li? I'd like you to handle this one personally. I may have another job for you later."

———

Ten minutes after Wynn left, Ty was updating Lieutenant Akins on what they had found. Akins listened with his fingers steepled in front of his lips. When Ty finished, Akins said, "So, for two years, the roommate not only thought that Wynn had set up his wife, but also had the hostess killed?"

"Yep."

"Any chance she's right?"

"No way, Lou. Wynn didn't do this. I know the guy. There's no way."

"Relax. I don't believe it either, but we've got to go through the process. And the process says we've got to look at him. What's your next move?"

"We need to expand the scope. Find Harris. Grueb may not like it, but he's the key."

"I'll talk to him. What else?"

"I'll go talk with Trish Johnson, Eunice's granddaughter. See if she knows anything about the money or where it came from, but the real key is Harris."

"Understood. Get on it," Akins said, ending the meeting.

———

Wynn was already on it.

The moment he walked down the steps outside the police headquarters, the fog lifted, replaced by clarity, purpose, and intention. Ty had promised he'd find the people who did this. Not if Wynn found them first. He'd bury their bodies so deep no one would ever find them.

Wynn cruised back to his place, stopping only long enough to pick up his Glock, then rode south on Harbor Boulevard, making his way back to Trish Johnson's place. He parked four blocks away, so as not to let the Harley's rumble alert them to his presence.

The dinner hour was in full swing as he set off down the sidewalk, the acrid scent of charcoal filling the air as he strode past people tending barbeques and drinking beer. Young kids played in the yards while groups of teenagers hung out near cars or in driveways, a different kind of neighborhood watch in action.

The Johnson place was the second house off the corner and backed up to an alley. Wynn approached from a cross-street on the opposite end of the block, hopefully far enough away not to be noticed. He needn't worry though, the home looked quiet as he hustled through the crosswalk. The tan Corolla sat parked in the driveway.

He turned up the alley and made his way past garages and chain-link fences, until he got to a wood-slat privacy fence surrounding the small backyard. He peered between the boards into the empty yard. The sound of a television came through an open back door, but the view inside was clouded by a flimsy screen door.

Wynn proceeded to the end of the alley, then turned toward the front street. Still seeing no activity, he walked up the sidewalk. He put his right hand on his hip, gripping the Glock but leaving it in the holster, then knocked on the front door.

The same kid of maybe thirteen or fourteen who'd threatened Wynn about the insurance the other day opened the door.

When he saw Wynn, the kid said, "What you want, man? She told you, she ain't selling."

"I'm not here about that. Is Trish home?"

"None of your damn business who's home."

Wynn pushed the kid backward and stepped inside, closing the door behind him. "Thanks for inviting me in."

"Hey! What the fuck?" the kid protested. "Get your ass out of here." Trish appeared from around a corner, presumably from the kitchen. Her eyes were red and puffy.

"Miss Johnson, the cops will be here in an hour, tops, unless you talk to me. I'm not here about the house, but I am here about your grandmother's cash. They know all about it. If you talk to me, I might be able to keep them away. If not, you're going to have some tough explaining to do."

"Don't tell him shit!" the kid yelled.

"Shut up, junior," Wynn said. "I've got a job for you, too. But the grown-ups are gonna talk first."

"Fuck you!"

"Jer!" Trish scolded. "Shut up and let the man talk."

"Is there anyone else here?" Wynn asked.

"Just the baby," Trish replied.

Wynn released his grip on the Glock and looked around the living room. There was a threadbare couch and a chair, a television, and toddler toys scattered on the floor. "How long have you lived here?"

"Six years."

"You were here when Jamaal went to prison?"

She nodded. Her eyes began to well with tears. Wynn realized she'd probably just heard about Johnson's death today, also.

"Was Jamaal your brother?"

She nodded again as tears streamed down her cheeks.

"Is this your brother?" he asked, indicating the kid.

Another nod.

"How old's your baby?"

"Sixteen months."

"You said your parents are gone?"

She nodded.

"Any other family you trust?"

She shook her head.

Wynn let out a long breath. "I'm sorry. I know what it's like to lose someone, but you need to listen to me. Someone was giving your grandmother a couple of grand in cash each month, right?"

She nodded again.

"The people who were doing that are the same ones who killed Jamaal. I need to know who was giving her that money."

"I don't know."

"C'mon," Wynn said, frustrated. "It didn't show up here on its own, and I doubt it came through the mail, so how'd you get it?"

"Doc brought it."

"Doc? As in DeAndre Renker?"

Trish nodded again.

"Why? Did he ever say why they were giving it to her?"

"Just that they wanted to take care of Grands now that Jamaal was no longer around to do it."

"Did they ever say it was part of a job? Maybe Jamaal's share?"

She shook her head, "No. I never heard anything like that."

"What about Jewel? I talked to Jamaal a couple of days ago. He said the ADs were dealing Jewel."

Trish hesitated, then nodded.

Wynn's mind raced. "Where can I find him?"

"Who? Doc?" Trish asked.

"Yeah. Either him or Harris."

The kid—apparently his name was Jer, Wynn didn't know if that was short for Jerry or Jeremiah or something else, and frankly, he didn't care—laughed. "Good luck with that."

Wynn turned to the kid. "Why?"

"They move around all the time. You don't find them. They find you."

Wynn paused, then to Trish, he said, "Do you have any money left?"

"Yeah."

"How much?"

"I don't know. Two, maybe three thousand."

"Okay," he said, handing her one of the cards with his phone number. "I don't think you're safe here. I want you to take the money and get out of town. Somewhere far away. Go spend a couple of days in a hotel. Call me at this number and let me know where you are, then lay low. I'll let you know when it's safe to come home."

"What are you talking about?"

"Jamaal snitched. That's why he got hit. And there's a good chance they're gonna come after anyone else who might know something. That's you. You need to go."

"You're not serious."

"Ask your bro, here," Wynn said, nodding to the kid. "Once the cops pull up outside, how long's it going to take for the ADs to find out? Ten minutes? Twenty?"

Jer looked at Trish and nodded.

"Why should I trust you?" she asked.

"If I wanted you dead, it'd be done by now. So you can either trust me, the cops, or the ADs. Take your pick."

"Shit," she said. "I gotta get the baby's stuff together."

"Grab the bare minimum. You can buy whatever you forget."

Jer spoke up again. "You said you had a job for me?"

"Time to choose sides, kid. Your sister or your gang?"

"The ADs are not my gang."

"Then you're choosing your sister?"

"Yeah."

"Go with her. Help her get packed, then get out of town and keep your mouth shut. You ever watch anyone die?"

Jer shook his head, his eyes opened wide, stunned by the question. "No."

"Don't let her be the first."

———

"You said to call if he didn't go home," Li's voice came over the phone.

"And?" Stuart replied.

"He left the PD shortly after we spoke and went to Oxnard."

"Where in Oxnard?"

"Looks like a residential neighborhood."

"You got an address?"

Li gave it to him. Stuart looked it up on Google Maps. *Shit. Four blocks from the Johnson place. He's up to something.* "Alright. Keep an eye on him and be ready to move. This may need to go from virtual to visual."

CHAPTER 14

WYNN HUNG AROUND outside while they packed a few things in the car. Like a good mom, Trish didn't appear to take much for herself, but grabbed a bunch of stuff for the baby. Jer hustled back and forth carrying loads out and stuffing them into the trunk. He didn't seem to worry about packing things for himself, either. Maybe there was hope for that kid.

When they had packed everything up and gotten the baby in a car seat, they backed out of the driveway and sped away. Wynn hustled around the corner and up the four blocks back to the Sportster.

Pulling out his phone, Wynn checked the time. It was too early for the ADs to be out yet, so he scrolled through his contacts until he found a name he hadn't called in almost two years. The call was picked up after three rings.

"Oh, wow. Sean, is that you?"

"Hi, Lisa."

"It's so good to hear your voice. How are you?"

"I'm fine. And you?"

"I'm good, I'm good. What's going on?"

"I've got something I want to ask you. Are you home? Would it be okay if I came over now?"

"Yeah. I'm home," she said cautiously, "but what is it?"

"I'll tell you when I get there. You still in Camarillo?"

"Yeah. Same place."

"Great. It'll take me about a half-hour. Is that okay?"

"Sure."

"Great. I'll see you in a bit."

Wynn could tell she was both startled and confused by his call. But he sure as hell wasn't going to ask one of Nicole's closest friends from work if his wife had had a lover over the phone. He needed to see her reaction.

Dusk had nearly settled as he strapped on his helmet and took the side streets east to Camarillo. At the tail end of rush hour, it was best to avoid the freeway if possible.

It'd been almost three years since he'd been to Lisa Montgomery's home. Like Nicole, she was a pharmaceutical researcher at Mynogen. Lisa was a couple of years older and had been there a few years longer. Her husband, Hal, was a psychologist, and together they had two kids, a boy and a girl, who were now, Wynn guessed, around seven and nine years old. One of them probably went to school in a classroom very similar to Vanessa Carow's.

He wasn't sure he'd remember exactly where she lived, or be able to find the place in the dark, but someone had turned on all the lights of the two-story brick home, making it stand out among the other dark houses on the block. He parked on the street and was making his way up the sidewalk when the front door opened. That seemed to happen a lot when you pulled a Harley up in front of someone's house.

"Sean, it's so good to see you." Lisa stepped from the doorway and hugged him.

"You too." Wynn returned the embrace. They separated, then she took him by the arm and led him inside.

Lisa was close to the same age as Wynn, thirty-six, five-foot-five, and slender, with shoulder-length blonde hair. Wynn remembered her cheerful smile and vibrant brown eyes, but tonight she looked tired. Hal came out of the kitchen wiping his hands on a dish towel, reminding Wynn he'd probably intruded on dinner.

"Sean, good to see you," Hal said, extending his hand.

Wynn shook it. "Good to see you, too. I'm sorry. I didn't even think I'd be interrupting your dinner. Where are the kids?"

"No worries. We're all done. The kids are up in their rooms. Supposed to be doing their homework, but ten-to-one says Jack's playing video games."

Wynn smiled. "They're doing well?"

"They're doing great."

"Good. Glad to hear it."

"Can I get you something?" Lisa asked.

"No, I'm good. Listen, I don't want to take much of your time, but some things have come up and I wanted to ask you a few questions."

Hal said, "Why don't you two go have a seat while I finish up." He excused himself and returned to the kitchen.

Lisa led him into a neat living room where she motioned him to a stuffed chair while she took a seat on a matching sofa. Wynn leaned forward across a glass coffee table to keep his voice down. Lisa picked up on it and did the same.

"What's going on, Sean? We haven't heard from you in two years, and all of a sudden you need to see us on barely a moment's notice?"

"Yeah. Sorry about that..." He paused, not knowing where to begin. "I don't know if you saw the news, but Jamaal Johnson was killed up in Corcoran yesterday."

"My God. No, I hadn't heard." Lisa well knew who Johnson was and why he was in prison. "What happened?"

"I don't know all the details, but I think it's less about what happened, and more about why it happened."

"What do you mean?"

"He sent me a letter a little over a week ago. Three words. 'It wasn't stray.'" He stopped there, looking for any reaction on Lisa's face. She stared at him blankly.

"It wasn't stray? What does that mean?"

Wynn shrugged. "Does it mean anything to you?"

Lisa paused and looked confused. "No. Does that mean Nicole's murder was intentional?"

"That's what I wanted to know, so I went up there a few days ago and asked him." He paused again, examining her face for a reaction.

Lisa stared blankly back as she waited for him to continue. "And?" she finally prompted.

"He said it was a hit. A setup. Johnson said someone paid the ADs a hundred grand to kill Nicole. I don't know if that's true, but I have confirmed that someone paid the hostess at Viacci's five thousand dollars to seat Nicole and me at that particular table that night."

Lisa was speechless. She stared at Wynn with her mouth slightly open.

"My question to you," Wynn continued, "is do you know of any reason someone might've wanted to kill Nicole?"

Lisa's face contorted into a look of pained confusion. "What?"

Wynn remained silent, letting the question hang.

"No! Of course not. I can't believe what you're telling me. That makes no sense."

Wynn exhaled heavily. "That was my reaction, but the evidence is starting to make it sound plausible. I've already been to the police and they've opened an investigation, but we're missing a motive. Why would someone want to kill Nicole?"

Lisa began to shake, her voice rising, "Why are you asking me? I have no idea."

"It's okay. Calm down." Wynn glanced toward the kitchen to see if Hal had heard, then up the stairs to see if the kids had come out of their rooms. No one appeared.

"I've been racking my brain all day trying to come up with a reason. Ty, uh, Detective Lenihan, says ninety-nine percent of the time it comes down to either money or sex. And no one's approached me in the last two years about Nicole owing them money, so I have to ask, was Nicole having an affair?"

Lisa stared blankly again. Her voice finally exploded in a high-pitched, barely contained whisper. "What? No! I... I don't know! Sean, she loved you. She'd have had to have been the greatest actor in the world. There's no way she was having an affair. We told each other everything and she never once said a bad word about you, let alone having an affair. Just... no... no..." Her voice finally trailed off.

Wynn sat back. *Damn. If she had been, she hid it well.* "Was there anyone else she was close to, that she might've confided in?"

"No. I mean, Janelle, her boss, maybe. They got along, but I didn't think they were close. Not enough for something like that."

He decided to try a different tack. "Do you know who all might have known we were even having dinner there that night?"

"I don't think it was a secret, but no, I have no idea who she might have told."

Dead end. Wynn paused and nodded. "What was she working on?"

"Two years ago? I have no idea. I mean, we were doing the same stuff, and there certainly wasn't anything interesting."

"But you don't remember what?"

"No. I can try and look back, but off the top of my head, I don't remember. Why? Are you thinking it might've had something to do with work?"

"I don't know. Have you ever heard of something called Jewel?"

"Jewel? No. What's that?"

"It's some kind of synthetic opioid. Becoming real popular on the street. I want you to think about this next question carefully." He paused, assuring he had her full attention. "Could someone at Mynogen, maybe working under the radar, use the labs and resources there to produce something like Jewel off the books?"

"A street drug? I don't see how. Everything we do is very controlled."

"Controlled how?"

"Every substance that comes in is verified and cataloged, then held under lock and key. Inventories are checked at the beginning and end of each shift, and whoever accesses them has to sign in and out. They've even got cameras covering all the storage areas. It'd be impossible."

Wynn paused as he took it in. "If it's not drugs, money, or sex, what else is there?"

"I have no idea."

"Well, if you can dig up what she was working on, I'm sure the cops would love to see it. Or if you come up with anyone she was spending time with, male or female, who she might've confided in, please let me know. I'm at a loss here. The evidence is starting to make this thing sound real, but I can't come up with any reason why."

"I can't believe this."

"You and me both."

They sat in silence for a few moments, unsure of what else to say, when Lisa finally spoke up. "I'll check around and ask a few questions, but right now I can't think of anything that would help."

"That'd be great. I appreciate your help. One last thing. I know you'll tell Hal, but other than that, probably best not to tell anyone else, especially at work. Ty's already come down on me for talking to the ADs. He thinks stealth is the best way to investigate, so better to stay quiet, you know?"

"Okay. Holy crap. This is unbelievable."

Wynn shook his head. "I'm gonna get out of here. Tell Hal goodbye for me. Maybe we can get together sometime."

"I'd like that."

She walked him to the door and gave him another hug, this time longer. After a moment, he pulled away and stepped into the night.

CHAPTER 15

STREETLIGHTS LIT THE freeway, creating a ribbon in the dark as Wynn raced the Sportster west to Ventura. Traffic had cleared and temperatures dropped, making the ride fast and cool. He took the exit just past the river wash basin, dumping him into the heart of AD turf.

It was almost two hours earlier than when he'd ridden these same streets two nights ago. He cruised past the same convenience stores, even stopping at the same gas station, in hopes of running into one or more members of the Acid Dawn. Harris was still at the top of his list, but a conversation with Doc would suit him just fine also. But whether it be the early hour, or perhaps word had gotten out to avoid him, there were no ADs to be found. Wynn cruised slowly, loudly, up and down the streets, revving the 1200cc engine for all to hear.

An hour later, Wynn pulled into the same all-night diner across from the strip mall. Bright light once again spilled from the windows, and while there were more guests than last time, the same waitress and cook were hard at work inside. He parked the Sportster in the wash of the exterior flood lamps, and smiled at the waitress as he walked down the side of the counter. He went all the way to the rear, where he slid into a booth with his back against the wall, facing forward, as far away from the front glass as possible.

No need to be an easy target.

Moments later, the cook, large and burly and closer to sixty than fifty, ambled over to his booth. "Coffee?"

"Please," Wynn replied. He knew why the cook had come over instead of the waitress. Noticing a tattoo of an anchor entwined in dog tags on the cook's forearm, he asked, "Navy?"

"Twenty years."

Wynn nodded. "Marines. Eight."

The cook finished pouring the coffee and stepped back. "Are you expecting your friends tonight?"

"I'm not sure. It's possible."

"We don't need any trouble."

"Understood."

The cook walked back to the kitchen, nodding to the waitress as he went, who then came over and took Wynn's order. A half-hour later she was clearing away his dishes and refilling his coffee when his phone rang. It was Ty.

Wynn answered with one syllable. "Hey."

"Hey, man. What's up?"

"You tell me. Did you talk to Akins?"

"Yeah, I talked to him. He's cool. We've got to follow procedure, but he knows you didn't have anything to do with it. I'm going to talk with Trish Johnson tomorrow."

Good luck with that, Wynn thought.

"How are you doing?" Ty asked.

"I'm good."

The waitress clinked some dishes in the background.

"Where are you?" Ty asked.

"At a restaurant. Didn't feel like cooking." He didn't bother to say who he was waiting for.

"Okay, that's good. Listen, I'm working with Grueb. We're going to try to bring Harris in tomorrow. Sweat him. See if we can get something. I'll let you know if anything comes of it."

"Sounds good."

"Alright, man. You take care. Go home and get a good night's sleep. We'll get these guys."

"I know. Thanks." Wynn disconnected the call.

Not if I get them first.

———

Li caught Xiang's attention and motioned him over as Stuart's voice came across the phone. "What's he been doing?"

"After he left Oxnard he rode over to Camarillo," Li said. "Stayed there for an hour, now he's back in Ventura, at a diner."

"What's the name?"

"Let's see." Li pulled up an internet browser and plugged in the address. "It's called Lucky's. Looks like a greasy-spoon place."

Xiang made a face.

"How long's he been there?" Stuart asked.

"A half an hour or so."

"Did he go straight there from Camarillo?"

"No. He rode kind of aimlessly around Ventura for almost an hour before stopping."

Stuart hesitated before responding. "He's trying to make contact with the ADs. Get over there and make sure that doesn't happen."

"How far do we go to stop it?" Li asked.

"As far as you need to."

———

Ninety minutes later, the diner had cleared and returned to its *Nighthawks* atmosphere while Wynn sat patiently. He'd paid his tab and added extra for a bottomless cup of coffee which he was well into. The cook had come over forty-five minutes ago and suggested his friends probably weren't going to show up tonight, and maybe he should go home. Wynn smiled and asked for a refill.

Finally, around midnight, a tapping on the glass came from across the room. Doc stood in the wash of light on the other side of the window, motioning Wynn to come outside.

"Not a good idea, son," the cook said from behind the counter.

Wynn remained seated and swept his hand toward the empty bench opposite himself, silently inviting Doc to come in.

Doc shook his head, pounded his fist on the glass, insisting Wynn come out.

Wynn turned back to his coffee as the cook made his way to the cash register and reached beneath the counter. Wynn was suddenly glad the place was empty.

Need to stop this before it gets out of hand. Wynn got up from his table.

"Don't do it," the cook said.

"He needs to save face. I'm going to invite him in." Wynn stepped into the foyer and opened the door leading outside. Doc stood on the sidewalk next to the window twenty feet away. "Doc, I know your guys are watching. The only thing I don't know is if you're the one who's supposed to pull the trigger or one of your boys. But either way, I'm not going anywhere, so why don't you come in and talk."

Doc hesitated and glanced into the darkness.

"C'mon, man. You can tell them you were assuring me it was safe."

Doc nodded, then followed as Wynn went back inside and slid into his booth.

"It seems I've touched a nerve," Wynn said when they were both settled.

"You don't know shit, man."

"I know that every month for the past two years you've been delivering two grand in cash to Jay-squared's grandmother."

"We take care of our own."

"Did you also take care of Jay-squared?"

"Fuck you."

"C'mon Doc. This isn't hard to figure out. You and I talk, Johnson winds up dead. If the Dawn didn't do it, that means there's a third party in play. Who is it?"

Doc sat silently.

"Who'd you tell about our conversation the other night? Harris, or someone else? Maybe Harris told someone?"

Doc remained silent as Wynn waited. Finally, Wynn said, "You realize this just got serious, right? I'm guessing you have instructions to put me down, but the question is where'd those instructions come from? If they originated with Harris, you're probably okay. But if Harris got 'em from someone else, that means they're trying to get rid of everyone involved. And guess what, Doc? You're involved. The moment you cap me, you're next."

"Harris doesn't know I'm here. We were told to stay away."

"So why are you here?"

"Trish called me. We've been hanging out. She said you thought she was in danger. She wanted to warn me."

Not that this was unexpected, but it did add a new twist. Trish and Doc were a couple. If the people behind Harris knew about it, that put Doc in serious danger.

"It's pretty simple, Doc. You and Harris took money from some pretty bad dudes. I don't know who they are or why they did it, but if you consider the lengths they've gone through and the money they've paid to keep this thing quiet, they won't think twice about getting rid of you."

Doc was about to say something when a pair of shadows emerged from the darkness outside the foyer. A glint of light off the short barrel of a semi-automatic caught Wynn's eye as the two figures swung open the front doors and rushed inside. The first took three steps toward Wynn. Two too many. Wynn's hand went to his hip and pulled out the Glock as he dove to the floor, bullets punching into the wall behind where he'd been sitting. The second gunman held the door open and fired toward the cash register, the cook ducking beneath the counter.

A bullet whistled past Wynn's ear as he landed shoulder-first on the floor between the booths. With both arms extended, he returned fire, punching three holes into the shooter. The guy staggered backward and dropped to the floor.

Wynn turned to the second guy, but the angle was wrong. From his position on the floor, the row of booths blocked his view of the doorway. Two massive explosions from a shotgun drowned out the other bursts of gunfire. The shooting stopped as the glass entryway shattered, the tinkling of tiny shards of glass hitting the tile floor audible as the blast's echo faded.

"Marine! Sitrep!" the cook called out.

"One hostile down in the aisle. Stand by," Wynn called back, providing his situation report.

"Second shooter is gone. Unknown if still in vicinity," the cook yelled. "Karen! You okay?"

"I think so," came the frightened voice of the waitress from somewhere to Wynn's right.

Wynn looked up at the booth and saw Doc leaning against the wall, blood flowing from an open wound on his neck and streaming from the seat onto the floor. He jumped up and grabbed a cloth placemat, applying pressure to the wound. Blood pulsed beneath his hand. Doc's eyes were open and searching, his breath raspy, blood drooling from his lips.

"One hit!" Wynn called out. "We need an ambulance!" Then to Doc, Wynn said quietly, "Hang in there, Doc. Help is coming, but you've got to tell me now, who are you working for?"

"Dunno... Harris," he whispered.

"Where can I find him?"

"Collin..."

"Collins? Lashika Collins? She knows where to find Harris?"

Doc blinked and gave an almost imperceptible nod. His eyes fluttered closed, and Wynn knew he wasn't going to get any more out of him. He pressed harder against the wound, the pulse weakening beneath his fingers, finally disappearing completely as wailing sirens approached.

CHAPTER 16

DEVON HARRIS SWITCHED the phone to his other hand so he could wipe the sweat from his palm onto his jeans. "How long ago?"

"Shit, man, like three minutes," Mikey said. "The uni's showed up but the suits ain't even here yet."

"Tell me again."

"That biker dude was trolling 'round the 'hood again, so me and Doc watched him. He stopped at Lucky's and sat there for over two hours, so Doc went in. A couple of minutes later two other dudes rush in and start shooting up the place. Doc ain't moved since."

"Are they working on him?"

"Nah, they just looking at him. I can see his foot sticking out from the booth."

"What about the biker? Did he get hit?"

"No way. He went all action-hero and got one of the shooters. He's talking to the cops now."

"One of the shooters is down?" Harris asked.

"Yeah."

"Is he dead?"

"I think so. They're not working on him either."

"What about the other one?"

"He ran, man. He's gone."

Harris paused as he processed the information, thinking about what it might mean. "Alright. Stay there and keep an eye on it. Let me know if something else happens."

"But Doc, man," Mikey's voice was faltering, on the edge of tears. "He's dead."

"If you don't want to be next, you stay low and keep your head straight, got it?"

Mikey sniffed. "Yeah, man."

"Okay. Good job, Mikey. Keep the intel coming." Harris disconnected.

This was not good. Harris wasn't surprised when Jay-squared got hit, but Doc was another matter. He knew Mr. S was connected and knew what his guys could do. It was a totally different league. Big time. They could reach anyone, including him.

Harris grabbed a duffel bag from his closet and stuffed a pile of clothes into it, along with some cash and a Smith & Wesson .380. It was time to disappear.

————

"What the hell happened here, Sean?" Lieutenant Akins looked down at Wynn, who sat in a booth close to the shattered doorway. Ty and Gruebauer were with him, all in a tight circle around Wynn, none of them happy. The lifeless body of the shooter lay a few feet away. Flashing red and blue police lights colored the darkness outside, illuminating a fifty-foot perimeter. At the edge of the light, a half-dozen media vans were setting up for live shots.

"He and his buddy came in, started shooting."

"According to the cook, you'd been here almost three hours, waiting for your friend there." He nodded toward Doc's body further back. "Said you did the same thing two nights ago. Said he also asked you to leave, that he didn't want any trouble."

Wynn was silent.

"I want to know, step-by-step, what you've done since you left the station this afternoon," Akins said.

"He's fucked up my investigation, is what he's done," Gruebauer said.

Wynn looked at Grueb. "I went to see Trish Johnson."

"Shit," Ty said, under his breath.

"I wanted to know if she knew where those cash payments were coming from."

"And?" Akins said.

"Not the original source. She said Doc had been delivering them for about two years."

"We should get someone over there," Ty said. "These guys are taking out all the links. She could be in danger."

"She's not there," Wynn said.

"How would you know that?" Akins asked.

"I figured the same thing. Told her to take whatever money she has left and get out of town."

Grueb threw up his hands and turned away while Akins chewed his bottom lip. "Where is she?"

"No idea. Told her to call me when she got to wherever she wanted to go, but I haven't heard from her."

"Great," Grueb muttered.

"Where'd you go after you left Johnson's?" Akins asked.

Wynn paused. He wasn't ready to give up Lisa Montgomery. "I came back here, to this neighborhood. Cruised around for a couple of hours to make sure they knew I wanted to talk, then came in here. Like Navy said, been here almost three hours."

"What were you hoping to do? Specifically."

"Find Harris and ask him who was behind this."

Grueb exploded. "Harris is mine, motherfucker!"

Wynn jumped up. "And you haven't done shit to find him!"

Ty stepped in between the two and held Wynn back.

"Cool it!" Akins yelled. When the two men calmed down, he asked, "Did this guy, Doc, say anything?"

"He didn't know who was behind it all, but he did say Lashika Collins would know where to find Harris."

"Why her?"

"He didn't say."

"You didn't ask?"

"He died before I got a chance."

Akins turned his back to Wynn so he could talk to Ty and Gruebauer but didn't bother stepping out of earshot. "We got an ID on the shooter yet?"

"Not yet," Ty replied.

"Get it. Asap."

Ty nodded.

"You know anything about Collins?" Akins asked Grueb. "Are they a couple?"

"Could be. Like I said, Harris has been laying low for the last couple of years. As long as they keep their noses clean, we don't give a shit who they're sleeping with."

"Track her down. If he's not with her, she might know where he is. Find him and bring him in."

Gruebauer nodded.

"As for you, Mr. Wynn," Akins said as he turned back around, "Detective Lenihan is going to take you over to county for a formal statement, then your ass is going in a cell until you learn to leave this alone."

———

Lights from the various TV crews lit up the area outside of Lucky's, giving Mikey a good view as he watched from the far side of the parking lot. Several of the cameras focused on the Harley. They seemed to like the image of the bike still standing among all the shattered glass. The reporters themselves flocked to the edge of the police tape when the biker came out, yelling questions and snapping pictures as he got into the back of an unmarked police car with one of the suits. Eventually, Doc's body was loaded into a coroner's van and driven away.

Earlier, a couple of the uniform cops had approached a group of bystanders off to his left, but Mikey had slipped into the shadows to avoid being questioned. Now, still hidden, he leaned over and tried to make himself throw up, hoping that would relieve the nausea he was feeling, but after a couple of dry heaves, he gave up. His pain wasn't physical.

He'd been debating making a phone call for the last hour, telling himself to wait until he knew for sure. Now that he did, he pulled up his contact list and tapped the name.

"Hello?" said a groggy female voice.

"Hey, Trish. It's Mikey." He was fighting back tears.

"Geez, Mikey. What time is it?"

"I... I don't know." He sobbed.

"What's wrong?"

He took a deep breath, trying to find his voice. "It's Doc. He was shot. He's dead."

———

Two hours later, after Wynn had given his statement, Ty cuffed him and put him in the back of his car for the ride over to the county holding facility. It was in the same complex where they had gotten Judge Thompson to sign off on the subpoena. Ty had calmed down, even going so far as apologizing for having to do it, then locked Wynn into a private jail cell. "The lieutenant never said you had to be in general lockup. At least this way you can get some sleep."

The setup was disturbingly familiar. A small room. A cot. Combination stainless steel commode and sink. "No worries," Wynn replied. "Not my first time."

Ty shook his head, "I don't want to know."

He paused. "Listen, Sean. I know you want to get these guys. But if you really want to help, you need to stop focusing on who gave the order, and more on why they gave the order. Grueb and I will eventually track down Harris, but we're past thinking he ordered this, right? He was hired, and he probably doesn't even know who hired him. Even if he does, he's not going to talk.

"The real question is why? That's the part that's bugging me. And no one knows more about Nicole's life than you. If it's not sex or money, then is it revenge? Jealousy? Did she take someone's job? Did she make someone look bad at work? Is there an old college crush? Hell, do you have an old crush who might've wanted to get her out of the way? That's where you need to spend your energy. We need to think our way through this, not bull our way through."

Wynn nodded as Ty closed the door. "Any idea how long Akins is gonna make me sit?"

"He didn't say, but I'm guessing overnight. He's trying to teach you a lesson. I'll come back and check on you in the morning."

"Thanks."

Wynn laid back on the cot and realized Ty was right. But nothing stood out. Nicole hadn't mentioned any problems at work and surely had no other enemies. The only woman he'd been with since then, he'd met only a couple of months ago, on a road trip to Sturgis. And if someone was trying to send him a message, wouldn't they have done so by now? Wouldn't they have tried to contact him? He had to start over. Wipe the slate clean. Look at everything in his own life, and Nicole's. The answer was in there. Somewhere.

CHAPTER 17

STUART LEGREA STOOD looking out his front window, sipping a cup of coffee with the lights off, hoping the ambient light wouldn't shine off his bald scalp. He'd been awakened by a phone call saying they'd be there in ten minutes. That was twelve minutes ago.

He couldn't remember if he'd ever given Chan or Li his home address, but he wasn't surprised they'd found it. Li was good at that kind of thing. Their last conversation played through his mind. *How far do we go to stop it?* Li had asked. *As far as you need to,* he'd replied.

Something must have gone wrong. Chan sounded angry, which was never good. The fact that he was making the hour drive north, at three a.m., told Stuart all he needed. The Ruger felt both heavy and comforting in his robe pocket.

Stuart was startled when he saw three men coming up the walk, a large, dark SUV now parked next to the curb. He hadn't seen it pull up without its headlights, its black paint blending with the shadows on the street. He stepped over and opened the door, allowing them to come inside without breaking stride. He didn't need his nosy, insomniac neighbors seeing he had visitors.

"What happened?" he asked when they were all inside and he'd closed the door.

Chan ignored his question while he turned and composed himself. "Who is this Sean Wynn?"

"He's an ex-Marine turned computer nerd. An unemployed loser."

"Ex-Marine?"

"He's been out for ten years. Can't be that dangerous."

"According to Li," Chan nodded toward the man-boy who was sulking several feet away, "he is quite dangerous."

"Why? What happened?"

"We lost a man this evening. Xiang Mao."

"How?"

"It seems you ordered Li and Xiang to stop a meeting Mr. Wynn was having. Mr. Wynn shot him."

"Uh-uh. You can't blame that on me. I can't help it if your guys ran up against someone better than they are. Not my fault."

"Since when do you give my men orders?"

Shit. He thinks I've disrespected him by going around the chain of command. "In this case, since you had already assigned Li and Xiang to the surveillance, I thought, as they did also, that we had your blessing."

"For surveillance."

"If I misunderstood, I apologize."

"We have enjoyed a mutually beneficial business arrangement for several years now," Chan said. "An equal exchange of services for compensation. But a man such as Xiang is difficult to replace. It may take many months to find a suitable replacement. I am afraid this is no longer an equal exchange."

There it is. He's using this to change our deal. "I have no doubt Xiang was a great asset and his loss will be felt deeply. He has my respect, and you, and his family, have my condolences."

Stuart paused, then continued. "But as you said, we have a mutually beneficial relationship precisely because it is mutually beneficial. To both our organizations. Which are bigger than one man, no matter how strong that man is. We will compensate you for Xiang's loss, but we must be careful not to upset the balance that makes this arrangement profitable to all of us."

Chan nodded. "What do you have in mind?"

"We'll discuss additional compensation when the job is done." He turned to Li. "I assume Mr. Wynn is still alive?"

Li nodded.

Turning back to Chan, Stuart said, "As I mentioned to Li earlier this evening, there may be a second job that could go a long way toward solving the issue we have with him."

"And what exactly is that issue? Why are my men putting their lives at risk to watch this man?"

"Because if we don't, he might just blow up our 'mutually beneficial arrangement.' Is that reason enough?"

"How would he do that?" Chan asked.

"It has nothing to do with Jewel. Something else entirely. But if he causes trouble for Carson, Jameson, or myself, that could affect all of us. Understand?"

Chan nodded.

"Good. Now about that other job. This one should be easy. It's a girl."

───────

The clock on the bedside table read 3:16 a.m.

Lashika Collins was awakened by the ringing of her phone inside the two-bedroom house she shared with her boyfriend and her parents. She picked it up quickly so as not to wake the baby in her crib a few feet away.

"Hello?" she said sleepily. Her boyfriend, Enrique, didn't move.

"Shik? Oh, thank God! It's Trish. Listen to me. You have to get out of your house. You have to leave."

"What?"

"You're in danger! You have to get out of your house!"

"What are you talking about?"

"It's that deal with Jamaal. They're coming after us. They killed Doc!"

Lashika sat up. "What?"

Enrique rolled over.

"They killed Doc. A few hours ago. This biker said they'd be coming after all of us. Anyone who knew anything."

"The biker killed Doc?" She immediately thought of the guy who'd come to the store a couple of days ago.

Enrique sat up.

"No! I don't know who he is, but he came by the house. Said Jamaal had snitched, and the cops would be coming around to talk to us. He said whoever hired Devon would be looking to get rid of anyone who knew anything. And he was right! They killed Doc!"

"Where are you? Are you at home?"

"No. The biker told me to leave town for a couple of days, so Jer and I are at a hotel. And that's what you need to do. You need to get out!"

Lashika thought about her former boyfriend. *Would Devon give me up like that? Yeah. He would.* "Thanks, Trish. I gotta go."

When she disconnected, Enrique asked, "What was that all about?"

"Trish's boyfriend was killed tonight. She's freaking out."

"Was he still running around with the ADs?"

"Yeah. I think so."

"Nothing good can ever come of that. I'm glad you cut ties."

A wave of guilt rolled through her stomach. *Not completely. There's still one secret.* "Yeah. Me too."

"Does she need something?"

"No. She just wanted to tell me."

"Are you okay?"

"Yeah. I'm fine. Go back to sleep."

———

Li had been forced to wait a couple of hours while his new partner, Huan, drove up from L.A. He'd tried to convince Chan that he could take care of this himself, but Chan insisted, never do a job alone.

After leaving Stuart's, Chan had dropped him off to pick up his own vehicle. He'd found Lashika Collins' house a few blocks from Trish Johnson's. He drove past once to get a feel for the neighborhood, then circled the block and parked two houses away.

———

Ty and Gruebauer were running on fumes. If Lashika Collins was the key to finding Harris, there was no time to waste, but it was bad PR to go pounding on a potential witness's door at four in the morning. Especially that of a young mother.

Instead, they asked the night patrol to do a drive-by of Collins' house every hour while they grabbed some shut-eye in the county break room. As the clock neared five a.m., Ty's phone rang, rousing him from a fitful sleep.

"Lenihan." Ty sat up and rubbed his hand across his face.

"Rise and shine, detective. This is Officer Hernandez. About that house you'd asked us to keep an eye on?"

"Yeah?" Ty was suddenly awake, alert.

"I've got a Cadillac SUV parked two houses away. Windows are tinted, so I can't tell if anyone's in it, but it wasn't there an hour ago."

"You said a Cadillac?"

"Yes, sir. Not too many of those in this neighborhood."

"Agreed. Good work, officer. Are you in a black-and-white?"

"That's affirmative, sir."

"Are you alone?"

"That's also affirmative."

"Okay. Where are you now?"

"Parked around the corner."

"Can they see you?"

"I don't think so."

"Good. I need you to keep an eye on the house but stay out of sight. If someone leaves the house and gets in the Caddy, try to follow them discreetly. Get plates if you can, but don't get too close. We'll be there in twenty minutes."

———

Li had seen the black-and-white cop car go by and turn the corner. He didn't like it. Too coincidental. He'd already missed one target tonight; he couldn't afford to abandon another unless he was absolutely sure. He picked up his phone and dialed Huan.

"Where are you?" Li asked.

"I'm off the freeway. A couple minutes out."

"Good. But hold on, we may have company. A cop came by a minute ago. I want you to circle the area on a three-block radius and see if he's still around."

"Black-and-white or unmarked?"

"Black-and-white. But look for either."

"Okay. Hold on."

Li kept the call connected. Neither spoke for the next few minutes, the only sound being Huan's engine purring softly across the line.

"Got him. He's parked a couple of blocks ahead of you on a side street."

"One guy or two?"

"I only see one."

"Alright. I need you to keep him pinned down while I go inside and do the job. Let me know when you're ready."

———

Hints of gray were lighting the eastern sky as Lashika lay awake, listening intently for any noise.

She slipped from beneath the covers and stepped over to the crib where Ayel slept peacefully. She put a hand on the baby's chest to make sure she was breathing, then pulled on a robe and tucked her phone into a pocket. She padded quietly down the hall into the living room. Light from the porch lamp lit up her face as she peeked through the curtains. The street was dark and quiet.

Shuddering as an imaginary chill swept the room, she stepped away from the window and sunk into her dad's favorite chair, facing the window and the TV.

It'll be okay, she thought as she closed her eyes.

———

With Grueb behind the wheel, Ty picked up the radio as they exited the 101 Freeway.

"Hernandez. You awake?"

"I'm here."

"Anything?"

"Nope. All quiet."

"Okay. We should be there in five."

———

Huan's voice was a whisper as it came over the open phone line. "In position."

Finally, Li thought. He pulled the black baseball cap low and slipped quietly out of the Caddy. He walked casually up the street until he came even with the Collins' front door, then darted up the sidewalk.

———

Officer Hernandez picked up his radio microphone. "We've got movement. Someone ran up to the house."

Ty's response was immediate. "Get over there but be careful. We're almost there."

In one fluid motion, Hernandez started the car, flipped on the lights and siren, and was instantly pelted by shattered glass as bullets ripped through the windows. He ducked beneath the dash and grabbed the mic. "Shots fired! Shots fired! I'm taking fire!"

———

Lashika's eyes snapped open as she sensed, more than saw, a flash of movement outside the window. It was followed a moment later by the sudden wail of a police siren and the distant popping of a handgun.

"Ricky!" she screamed just before a gunshot blasted through the front door. She bolted from the chair and ran down the hall as the door smashed open.

———

When they heard Hernandez's frantic call, Ty reached over and hit the lights and siren, then braced himself as Grueb stomped on the gas. "Turn left!"

Tires squealed as Grueb cranked the wheel, fishtailing through the tight turn.

"There!" Ty yelled. Taillights flared a few blocks ahead as a large SUV peeled away from the curb. It accelerated quickly until the brake lights flashed, then turned hard and disappeared out of sight two blocks ahead. Moments later, they raced past the Collins house, the front door hanging awkwardly from its hinges.

"Shit. Someone got in," Ty said.

"Pursue or assist?" Grueb asked.

"Pursue." Ty picked up the radio and called for assistance to the house.

Grueb twisted the wheel to follow the SUV and raced up the side street. The road ahead was empty.

"Toward the freeway?" Grueb asked.

"Try it."

They sped through the neighborhood, scanning the parked cars along the side as well as up and down the cross streets, but there was nothing. The SUV was gone.

Ty picked up the radio. "Hernandez. What's your status?"

A terrifying moment of dead air was followed by a shaky voice. "I'm here. I'm okay. The shooter's gone. Car's shot to shit but I'm okay."

"Good to hear. We're heading to the witness's house."

"I'll meet you there."

"Roger that."

Hernandez was already on the scene by the time Ty and Grueb pulled to the curb. He was standing in the front yard with one man, while a younger man and two women stood under the shelter of a front porch. The older man wore blue jeans and a white wife-beater made gray in the breaking dawn; the younger, a t-shirt and athletic shorts. Both women wore robes. The younger held a baby.

"The scene is secure," Hernandez said as Ty and Grueb got out of the car and approached.

"Is anyone hurt?" Grueb asked.

"No. Everyone's fine."

"Mr. Collins?" Ty asked, addressing the older man.

"Yeah," he said cautiously.

"I'm Detective Lenihan, Ventura Police. I'm assuming that's your wife and daughter?" Ty nodded toward the two women.

"And my granddaughter."

"Uh-huh. And the gentleman?"

"My daughter's boyfriend. Enrique."

Ty nodded. "What happened?"

"One moment I'm sound asleep, and the next thing I hear is my daughter screaming and gunshots coming through the front door."

"Your daughter, Lashika?"

"Yeah."

"Did anyone enter the house?"

"No. I think he hesitated when he heard your sirens, then took off when he heard my shotgun."

"You fired a weapon?"

"Damn right."

"Did you hit him?"

"Not unless there was another one outside my window. I don't aim to kill, detective. I just want them to know I can."

Ty smiled and nodded. "This is Detective Gruebauer. He's going to ask you some more questions." With that, Ty stepped away and walked over to the other three, who were huddling together beneath the porch roof.

"Lashika Collins?"

"Yeah?" the younger woman replied.

"I need you to leave the baby here, with your parents, and the two of you to come with us."

CHAPTER 18

WYNN WOKE TO the sound of metal sliding on metal. A hinged tray set in the cell door folded down, revealing a slot through which a tray of biscuits and gravy had been passed, along with a single cup of weak, lukewarm coffee. Breakfast was served.

Expecting to be released at any time, Wynn skipped his morning kata and waited for Ty to come by and let him out.

Two hours later, he was still waiting.

———

A hundred feet away, Ty and Gruebauer stood in a hallway between two doors. Lashika Collins sat in a small interrogation room behind one. Her boyfriend, Enrique Garcia, sat behind the other.

Lieutenant Akins approached from down the hall. "What do we have?"

"Not what we expected," Ty said. "And probably not what Devon Harris expected, either."

Akins raised his eyebrows. "Explain."

"The part of the story we can confirm," Ty said, "is that Harris did indeed ask her to lure those three guys to the waterfall outside of

Viacci's the night Nicole Wynn was murdered. But that's where it stops. According to Lashika, she had no idea it was set up to be a diversion for a hit. She claims to have been pissed as hell when she confronted Harris about it afterward, but he told her to grow up, and basically blew her off."

"What's unexpected about that?" Akins asked.

"That she would dump him and shack up with one of the guys she lured there."

"Garcia?"

"None other."

"What's his story?"

Grueb jumped in. "He claims not to know anything about it. Collins says she hasn't told him, and it appears he didn't know."

"The secrets of young love," Akins said.

Grueb rolled his eyes. "It would seem so."

"Does she have any idea where we might find Harris?"

Ty took that one. "She says no. She's afraid."

"But you think she does?"

"I wouldn't bet my pension on it, but yeah."

Akins sighed. "She's in far more danger if she doesn't tell us. They'll try again."

Ty nodded. "Told her that. She doesn't know what to do."

"What about her parents?"

Ty and Grueb looked at each other. "What about 'em?" Ty asked.

"If their relationship is good, if she trusts them, maybe they can convince her."

"It's worth a shot," Ty said. "We'll get on it. On another note, when can I release Wynn?"

"Now," Akins said. "On one condition."

———

"You have got to be shitting me," Wynn said.

"It's either this," Ty held up an ankle bracelet, "or stay here another couple of days."

"What the hell's he trying to prove with this?"

"Dude, you killed a guy last night. Total self-defense. I get it. But he's trying to rein you in before something else happens. Considering the alternative, house arrest isn't so bad. Would you rather stay here?"

"I'd rather be out finding Harris."

"Don't let Grueb hear you say that. Pull your pant leg up." Ty knelt in front of Wynn and began securing the monitor to his ankle. "Besides, for once, we might be ahead of you. We picked up Lashika Collins this morning."

"Really? Did she tell you where to find Harris?"

"Not yet. So far she's not talking, but her parents are with her now. They seem like good folks. I think they'll get her to cooperate."

"Let's hope. So what are the rules with this thing?"

Ty stood, the ankle bracelet firmly in place. "Pretty simple, even for you. Go home and stay home."

"Shit."

"Did you listen to anything I told you last night? If you want to be useful, figure out why someone would want to kill Nicole. Do you still have her old phone?"

"Yeah."

"Start there. I assume you've got her password. Go through her contacts. See if there's anyone you don't recognize. Check her texts and email. Find us another investigative path. Grabbing Harris only helps if we can get him to talk, and those odds aren't good."

"I'll make him talk."

Ty rolled his eyes. "Don't let Akins hear you say *that*. He'll keep you in here."

"Oh, hell no. Where's my bike?"

"We had it towed back here. I was able to keep it out of impound so it's outside. You'll get the keys along with the rest of your stuff when you're released. You ready?"

"Definitely."

"Alright. Let's get you out of here."

———

Li slammed the door as he stormed out of the warehouse. Losing Xiang was bad enough, but missing the girl was worse. And then having to sit there and endure both Chan's disappointment and Stuart's contempt when he told them what happened. He wanted to scream. No, he wanted to kill something.

Someone.

Wynn.

———

An hour later, Wynn was at home, the weight on his ankle as much psychological as physical. He went upstairs and found a box in the bedroom closet that had a lot of Nicole's old things, including her cell phone. Knowing the battery would be dead, he found a charger and took them both downstairs and plugged them in.

Next, he pulled out his own cell phone. He'd been in such a hurry to get out of jail he hadn't bothered to check it until now. He had one voice message. Hoping it was from Trish Johnson, telling him where she was, he was surprised at the actual message.

Hi Sean... this is Vanessa... Carow. I saw you and Detective Lenihan on TV with that shooting last night. Are you okay? Did that have anything to do with Diana or your wife? Is there something going on I should know? Please call me when you can.

He lowered the phone from his ear. *Shit. We didn't need this all over the news. Probably part of what got Akins pissed.* Pushing the redial button, he waited for her to pick up.

"Hello?"

"Hi, Vanessa. Sean Wynn. Returning your call."

Her voice rushed out. "Oh my God! Sean. Are you okay?"

"Yeah, I'm fine."

"Oh, thank goodness. I was worried."

"I appreciate that, but there's nothing to worry about. Detective Lenihan and I are both fine."

"Oh good. I saw you on TV. What was that all about? Did it have anything to do with Diana or your wife?"

"I can't comment."

"It did, huh? No comment always means the worst."

Wynn laughed softly. "No comment."

"Were those the guys that gave Diana the money? That set it up?"

"I honestly don't know."

"Shit. So that guy, or those guys, could still be out there?"

"All I can tell you is I have no reason to believe those two from last night were directly involved."

"That doesn't make me feel very safe," Vanessa said. "Are the police still looking?"

"As much as they ever were."

"What about you?"

Wynn felt the weight on his ankle. "Not today."

"Why not? I mean, you found Diana, talked to her mom. You found me. Seems to me the police would be nowhere without what you've done."

"Let's just say I'm indisposed."

"Are you hurt?"

"No, I'm fine. I'm just not going anywhere."

"What? Like they put you under house arrest?"

Wynn stayed silent.

A beat longer.

And another.

"Oh my God! Are you serious?" She laughed. "I was joking! They really put you under house arrest?"

Wynn smiled. "I'm glad you see the humor in it."

"Do you have one of those ankle bracelets?"

Wynn stayed silent.

"You do! Oh my God!"

Wynn let her laugh herself out, then said, "As long as you're not worried anymore..."

"No, no. I'm sorry." She composed herself. "I know this isn't funny. I guess I was so worried, and now relieved, that my reaction was inappropriate. I'm sorry."

"It's not a problem."

"Can I make it up to you?"

"That's not necessary."

"No, I want to. Tell you what. If you can't go anywhere, let me at least bring you some groceries. You have to eat, right?"

"That's truly not necessary. I'm fine."

"Maybe some takeout?"

Wynn had to admit that besides Corona, the fridge was pretty bare. "It's really not necessary," he said weakly.

"Yeah, but I insist. Do you like Greek?"

"Sure." Wynn relented, then gave her his address. She said she'd be there between four and five o'clock this afternoon.

Better than ordering a pizza.

Wynn spent the rest of the afternoon going through his contacts, making lists, trying to remember his last interactions with people, and jotting it all down. He then began prioritizing each name by assigning it a number. "Fours" were those he immediately eliminated as having no possible motivation, as he or Nicole didn't know them well enough. That was forty percent of the list.

"Threes" were people who at least ran in their circles. Not that he would call close friends, but did have some degree of attachment. It was doubtful they would know anything. This was another forty percent.

"Twos" were friends or co-workers who might have been considered trusted confidants. If something was going on, Nicole might have told one of them about it. That was twenty percent. "Ones," were those who had a beef with either him or Nicole and could be considered an immediate suspect. No one rose to that level.

While he knew a lot of his contacts would also be on Nicole's phone, he also knew he'd have to do this same exercise all over again when he got to her list.

About a quarter to five in the afternoon, his doorbell rang. He glanced at the camera monitor on the counter. Vanessa Carow stood at the entry with plastic grocery bags hanging from each arm.

Shit! He'd forgotten she'd be stopping by.

Leaving his notepad and phone on the kitchen table, he quickly scanned the living room to make sure it wasn't too messy. *Not great, but acceptable.*

"Vanessa," he said as he opened the door. "Please come in. Let me help you with those." He reached out and took the bags from her left hand.

She stepped inside. "Thanks. How are you doing?"

"I'm good. Better than being in jail."

She glanced around the house, to the windows and harbor out back. "Wow. I should say so. Nice place."

"Thanks. Come on back." Wynn led her through the house to the kitchen, where they placed the bags on the counter. "You really didn't have to do this."

"I know. But honestly, I feel bad about having misjudged you all this time. And when you told me you were cooped up, well, if you're like most bachelors I know, you probably couldn't live very long on what's in your refrigerator."

He smiled sheepishly.

"I thought so. Anyway. I stopped by this great little Mediterranean place and got enough for two because for one thing, I love it, and two, I figured you could use the company. And then I picked up some things for breakfast in the morning."

"Breakfast?"

She looked at him quizzically, and then a wave of embarrassment flushed across her face. "Oh my God, no! *Your* breakfast. You. Alone.

Or, with whomever. But without me. Oh, crap. Look at me. I'm not here five minutes and already putting my foot in my mouth. I should leave."

Wynn laughed. "No, it's alright. This is all very sweet. I appreciate it."

"Ugh. I'm such a dunce."

"You're very thoughtful. Tell you what. Let's warm up dinner in the oven, put the groceries away, and then we can eat on the patio. And you're right. I would love the company."

"You sure?"

"I'm sure."

"Okay, but I've got one favor to ask." A smirky smile crept across her face.

"What's that?"

"Show me that ankle bracelet."

Wynn rolled his eyes. "Seriously?"

"It's the whole reason I'm here. A girl can't be too careful."

He pulled up his pant leg and stuck his foot out, revealing the tracker. "Satisfied?"

She laughed. "It's all good. I've never had dinner with a guy wearing an ankle bracelet before."

Wynn smiled as he let his pant leg fall, then turned serious. "Vanessa, I have to ask. Twenty-four hours ago, you were terrified of me. Now you're bringing me groceries. What gives?"

"Well," she said thoughtfully. "The fact that you brought a cop with you yesterday didn't hurt, but when I saw how you reacted to those finger paintings, I was touched. I knew you couldn't have had anything to do with it."

"That's it?"

She sighed and her shoulders fell. Looking down, she said, "I realized how much pain I caused you by not going to the police right away. They might've caught these guys and you might've gotten closure two years ago if I hadn't been so afraid. I'm sorry. I'm really, really sorry."

Wynn was silent a moment. *She's not wrong. But she is trying to make amends.* "Nothing to be sorry for," he said. "Anyone might've reacted that way."

"You're sure?"

He knew what she needed to hear. "Not that you need it, but you're forgiven. It's all good."

"Thanks."

He could see the relief wash over her. "Here," he said, handing her a cutting board and nodding toward the takeout bag. "Get that ready for the oven." He put the groceries away while Vanessa prepped dinner. "Would you like a glass of wine?"

"Sure."

He opened a bottle of Cabernet and poured them each a glass, then led the way out to the patio. They made small talk as a warm breeze wafted off the ocean. The late afternoon sun cast an orange glow on the horizon that lit up the boats in the harbor. Eventually, they brought dinner outside.

"This is gorgeous." Vanessa settled into her chair. "How long have you lived here?"

"I've owned it about a year and a half. Haven't spent much time here, though."

"Why not?"

Wynn paused between bites. "Been on the road a lot."

"After your wife died?"

"Yeah. Couldn't stay in the old place. Then realized it was as much about the town as it was the house."

"Tell me about her."

He smiled sadly and exhaled. "What's to tell? She was smart, funny, sexy. Everything a guy could want."

Vanessa matched his smile. "How'd you meet?"

"In college. USC."

"College sweethearts?"

"Sort of. She went right out of high school. I spent eight years in the Marines first."

"Marines? Doing what?" Vanessa took a sip of wine.

"Mostly waiting for something to happen."

"Pretty boring?"

"It had its moments, but yeah, for the most part, pretty boring."

"How long were you married?"

"Four years. We were celebrating our anniversary the night she was killed."

"I'm sorry."

"Thanks." Wanting to change the subject, Wynn asked, "What about you?"

She sat back. "My life is boring. I'm twenty-five years old, went to high school in Santa Clarita, college and grad school here in Ventura, and now a year of teaching. A third of my life is gone, but it feels like I haven't done anything yet."

"Adventure is overrated."

"I thought you said the Marines were boring?"

"That's not the only place adventure happens."

"Where else?"

He looked at her and raised his eyebrows.

"Oh. Sorry," she said.

"Speaking of that, I was wondering if you remembered the name of the waitress Diana had to pay off?"

"No, sorry. Diana told me about it, but if she ever mentioned a name, it wasn't someone I knew, so it didn't stick."

"I wonder how many wait staff they had back then? If we could get a list, maybe I could get Ty to send someone out to talk to them."

"You'd just need those who were working that night. Heck, you'd really only need to know who *your* waitress was. She'd be the one complaining about the table sitting empty."

Damn. She's right. I wonder if that's in the files...

They continued to make small talk until the sun went down and lights began to twinkle on the masts in the harbor. It was beautiful. And romantic. And if he remembered anything at all about dating, he'd swear she was giving him signals, twirling her hair, touching his arm, laughing at his lame jokes. But he wasn't ready to go down that road. He tried to walk the line between friendly and flirty, and hoped she understood. In reality, he was more interested in checking the files for the name of the waitress.

After a while, as the conversation lulled, she said, "This is so beautiful I could sit here all night, but I should get going."

"I want to thank you for dinner tonight, and groceries for the morning. It's very thoughtful."

Vanessa shrugged. "I felt like I owed you."

"Consider us even. I'll even owe you if I can find the name of that waitress."

"Anything I can do to help."

Vanessa got up and placed Wynn's empty plate on top of her own and carried them into the house. He picked up the wine glasses and followed her in. She set the dishes in the sink then walked around the counter and picked up her purse and dug out her keys.

"Are you okay to drive? Would you like me to call an Uber?"

"After one glass of wine with dinner? I'm fine. Thank you, though."

He followed her as she walked to the door and opened it. It felt awkward, like he should say something, but he didn't know what. "Maybe we can do this again sometime, after all this settles down."

"I'd like that. You can take me for a ride on your bike. *After* all this settles down."

One corner of Wynn's mouth curled up in a poignant smile. He nodded. "You got it."

"Good night, Sean."

"Good night, Vanessa."

He closed the door and went straight to his computer, opened the case files, and began scanning the reports for the name of the waitress.

———

Well now, who's this? Li watched the girl come out of Wynn's front door and walk to her car. In the couple of days he'd been tracking Wynn, it was unusual for him to spend a full day at home. On a hunch, he'd driven past Wynn's house more than an hour ago and saw the car parked in the driveway. He'd pulled to the curb a block away. Maybe that hunch would pay off.

He turned the ignition and followed as the girl drove away.

————

After a fruitless half-hour of searching the case files for the waitress's name, Wynn's phone rang. It was Ty.

"How you doing, Sean?"

"Good," Wynn replied. "I'm glad you called. I've got a question for you."

"Go for it."

"Do you guys have the name of the waitress who was serving Nicole and me that night?"

"I'm sure it's in the file."

"Great. Can you get it?"

"Tomorrow, probably."

"Not tonight?"

"I'm going to be busy," Ty said. "That's why I called. Lashika talked. We're going after Harris tonight."

CHAPTER 19

THE RIVERSIDE APARTMENT complex consisted of eight two-story buildings situated along the banks of the Santa Clara River. Like the trickling river itself, the apartments appeared to be well past their prime. The structures were laid out in a large "U" shape with a parking lot, clubhouse, and swimming pool in the middle. Each building contained eight units, four on the first floor, four on the second. According to Lashika, Harris had been tight with her cousin, Lon, who lived in apartment 2D of building six, which backed up to the river.

The headlights of Ty's unmarked Ford lit up the black-and-white police cruiser parked a block away from the complex's main entrance. He pulled to a stop behind it, then he and Gruebauer got out and went around to the back of his car. Ty opened the trunk and handed Grueb a bulletproof vest, then put one on himself as a uniformed officer approached.

"What do you have?" Gruebauer asked.

"Not much," the officer replied. "A few cars have come and gone. Impossible to know if he might've been hiding in one of them. Plus, there's a lot of open space on either side. He could've run out the back and we'd never see him."

"Did you bother to get off your ass and go look?" Ty scowled. Lashika had played coy with the information. Pretended she wasn't sure exactly which building or apartment, and a judge sure as hell wasn't going to give him a warrant to search the whole complex.

"Yeah, we did, fuck you very much," the officer replied. "My partner's walking it right now. But our instructions were to lay low, be inconspicuous. Couldn't hardly hang out in the yard all day."

Ty stared him down.

"Where's your partner now?" Gruebauer asked.

The uniformed officer squeezed the button on his shoulder radio. "Frankie, what's your twenty?"

"On the path behind building five," a male voice came back. "What's up?"

"The dicks are here. Hold on."

"He's behind and slightly west of the target."

"Have him get in position to watch the back in case he runs," Gruebauer said. "Let's go find out if he's in there." He turned and started walking toward the complex.

———

Inside apartment 2D, Lon Collins' cell phone rang. He answered quickly. "Yeah?"

"He's been joined by two suits. Three of them coming this way. Not sure where the fourth is. Probably behind your ass."

"Anyone else?"

"No, man. That's all I see."

"Thanks." Lon disconnected the call and looked at Harris. "When we got more time, you can tell me what you're messed up in, boy. But for now, you need to get your ass out of here. Come on."

Lon cracked open the front door and looked past the swimming pool out toward the parking lot. A couple of guys who had been drinking beer in the pool all afternoon were talking up some girls, but the cops hadn't appeared around the corner of the clubhouse yet. He stepped out onto the second-floor walkway and looked around the corner, searching for the fourth cop. Seeing no one, he leaned back inside the apartment. "Quick now." Lon hustled past two doors, finally stopping at apartment 2A. He knocked quietly.

The door opened immediately, and a young woman stepped aside. Harris slid quietly through the door.

"Thanks, bae," Lon said. He gave her a quick kiss, then darted back to his own apartment.

———

Not a coincidence, Ty thought when he saw the darkness shrouding building six. The porchlights outside each unit were out, as were those in the stairwell that went up through the center of the building.

"You got a torch?" he asked.

The officer grunted and pulled a flashlight off his belt, then played the light across the front of the building. Apartment 2D was on the second floor, far right. The stairwell looked clear.

Ty pulled out his phone and smiled as he read an incoming text. "Can you confirm your partner's position for us, please?" he asked.

The cop triggered his radio. "Frankie, what's your exact position?"

"In the bushes. Twenty yards from the southwest corner of the target building."

The cop looked at Ty. "Is that where you want him?"

"That'll work." He nodded to Gruebauer, who took off jogging around the east end of the building, disappearing into the darkness. "Let him know we have a detective coming around to take an opposite position on the east side."

"Hey, Frankie. Be advised there's a suit taking up a position directly east of you. He's a friendly."

"Roger that."

Ty pulled his Glock from the shoulder holster under his jacket and led the way up the stairwell. He stayed to the left while the officer followed behind on the right, shining the beam past Ty and lighting the way ahead.

When they reached the second-floor walkway, Ty stopped. "Hold a second."

Gliding silently up the stairs behind the officer was one of the guys from the pool. He was barefoot, wearing only swim trunks and a black bulletproof vest with "VPD" emblazoned in bright yellow letters across the back. He was also carrying a Glock.

"That's how you do inconspicuous," Ty told the officer. "Stay here, just in case he gets past us. And make sure no one comes out from behind. Especially watch 2D."

Ty turned toward 2A and crept down the walkway.

———

Harris stood inside the door, his phone in one hand, the .380 Smith & Wesson in the other. He strained to hear the knocking on a door at the other end of the building, then nearly jumped out of his shoes when he felt his phone vibrate. Even the muted vibration seemed like a scream in the silence. He looked down at the one-word text from Lon:

Run

A loud pounding erupted from the other side of the door next to him. "Police! Open the door!"

Harris sprinted through the apartment. As he stuffed the phone in his pocket, he knocked over a chair, then yanked open the glass slider to the balcony. The sound of the front door being kicked open behind him was the last thing he heard as he launched himself over the railing. A long second later his ankles exploded with sharp stingers as he hit the ground and rolled through the damp grass.

From very close by he heard a voice yell, "Stop! Po—" but the voice was cut off as he rolled into someone's legs, knocking them from their feet. Suddenly, someone—a cop, he assumed—was on top of him, a tangle of arms and legs. He flailed his left fist and connected with something hard, pushed away, then fired three shots blindly in that general direction.

Climbing to his feet, he saw another cop rushing toward him out of the bushes. He pointed the gun toward the oncoming cop, fired four more shots, then turned and ran.

———

Ty heard the gunshots from inside the apartment and raced out to the balcony as the uniformed officer, Frankie, ran up to Gruebauer, who was lying in the grass.

"You hit?" Frankie asked, slowing as he approached.

"I'm good. Go after him!" Gruebauer yelled.

Frankie ran down the dirt path along the edge of the river, disappearing into the tall grass and shrubs along the riverbank. Ty strained to see, but there was nothing but darkness. "Grueb, talk to me. You okay?"

"I'm hit," he wheezed. "But I think the vest stopped it."

Ty raced back through the apartment, then ran down the stairs and around the building to where Gruebauer now sat up in the grass, a handkerchief, stained dark with blood, held to his face. "Where?" Ty asked as he knelt next to Grueb.

"Chest. But I don't think it got through."

"Lie back," Ty instructed, then took out his phone and turned on the flashlight. He found three bullets embedded in Grueb's vest. He zipped it open and looked underneath. Grueb's shirt was clean. No bullet holes. No red stains. "Looks like you're good here. Let's check the rest of you."

Grueb waved him away and sat up. "Fucker got me with a lucky punch." He removed the handkerchief from his face to reveal a bloody nose. "Don't start."

Ty smiled. "I'm glad it's not worse. Let's hope Frankie has better luck."

The words were barely out of his mouth when Frankie emerged from the dark bushes. Alone.

Harris was gone.

CHAPTER 20

Ty called on Sunday morning. Wynn was finishing the contact review he'd been working on yesterday afternoon before Vanessa arrived.

"How'd it go?" Wynn asked.

"No good."

"What happened?"

"The asshole jumped off a second-story balcony and almost took out Grueb at close range. Dude's lucky to be alive."

"But Harris is gone?"

"Like the wind."

"Shit. What next?"

"You want that bracelet off?"

"Damn right."

"Get your butt down here."

Wynn hopped on the Sportster and within twenty minutes was at the police station. He walked straight past the receptionist and directly to Ty's office where he knocked on the open door. "Hey."

"Hey, yourself. Thanks for coming down."

"Anything to get this thing off."

"Couldn't have been that bad."

Wynn thought about his evening with Vanessa. "Maybe not terrible," he admitted.

"Before I take that off, Akins wants a word."

Ty led the way to another office where Akins sat behind a desk opposite Gruebauer. Akins motioned Wynn to sit in an empty chair next to the gang detective.

"Mr. Wynn," Akins said, "I do hope you enjoyed your evening."

"Your tactics are a little too Hotel California-ish for my tastes, Lieutenant, but otherwise charming." Wynn turned to Gruebauer, hoping to thaw the ice that had formed between them. "Ty told me what happened. You okay?"

Grueb shrugged. "Still here."

Wynn nodded, then turned back to Akins. "Any other progress?"

"Well, yes. But before we talk about that, I want you to understand why I put that thing on you." Akins paused until Wynn looked him in the eye. "Sean, you've proven to be damn resourceful. And dangerous. Since you've gotten involved, we've got two people dead, two more on the run, including Harris, and one of my detectives nearly killed.

"Believe it or not, we do know what we're doing, and eventually, we'll get Harris. But in the meantime, I can't afford to have you chasing after him only to have him, you, or anyone else end up dead. Despite the fact he got away, I consider what happened last night a success because all my officers are alive. I'd like to keep it that way."

A flush of embarrassment he hadn't felt since his own dad last scolded him in high school washed down Wynn's face. "Understood, Lieutenant. It won't happen again."

"I'd appreciate that." He nodded to Ty. "Take it off."

While Ty removed the bracelet, Akins continued. "Now normally we'd send you home at this point, hoping you'd learned your lesson, but we do have some new information that I think is important for you to hear. Ty, bring him up to speed."

Ty stood and set the bracelet on the desk. "We finally got an ID on the dude you shot the other night. Xiang Mao. He's part of a

Chinese American gang based down in L.A. No known connection to the ADs, which lends credence to the theory that Harris and Johnson were simply hired to do a job, but someone else ordered it. Grueb can tell you more."

"Ty used the word gang," Grueb said, "but the reality is these guys operate more like organized crime. They're known as the Silent Mafia, and they're big-time. Run by a guy named Ishan Chan, they're into drugs, racketeering, and human trafficking. A bad reputation that seems to be well-deserved."

"What kind of drugs?" Wynn asked.

"Cocaine, heroin, other opioids."

"Jewel?"

Grueb shrugged. "Maybe." Apparently, the ice hadn't completely thawed.

Akins stepped in. "The takeaway from this is that with the way you've been stirring things up, it is very likely that you, not DeAndre Renker, were their primary target the other night."

Everyone nodded their agreement, but Wynn was more confused than ever. *How in the world would Nicole have even been known to the Silent Mafia?*

Akins' voice brought him back to the conversation. "All that said, Sean, I want you to do three things. One, you need to drop this cowboy shit you've been pulling. Two, do what Ty told you, which is to work on finding us a motive as to why someone would want to kill your wife."

Wynn nodded. That's what he'd been planning anyway. For now, at least. The addition of the Silent Mafia to the equation made it that much more important. "And the third thing?"

Akins' voice softened. "You need to watch your back, son. Just because they missed this time doesn't mean they won't try again."

———

Stuart Legrea waited patiently inside his golf cart under the shade of a massive oak tree just off the island green of the beautiful, par-five eleventh hole at Lockdale Country Club. The morning air was crisp as the water surrounding the green reflected the clear blue sky above. Birds fluttered in the trees. The smell of freshly cut grass filled the air as groundskeepers mowed the rough on the next hole across the pond. It was a perfect day to get in eighteen holes, or maybe even thirty-six, but that wasn't in the cards. Not for him, anyway.

Back on the island, Alexander Jameson crouched at the edge of the green, studying the contours, picking his line. One of his three playing partners was chipping from the fairway a few yards short of the green. His ball rolled several feet past the hole.

All four of them were dressed in light-colored pants and shirts, an air of snooty haughtiness emanating from each. Finally settling on his mark, Jameson walked slowly to his ball and leaned over a nine-foot putt. Stuart hoped he'd make it. He'd be easier to talk to.

Jameson rocked his shoulders and drew back the putter, then slid through the stroke like a pendulum, gently tapping the ball. Stuart smiled when he heard the satisfying "pa-lunk" of the ball dropping into the cup, followed by the polite congratulations of Jameson's fellow golfers.

Stuart heaved himself out of the cart and stood next to it as Jameson strode across the bridge, veering away from his cart and over to Stuart.

"Nice putt," Stuart said. "Good round?"

"Two under with that birdie."

"Nice."

"What's the situation?"

"In a word? It's a clusterfuck."

Jameson sighed. "While I do love your ability to boil a complex situation down to a concise description, Stuart, more details would be helpful."

Stuart leaned against the cart. "You already know that Wynn killed one of Chan's men in a shootout two nights ago. Besides that, Harris gave me the name of a girl he used to help set up the hit at Viacci's. I sent Li after her yesterday morning, but he missed. The cops have her. Harris says she doesn't know enough to hurt us, but she can verify at least one part of Johnson's story. Enough to verify it was set up."

"And where's Harris?"

"I haven't heard from him since Friday," Stuart said. "He's not answering his phone."

"I don't suppose I need to remind you that right at the very beginning I suggested the easiest way to handle this was to take him out."

"I'm well aware."

"Find him." Jameson jammed his putter into the ground for emphasis. "I assume you're aware of the consequences if the cops find him first?"

"Of course. We'll get him."

"And Wynn?"

"I think he might have given it up. He spent Friday night in jail after the shooting but stayed home all day yesterday. Chan's guys are still monitoring him."

"Make sure they do."

"Speaking of Chan." Stuart cleared his throat. "He tried to use Xiang's death as a way to change our arrangement. Says we owe him additional compensation."

"Why? Because his guy screwed up and got himself killed?"

"Because it happened on a job for us. Therefore, he says we're responsible. It's fucked up, but that's how he sees it."

"You didn't agree to anything, did you?" Jameson looked across the pond to the next tee box. The first of his playing partners was teeing off.

"Of course not," Stuart said. "I told him we'd look at additional compensation after the job is done. But Chan's boy Li is pissed. He wants revenge. He wants to take Wynn out."

"Why not?" Jameson said, turning his attention back to Stuart. "You called it poetic tragedy."

"In time, but not yet. Wynn's been spending a lot of time with the cops lately. If he goes down, they'll be all over it. They'll know he was on the right track. And if they haven't gotten an ID on Xiang yet, they soon will. Then they'll be coming at this from both directions, the ADs on one side, Chan's crew on the other, and us in the middle. We can take out the ADs, but trying to cut ties with Chan is not a war I want to get into. Li will get his chance, but not yet. Agreed?"

"Sure. Is that it?"

"For now."

"Okay, good," Jameson began walking to his cart, then stopped and turned back. "And Stuart?"

"Yes?"

"Find Harris."

Despite his lack of sleep the night before, Ishan Chan was up early Sunday morning. Stuart's comments during his three a.m. visit two nights ago had bothered him all day yesterday. If Wynn was in a position to *blow up our mutually beneficial arrangement*, as Stuart had said, that meant Jameson and Stuart were vulnerable.

If my supplier is vulnerable, am I not also?

The simple answer, the one Stuart was pursuing, was to watch and potentially get rid of Wynn. But Chan was a businessman. And the rules of business had taught him that if he couldn't rely on his supplier, he had two choices.

Find a new supplier, or take over the manufacturing of the product myself.

Wynn sat at his kitchen table going through Nicole's Facebook profile while a Sunday morning NFL pre-game show played on the television in the background. Nicole's sister Julia had provided the required proof of death, so Nicole's profile, like Diana Williams, contained the gentle heading "Remembering," which allowed him to continue to view all of her connections. As he had done with his own contacts, Wynn made a list of Nicole's friends and prioritized them on his scale of one to four. Once again, not a single name rose to the level of an immediate suspect.

Pulling out her phone, he reviewed her contact list, suddenly realizing there were many names he didn't recognize. He made a separate list of those.

Around noon, he finished up the last of the contacts and examined the long list of unrecognized names.

She really did have a life I knew nothing about.

Assuming most of the names were from work, he picked up his phone and dialed Lisa Montgomery. After exchanging greetings and pleasantries, he went straight to the reason he'd called. "I was wondering if you'd had a chance to find out what Nicky was working on back then, or come up with any more names of people she might've confided in?"

"I'm sorry, Sean. I haven't been back in the office since we spoke on Friday so no, not yet. In terms of who she might've confided in, maybe her boss, Janelle Evans. She could probably also tell you what Nicole was working on, but she doesn't work there anymore."

Wynn well remembered Janelle. She was at the restaurant the night of the shooting. She'd rushed over to help but ended up mostly holding Wynn back as an off-duty doctor performed first aid. "Is she still in the area?"

"I have no idea. I was never that close with her."

"Okay. I'll give her a call. On another note, I was wondering if you could do me a favor."

"I'll try. What is it?"

"I've got a list of maybe thirty names from the contacts in

Nicole's phone that I don't recognize. I'm assuming most of them are co-workers but was wondering if you'd look at it and confirm."

"Sure. Send it over."

"Great, thanks."

Wynn disconnected the call and snapped a picture of the list, then texted the photo to Lisa. Next, he pulled up Janelle's name from Nicole's phone and copied the contact to his own phone, then tapped the call button.

It was answered on the second ring. "Hello?"

"Hi. Is this Janelle Evans?"

"Yes?"

"Hi, Janelle. This is Sean Wynn, Nicole Wynn's husband."

There was a pause, then, "Yes, Sean. What can I do for you?"

He hesitated, unsure of what to say. "Well... it's taken me a while, but I'm finally coming to terms with what happened to Nicole, and I'm realizing I knew very little about the work she did or the people she worked with. I was wondering if you'd be willing to talk with me about it."

Janelle paused. "Is this some kind of therapy thing?"

Wynn let out a small laugh. "Not officially, but yeah, I suppose so."

"Hmm. You know, I still think about it almost every day. Maybe it'll help both of us. What were you thinking?"

"Can I buy you a cup of coffee? The sooner the better for me."

"I have to work in the morning, but I'm free this afternoon. Say four o'clock?"

CHAPTER 21

Wynn spent the next couple of hours calling a few of Nicole's old friends. Inevitably, each call turned into an awkward conversation. After some perfunctory catching up and polite banter, he got down to it: Was Nicole seeing anyone on the side? Was she into something sketchy? Was she doing anything that might have made her an enemy? He was sure it made him sound pathetic, like he was spiraling into an emotional abyss, pleading for someone to give him a reason to blame her and not himself. But there was nothing. Each of them confirmed what he already knew; Nicole was as close to perfect as there ever was.

At half-past three, he hopped on the Street Glide and hit the freeway for the twenty-minute ride to a Starbucks in Camarillo. He'd gotten Janelle's order and wanted to get there early to make sure they could get a table. At four o'clock on a Sunday afternoon, it wasn't a problem. The place was practically empty.

He placed the order and found a table in a quiet corner. Janelle came in as the barista called his name. Getting up, he extended his hand as she approached, but she ignored it and pulled him into a polite embrace.

"Oh, I think we're past the handshake phase," she said. "It's good to see you again, Sean."

"Good to see you, too." He took the coffees off the counter and handed one to her, then motioned her to the corner table and slid into a chair while she removed her jacket and settled in.

"I have to admit," Janelle began, "I've been looking forward to this all afternoon."

"Oh yeah? Why is that?"

"It's the odd day that goes by that I don't think about Nicole. I guess I'm hoping this might be therapeutic for me, too."

Wynn felt an ache in the pit of his stomach. He hoped she'd still feel that way after he asked his questions. "I hope so, too."

"So, what do you want to know?"

"As much as she talked about her work, I realize I don't know much about the kinds of things she worked on or who she worked with, what her days were like. Just hoping we could talk about that for a while."

"Hmm, good old Mynogen. Where to start?" she asked herself. "Obviously you know the big picture, pharmaceutical research and development, right? My group reviewed clinical trials. It was our job to confirm the trial data before moving to the next phase of development. It was pretty boring and monotonous to tell you the truth. Just compiled and examined data all day, comparing test groups to one another. Looking for discrepancies among the different groups and then comparing their results to the placebo groups."

"What happened if you found a discrepancy?"

"We'd look for anomalies among the subjects. Different races, ages, sexes, health conditions. We'd slice and dice the data every different way we could think of to try to find a pattern. To give you an example, we might have a blood pressure medicine that initially looks great. But when we analyze the data, we might find it works great on men but has some nasty side effects on women. We'd give the researchers this feedback and they would modify the treatment regimen, maybe change the dosage, for example. They'll run it again on this more targeted group to see if the changes make a difference."

She sounds just like Nicole, Wynn thought. They both had a way of taking something complicated and simplifying it so that even a dummy like himself could understand. He was struck for a moment by how alike they were. Janelle was maybe twenty pounds heavier and fifteen years older, but they were roughly the same height, same hair color. *She's what Nicole would've been.*

"Is that what you were working on, this blood pressure medicine, when Nicole was killed?" he asked.

"I wish," Janelle said. "No, we were working on something called hydrexachloromine, HCM for short."

"What's that?"

"The drug from hell that was supposed to cure the disease from hell. Remember a few years ago there was an outbreak of the Marburg 2 virus in Africa? They called it MV2. It was a mutation of the Marburg hemorrhagic fever. Had a fatality rate near ninety percent and was spread both airborne and on surfaces."

Wynn nodded. He recalled a little about it.

"Yeah, well, this was bad stuff. Some little company down in the valley claimed they were miles ahead in the race for a vaccine, but they were too small to develop and manufacture it on their own, so Mynogen bought them out. But the vaccine had some nasty side effects among the indigenous population. They couldn't seem to get the formula quite right. They were still running targeted trials when I left."

"That's what Nicole was working on?"

"She'd started on it a week or two earlier. I pulled her off another study to help with this one. We had a couple of trials that didn't match up, and I was hoping a fresh set of eyes could figure out why."

"Did she?"

Janelle shook her head slowly. "She never got the chance."

Wynn sat back. A vaccine like that had to be worth a fortune.

Especially to a small company that was looking to be bought out by a larger one.

"What was the name of the little company down in the valley?"

"Oh gosh, I don't remember." Janelle put her hand to her forehead and looked down at the table, hiding her eyes. "A.L.K., A.M. something. I don't remember, but it was like three initials and then research, or pharmaceuticals, or something like that."

"Do you know who owned it?"

Janelle laughed. "No, that was above my pay grade."

"And you say they were still working on it when you left?"

"Yeah," she said bitterly.

Wynn suspected more to the story. "Why'd you leave?"

"My boss was an asshole."

"Who was your boss?"

"Neil Carson. He was in charge of the HCM trial. He blamed me for the fact that the numbers didn't line up but hey, numbers are numbers. They either line up or they don't. Not my fault. The dipshit probably said the same thing when they fired his ass six months later."

"Carson was fired?"

"Yep. I heard they still couldn't get it figured out."

"And that's why I've never heard of HCM," Wynn said.

"Probably."

Wynn paused for a moment. "What about something called Jewel? Have you ever heard of that?"

"That's the street name for some kind of opioid, isn't it?"

"Yeah. Does Mynogen do any work in that area?"

"Opioids in general? Sure. All major drug companies do."

"Was Nicole working on anything related to that?"

"No. My group hadn't touched an opioid-based drug in years."

They sat in silence for a few moments while Wynn sipped his now lukewarm coffee and mulled over everything he was learning. "Did Nicole know Neil Carson?"

"Probably. I worked pretty closely with both of them, so I'm sure their paths crossed."

"Did they ever work together directly?"

"I don't think so. As I said, I had just pulled her into it."

Wynn paused again. Took another sip. "Was Nicky close with anyone at work?"

"Hmm. She and Lisa Montgomery seemed to get along pretty well."

"Yeah, I know Lisa. Was there anyone else, maybe any guys she seemed to hang out with a lot?"

Janelle straightened up, suddenly looking very alert. "What do you mean?"

Wynn didn't want to lay all his cards on the table, but he needed an honest answer. "Listen. I can't go into detail, but there's a chance... I mean, I'm hearing rumors... that Nicole may have been having an affair. I need to know if it's true. Did you see or know anything about something like that?"

Her shoulders fell. "Oh, Sean. No. I remember she was so excited about your dinner that night. It was your anniversary, right?"

"We were celebrating it, yeah."

"She talked about it for two days. Said she had a big surprise for you at Viacci's. In fact, that's what gave Alan and me the idea to go there for our anniversary that night."

It killed Wynn to make people think he didn't trust Nicole, that his last memory of her would be that she was unfaithful. He didn't believe it, but there had to be some reason she was targeted. "I don't want to believe it, but..."

"I know affairs happen in the workplace all the time," Janelle said. "And Mynogen had its share of romances, but those were among the single folks. When it came to the flirting and all that, there were two distinct cultures. Those who did it, and those who wouldn't touch it. Nicole didn't touch it. Besides, the single girls outnumbered the single guys by at least two-to-one. The guys had more than their share to pick from."

"What about the married guys? Anyone there she seemed close to?"

Janelle paused and looked down, thinking. "No. I mean, we didn't have that many guys in our group. Carson was a creep, but I was under the impression they barely knew each other."

"What do you mean, he was a creep?"

Janelle hesitated. "Well," she finally said. "I heard that after he was fired, his wife divorced him because he was having an affair with someone at work."

CHAPTER 22

WYNN TOOK HIS laptop and a Corona out to the patio overlooking the harbor. The night was cool but comfortable as stars twinkled beyond the glimmering forest of sailboat masts. His mind wandered back twenty-four hours as he pictured Vanessa Carow sitting at the table. She was bright, caring, beautiful...

And right.

Anything more with her would have to wait until after he had his answers. And maybe not even then.

He still didn't believe that Nicole had been unfaithful, but he could use that idea as a premise to find out more about Neil Carson. The rumor that he'd had an affair with someone, if true, did say something about his character. Combined with the fact that Carson had been in charge of studying a drug potentially worth billions, which then resulted in the buyout of some smaller company by Mynogen, was worth looking into.

Janelle had said Carson moved to Palm Springs after being fired from Mynogen, so the first thing he did was to look up Carson's address, which he found quickly. Janelle couldn't remember the ex-Mrs. Carson's first name, so Wynn opened a browser to Intelius, a public records search website, and soon found her name to be

Amanda, and that she currently lived in Thousand Oaks. A few more clicks and he had her phone number.

Leaning back, he debated if he should call her. On the one hand, Akins had specifically warned him off. But on the other, Ty had pressed him to find out why someone might target Nicole. The whole HCM debacle seemed to smell of high stakes, and a conversation with Amanda Carson could either solidify or dismiss Neil Carson as a lead. That alone was enough to justify having a conversation with her.

He dialed the number, but after six rings it went to voicemail. He left an intriguingly vague message saying only that his wife may have worked with her ex-husband at Mynogen, and would she please give him a call.

Moments after disconnecting, the phone buzzed in his hand. It was Ty.

"Hey," Wynn said by way of greeting.

"Hey, yourself," Ty said. "How are you feeling?"

"Like I've been cheating on my wife."

"How's that?"

"It's been a strange day. I talked to some of Nicky's friends and co-workers. Felt like I was trashing her, asking about affairs or if she was into something sketchy. Not particularly proud of myself at the moment."

"Did you come up with anything?"

"One interesting thing going on at work. Nothing solid, but I'm hoping to find out more tomorrow. I'll let you know. Anything new on Harris?"

"Not yet."

Wynn's phone beeped to indicate an incoming call. He looked at the screen and recognized Amanda Carson's number. "I'm getting a call on the other line. Let me take this. Call me the minute you get a line on Harris."

Wynn disconnected from Ty and picked up the incoming call. "This is Sean."

"Hi, Mr. Wynn. This is Amanda Carson, returning your call."

————

First thing Monday morning, Wynn rolled his gray and black Harley Street Glide onto the eastbound 101 freeway toward Thousand Oaks. The overnight low had touched fifty, his limit for trading two wheels for four. While he knew it would warm up nicely later in the day, the Street Glide, with its large front fairing, helped protect him from the cool morning air. He also put on an additional layer of thin riding armor underneath his clothes to help combat the chill.

On the phone last night, he'd remained vague as to why he was reaching out to Amanda Carson, preferring to have the conversation with her in person. She was initially hesitant, but finally agreed to let him come over.

He pulled into her gated community a little after nine o'clock, and punched a code she had given him into a digital call box, then waited as the intricate dual gates slowly swung open. Being a few minutes late, he squeezed through the narrow opening and accelerated up the palm tree-lined boulevard, sure his rumbling Harley would scandalize the neighborhood busybodies.

The ex-Mrs. Carson lived in a large, white stucco two-story home, with a looping driveway and four-car garage nestled among large oak and acacia trees at the end of a long cul-de-sac. Wynn pulled to a stop next to the curb and took off his helmet and jacket before walking up the driveway, where a black Mercedes convertible sat parked outside. A path of brown brick pavers led to the front door where he rang the bell.

The door was opened a moment later by a woman Wynn guessed to be in her early fifties, with short, reddish-brown hair. She was slender, dressed in a flowing green top, white yoga pants, and high-heeled sandals.

"Mrs. Carson? I'm Sean Wynn."

She looked him over. From head to toe. Like a piece of meat.

Deciding if it's safe to invite me in.

He was wearing blue jeans and an untucked button-down shirt. The riding armor he wore underneath tended to exaggerate his already athletic frame. He quickly removed his dark sunglasses so she could see his eyes.

"It's Miss Carson, now. But you can call me Amanda." She looked past him toward his bike on the street. "Come on in."

She stepped back, allowing Wynn to enter. She closed the door behind him and led him down a short hallway into the kitchen where another woman sat on a barstool next to a large granite island. "This is my friend, Kathy," Amanda said. "I hope you don't mind, but I asked her to come over. We share everything. At least from my side, she's heard it all, so I doubt there's anything you can ask that she hasn't already heard from me."

Safety in numbers. Doesn't want to be alone with a strange guy in her house. "No, that's fine." He shook Kathy's hand, then sat down at the island, leaving an empty chair between them.

"Would you like some coffee?" Amanda asked.

"That'd be great. Thank you."

"Cream or sugar?"

"No, thanks. Black is fine."

"So, what can I do for you, Mr. Wynn?" She poured the coffee then handed him the steaming cup. "You said your wife worked with Neil at Mynogen?"

"Yeah."

"Forgive me for being blunt, but are you trying to find out if she slept with him? Or maybe if she's still sleeping with him?" She leaned forward, placing her elbows on the granite, the loose neckline of her shirt dangling dangerously low. She wasn't wearing a bra.

"Maybe yes to the first part, but no to the second." Wynn willed his eyes to remain on hers. "She died a couple of years ago."

"Oh. Sorry." Amanda straightened up. "Maybe I should stop assuming and let you tell me why you're here."

"It's okay. No offense taken." He decided to go with the same story he'd told Janelle. "My wife was killed in a drive-by shooting in Ventura a couple of years ago..."

"That was your wife?" Amanda said. "I heard about that."

Kathy moved to the stool next to him and put her hand on his arm.

He paused, slightly taken aback by Kathy's show of concern. "Yeah. Well, I'm finally coming to terms with it and trying to get an understanding of what her last days were like, including what she was doing at work. In talking to some of her co-workers, Neil's name came up. And yeah, so did the possibility of them having an affair. I'm trying to find out if there was any truth to it."

"Did you ask him?" Amanda said.

"Not yet. I will, but figured he'd deny it without any proof. Was hoping you might be able to shed some light on it."

"What was your wife's name?"

"Nicole."

"Hmm. If it makes you feel any better, no, I'm not aware of Neil having an affair with anyone named Nicole. What did she look like?"

Wynn got out his phone and pulled up a photo. Amanda walked around the island and sat on a stool next to him. Wynn handed her his phone. She looked at it as Kathy stood and removed her hand from his arm. She walked behind them and looked over their shoulders, once again placing a hand on Wynn's back. His spider-sense stirred.

"She's pretty," Kathy said.

"What did she do at Mynogen?" Amanda asked.

"Research analyst."

"Doctorate?"

"Master's degree. Why?"

Amanda handed the phone back. "How would you describe her body type?"

Wynn was confused. He answered slowly. "Slender. Athletic."

Kathy slid back onto the stool on the other side of him, dragging her hand across his back, allowing it to linger a little longer than necessary.

"Not voluptuous?" Amanda said, raising her eyebrows.

"No..."

"Neil had a very specific type, Sean. Small brains and big tits. I know of three different women he cheated with, and they were all stupid as hell and looked like they'd just come off a porn set. Your wife was very pretty, but based on that picture and the fact she had a job that required brain cells, I don't see it."

"I guess that's good news, but then, who was he having the affair with?"

"Some bimbo secretary. Does it matter?"

"If that's what got him fired..."

"It wasn't. He was fired because he's a lying, deceitful asshole. I'm surprised you don't remember. It was in all the papers."

"When was this?"

"About a year ago. Maybe a little more."

A year ago, Wynn had been riding the Street Glide across the country, staying in dive hotels, and doing everything he could to stay away from Ventura. "I was traveling a lot back then. What did he lie about?"

"He didn't tell Mynogen he was an indirect shareholder in ALJ and as such, his role in the Hydrexa-whatever study was a total conflict of interest."

"I don't understand. Who's ALJ?"

"ALJ Pharmaceutical Research. He worked for them when they were a small startup. He was part of a private equity group that owned forty percent. He left them to go work for Mynogen. When ALJ came up with this great new drug, Neil vouched for them. Told the folks at Mynogen that ALJ was the real deal, that they'd be a great acquisition and he'd personally oversee the HCM study. He failed to tell them that he owned part of ALJ. Stood to make millions if Mynogen bought them out. Fucking asshole. All he had to do was tell them and he'd have been taken off the study, kept at arm's length, and everything would have been fine. As it is, Mynogen is pissed and wants their money back. They can have his, but I'm keeping mine."

Wynn's mind raced as he processed what he'd heard. Nicole had been brought in to analyze trial results that could mean millions of dollars to her boss two levels up. He recalled Ty's comment, *It's either sex or money.* "I don't mean to pry, but how much are we talking about here?"

"What kind of girl do you think I am?" she said flirtingly. "Talking money with a man I've just met."

He blushed. "I'm sorry. I didn't mean to..."

"It's alright!" She laughed. "The papers got pretty close this time. His share was thirty-six million."

"Thirty-six million?"

"Well, that's how much it was supposed to be. They were paying it out in four installments. We'd gotten two before they found out but then they held back the other two. My attorney said it wasn't likely Neil would get any more and there was a possibility he'd have to pay it all back. He suggested I settle for half of what we had at that time, along with a release that Neil would be responsible if we had to pay anything back. In return, I'd release him from any future claims if they eventually paid out the rest. It was probably foolish, but the lawyer convinced me something was better than nothing. As far as I know, he hasn't gotten anything more, so that by itself is pretty sweet revenge. Let's see how long his little whores stick around once the money runs out."

"And all this is common knowledge?"

"Most of it. I mean, I haven't confirmed anything for the papers and of course, the divorce settlement is private, but someone at Mynogen leaked the numbers. When a reporter asks, I tell them they're way off, but they're usually pretty close. But with you, it's weird. I feel like I can trust you." She leaned in close. "Like I can share anything with you."

Wynn paused as his spider-sense flew off the charts. "Thank you. I appreciate that."

"As I said, Kathy and I are close, too. We share everything."

Kathy leaned in and once again placed her hand on his back. Lower.

Wynn paused. "Uh-huh. Where's Neil now?"

"Oh, he's shacked up with his latest bimbo in Palm Springs, I think. You gonna pay him a visit?"

"Yeah. I think so."

"You know..." Amanda said, drawing out the syllables and tracing a finger slowly along Wynn's arm. "They say living well is the best revenge. And there are a lot of ways to live well, aren't there, Kathy?"

"Lots of ways," Kathy said. She raised her eyebrows and slid her hand to his thigh.

Wynn was momentarily dumbstruck, the intent finally becoming clear. "Well, it's a good thing he and Nicole weren't messing around. Otherwise, I might have to consider that. As it is, I think I'll just go talk to him."

Amanda gave him a pouty look. "Are you sure that's all you want to do?"

"I'll kick his ass if I have to."

"Fine," she said firmly, getting the message. "If you do, make sure you get in a good shot for me."

CHAPTER 23

"I DOUBLE-CHECKED EVERYTHING." Li stood inside Chan's office. "The address, the property owner, and the relationship. There's no doubt. Wynn is visiting Neil Carson's ex-wife right now. Whatever reason Jameson and Stuart have for tracking Wynn, it has something to do with Carson."

Chan nodded. "It would seem so. Let's give Stuart an update. See what he has to say."

Li took out his phone and dialed Stuart's number. He put it on speaker.

Stuart picked up with one word. "Yeah."

"I have an update for you," Li said. "Maybe it's more of a question."

"Okay..."

"Why is Mr. Wynn talking to Neil Carson's ex-wife?"

"What? When?"

"Right now. One of Wynn's motorcycles is parked outside of her house. Why is that?"

"It doesn't matter. But it's not good."

Li looked at Chan, who said, "But it does matter, Stuart. We can only assume Wynn is attempting to contact Neil Carson. We can further assume that doing so may, to use your words, blow up our arrangement. Do we understand correctly?"

"Close enough, yes."

"Then I think it's time you tell us exactly what risk this man poses."

"I've already told you. It has nothing to do with Jewel."

"Then I would suggest it's time to take Mr. Wynn off the board. Since this is beyond the scope of our normal arrangement, we will charge extra, but I believe I have someone..." Chan glanced at Li, who stared back at him with hard eyes, "who can take care of that for you."

The corners of Li's mouth turned up in a grim smile.

"Fine. Do it." The line clicked and went dead as Stuart hung up.

Chan sat back and steepled his fingers in front of his chin. "Wait for my instructions," he said to Li, "but be prepared to take Mr. Carson off the board, also."

———

Wynn was happy to get out the door with his dignity intact. He'd experienced a lot of strange things over the years, but the proposition from Amanda Carson and her friend ranked right up there.

The map app on his phone indicated a three-hour ride across the city to Palm Springs, but he knew it could be twice that if he got caught in traffic. Thankfully, he was able to escape the ex-Mrs. Carson's home before ten a.m., meaning he might make it to Neil Carson's by one.

The Street Glide purred like a big cat as he cruised east, weaving through the heavy mid-day traffic. He took the exit onto Bob Hope Drive and grabbed lunch at an In-N-Out Burger, then plugged in Carson's address and followed the directions through town.

Talk about your time warp, he thought as he rode past streets named after Frank Sinatra, Dinah Shore, Gerald Ford, and dozens of forgotten others. He'd never been to Palm Springs, but could see what it had once been, a playground for the rich and famous. Whether it was still that today was debatable.

Neil Carson lived in a golf course community in the central part of town. The house was a Spanish-style two-story with white brick and a red tile roof, similar to his ex-wife's in some respects, but older.

He parked in the driveway, then made his way to the front door and rang the bell. Moments later the door was opened by a woman who, if the description given by Amanda Carson was to be believed, was the "latest bimbo."

She was tall with long blonde hair, wearing a white string bikini beneath a sheer white cover-up, that failed miserably at covering much of anything. The tan skin of her obviously enhanced breasts swelled against her bikini top, while a dangling diamond pendant hung from her pierced navel above a matchbook-sized bikini bottom. Six-inch stiletto heels appropriately completed the look.

She was in a word, voluptuous.

"Can I help you?" she asked.

Wynn paused a beat, waiting for the inevitable gum-smacking to complete the stereotype. When none came, he asked, "Is Neil home?"

"Can I tell him who's here?"

"Sean Wynn. I'm an old friend. Neil and my wife used to work together."

She stepped back, opening the door wider, "In that case, come on in. He's in back by the pool."

She closed the door, then led him through the house. "I'm Jasmine, by the way. Can I get you anything?"

"No, thanks. I'm good." He couldn't help but notice that from behind, three pieces of string covered very little. He was pretty sure by the way she moved her hips that she knew it, too.

"You knew Neil from work?" she asked.

"My wife worked with him."

"Where at?"

"Mynogen."

"Oh."

Wynn sensed an opportunity. "Did you ever work there?"

"Yeah." She giggled a little. "That's where we met."

Jasmine pulled open a sliding glass door and stepped out to a back patio where a man sat at a table beneath a large umbrella, next to a glimmering blue pool. The man looked up from his laptop when he heard the door open.

"Hey, babe," Jasmine called out. "You've got a visitor."

Wynn strode over to Carson and extended his hand, "Sean Wynn, Neil. It's good to see you again."

Carson cautiously shook Wynn's hand. "Jaz, could you bring us some iced tea?"

"He said he didn't want anything."

"Yeah, but he will in a minute. You know how hot it gets. And I could use a refill myself. Be a doll, huh?"

The two men watched as Jasmine went inside. It was hard not to. When she was gone, Wynn turned to Carson, who said, "Forgive me, have we met?"

"Several years ago. At a Mynogen event. My wife, Nicole Wynn, introduced us."

"Uh-huh." Carson leaned back. "And what can I do for you, Mr. Wynn?"

"Call me Sean. May I sit?"

"No. Tell me why you're here."

Wynn ignored him, pulled out a chair, and sat down anyway. "I want to know if you were fucking my wife."

Carson smiled. He was about the same general size as Wynn. Maybe six feet tall, two hundred pounds. But he was twenty years older and looked like he hadn't seen the inside of a gym in a decade. His salt-and-pepper hair was slicked back and tapered down the sides into a short beard. *Going for the George Clooney look.* He was wearing swim trunks and a short sleeve Hawaiian shirt, unbuttoned to reveal a flabby midsection.

"And why would you think that?" Carson asked.

"Rumor is that's why you were fired."

"Don't believe everything you hear, Mr. Wynn."

"So why were you fired?"

"First of all," Carson said, leaning forward, "I wasn't. But my reasons for leaving are none of your business."

"Well, if it wasn't that, maybe it had something to do with HCM?"

"And what do you know of HCM?"

"I know Mynogen paid a boatload of money for it. Probably even bought this place, but it never went anywhere."

"You ever work for a Fortune 1000 company, Mr. Wynn?"

"Haven't had the pleasure."

"Oh, it's a pleasure alright. Politics, bureaucracies..."

"I was a Marine. I know all about politics and bureaucracies."

"Then you should also know that sometimes you can do everything right and still get blamed when things go to shit. When that happens, you part ways. Nothing more."

Wynn stayed silent.

"Nicole Wynn. She was the one killed in that drive-by a couple of years ago, right?"

"Yeah."

"If I remember, she was what, about five-six, maybe five-seven, mousey blonde hair, thin as a rail, and tits out to... well, nowhere, right?"

Wynn didn't respond.

"Look behind you." Carson nodded toward the house. Jasmine had come out of the sliding glass doors carrying a tray with two glasses and a bowl of lemons toward them. Her breasts bounced noticeably as she approached. "Why the fuck would I mess around with your hamburger when I'm eating filet mignon every night? Now I don't know what you heard, but I can tell you categorically I never touched your wife. I barely knew her. Yeah, I dipped my line in the company pond a couple of times, but not her, and that's not why I left. So, if there's nothing else..."

He paused as Jasmine walked up and bent down to place the tray on the table. "Would you like some sweetener, Sean?" she asked.

Wynn pushed up from the table. "No, thanks. I need to get going."

"But you just got here."

"Sorry about that, babe," Carson said. "I was hoping to convince him to stick around a little longer, but Sean here's a busy man."

"I'm sorry for your trouble," Wynn said.

"Oh, that's okay," she said. "Will we see you again?"

"Probably." Wynn looked Carson in the eye. "Probably soon."

———

"You couldn't stop him?" Stuart's voice boomed over the speakers in the car.

"Traffic. He was on a bike. He was able to get through spots we couldn't," Li explained.

"How long's he been in there?"

"Ten minutes."

"But you've got eyes on him now, right? You're sure you've got him?

"Yeah, we got him."

"Good. Don't let him make it back."

CHAPTER 24

WYNN SHOWED HIMSELF out of Carson's house and was soon back on the freeway, headed west toward Los Angeles. The clock on his bike read a little after two o'clock, meaning he'd hit the heart of L.A. rush hour. Taking advantage of the relatively open freeway east of Beaumont, he twisted the Street Glide's throttle until his speedometer touched eighty.

He wasn't the only one hoping to beat traffic. A black Cadillac SUV with tinted windows followed him onto the freeway and kept pace mile for mile. It hung back, but mimicked his every move as Wynn weaved back and forth across the four lanes.

A momentary backup forced Wynn to slow, allowing the Caddy ease up beside him. The passenger window slid down. Movement inside the Caddy caused Wynn to glance over, just in time to see a handgun pointed out the window.

Wynn slammed on the brakes, his left hand pulling the clutch while his right foot jammed down on the rear brake pedal. His right hand grabbed the front brake lever, causing the Street Glide to sink into its forks and wobble precariously as the Caddy screamed past. Horns blared and tires screeched as the drivers behind Wynn stomped on their brakes, attempting to avoid him.

Smoke rose from the Caddy's tires as it too, jammed on its brakes, then swerved into Wynn's lane and came to a complete stop fifty yards ahead.

Wynn managed to control the fishtailing Street Glide and stopped twenty yards short. Cars continued to speed past in the outside lanes, but the sounds of squealing tires and crunching metal told Wynn that wouldn't continue for long.

The Caddy's passenger door opened and a young Asian man stepped out. His right hand was hidden behind his back.

Wynn glanced right, looking for an exit.

The Asian guy took two familiar steps forward. *Just like the other night at the diner.* His right arm swung around.

Wynn didn't wait for visual confirmation. He'd already seen the gun. He twisted his right hand on the throttle and popped the clutch, then swung the bike to the left, around the driver's side of the Caddy, using it as a shield from the passenger.

He sped away down the freeway, the immediate traffic now light. A quick glance in the mirror showed the Caddy already moving, in pursuit. A half-mile ahead, brake lights flared. He'd catch up with the heavier traffic in no time.

Two options. Split lanes, or get off the freeway.

The problem with splitting lanes wasn't just that drivers might unexpectedly change lanes, they also tended to drift. But there was a reason it was legal in California: it allowed cycles to move faster. Wynn eased to the left, pointed his front wheel along the dashed white line between the third and fourth lanes, and sped between a pickup and a sedan.

He shifted his gaze back and forth between the road ahead, and his side mirror, keeping an eye on the Caddy. It had pulled onto the left shoulder and was using it as a lane to keep pace. It was now barely two cars behind.

Ahead of him, a car changed lanes.

Wynn slammed on the brakes, then swerved to the right, taking the space the car had just vacated. The Caddy was almost even with him now, one lane between them. A sign overhead indicated an upcoming exit. Wynn downshifted with his left toe and accelerated hard, slicing between two cars on his right, and prompting a new chorus of angry, blaring horns. He glanced over his shoulder and repeated the maneuver, sliding into the right lane, but then was forced to let up on the throttle, slowing among the long line of exiting vehicles.

The Caddy rolled off the shoulder. It crossed two lanes, causing other drivers to brake or swerve, but it stayed with him. The window lowered and a gun appeared.

Wynn swerved to the right and twisted the throttle. A rapid pop-bang sounded. The nose of the bike dipped, the front tire suddenly unresponsive, as if plowing through wet cement.

He lurched forward as the bike slowed, rubber peeling away and flying past his face. Sparks burst as the rim caught on the asphalt and ground to a sudden stop, launching Wynn over the handlebars and sending the bike cartwheeling down the freeway while the Caddy roared away. Wynn tucked his chin and rounded his shoulders, then landed hard on his back and rolled across the pavement as cars raced past. He came to a stop face down, the sound of tires squealing and metal crunching all around.

———

Carson picked up his ringing phone without looking at the screen. "Yeah, this is Neil."

"Carsonnnn." The voice was soft and velvety and drew out the final consonant.

Stuart.

Carson looked across the pool to where Jasmine lay in a recliner, sunning herself. Topless. Earlier, he'd had to run off some of the neighborhood ten-year-old boys who'd been peeking over the privacy wall. He rubbed a hand over his face. "What do you want?"

"I'm curious what you and Sean Wynn talked about."

That was fast. Wynn had only left a half-hour ago. No use denying it. "He wanted to know if I'd been sleeping with his wife."

"What'd you tell him?"

"What do you think? I told him she wasn't my type."

"What else?"

"Nothing else. The guy was only here a few minutes."

"Nothing about Mynogen or HCM?"

There it is. The golden goose and its toxic egg. "No," he lied. "The guy thinks his wife was fucking around. My name came up, so he paid me a visit. Had nothing to do with HCM."

"You're sure?"

"Yes, Stuart. I'm sure."

"Cause I'd hate to have Li pay you a visit also."

Carson leaped up, tipping over his chair. "Don't you fucking threaten me!"

Jasmine raised her head and looked in his direction.

He turned away and lowered his voice. "You know what'll happen if something happens to me, you bastard. My attorney's got very explicit instructions and enough documentation to put you and Jameson away forever. You leave me alone and those docs will never see the light of day, but if something happens to me..."

"Neil, Neil, calm down. You misunderstood. I'm not threatening you. I just want to make sure Wynn doesn't cause any trouble that might hinder your production capabilities. As you know, Li and Chan have expressed some concern."

"I've been alternating shifts with Rick and Howard around the clock since last week. We're good."

"Excellent. I'm sure Chan will be pleased. And regarding HCM, Mr. Jameson and I understand your position perfectly."

"Good."

"Of course, if Mr. Wynn does make contact again, I'm sure you'll let us know right away, correct?"

Carson gritted his teeth. "Yes, Stuart."

"Okay. You take care now, Neil. We'll be in touch if something comes up."

Carson disconnected and dropped the phone back on the table. Black spots filled his vision.

"Baby, I'm bored," Jasmine called from across the pool.

Carson let out a deep breath and closed his eyes.

———

"If nothing else, he should be slowed down for a couple of days," Li said. He and Huan sat stuck in traffic.

"Good." Chan's voice filled the cabin from the Caddy's speakers. "When you get back, come to the warehouse. I've set up interviews with two people you know. We have a choice to make."

"About Carson?"

"That decision's been made. We need to decide who will replace him."

———

"You are one lucky son of a bitch," Ty said as Wynn gingerly reached for his pants in the emergency center exam room. "How often do you wear that shit?"

"As of today, it's gonna be more," Wynn said.

They were referring to the Bohn riding armor that Wynn had worn underneath his clothes to protect himself from the morning chill. The undershirt and pants, with the armor pads still in them, lay crumpled in a pile on the floor. They'd been cut off when he was brought in. His heavily scuffed jacket and helmet sat on a chair next to the bed.

He'd come out of the accident in remarkably good condition. Several bumps and bruises, but no broken bones or road rash. After the front tire blew, he'd been able to reduce his speed enough so that by the time he went airborne the impact wasn't significant. His leather jacket and the armor cushioned the blow when he hit the road, but left his jeans torn with one of those fashionable knee holes the young girls paid hundreds for.

The Beaumont police had arrived at the emergency center about an hour after Wynn was brought in, and Ty an hour after that. He'd shared the description of the Caddy and the chase with everyone, but kept any mention that the men were Asian and that one of them had shot out his front tire until he was alone with Ty. They both knew what that meant.

He reached down to pull up his jeans, his left shoulder protesting harshly despite the heavy dose of pain killer he'd already received.

Get this filled in the next two hours, the doctor had said, handing him a prescription. *You're gonna need it.*

The problem was it took almost an hour to get checked out of the hospital and he could already feel the drugs wearing off. An admin finally came in and had him sign a few forms, then said he was free to leave, as long as he wasn't driving.

"I got him," Ty told her.

They stopped at a pharmacy on their way out, and found a drive-through to get something to eat before finally getting back on the road a little before eight in the evening. Wynn wasn't overly hungry, but the doctor told him to take the meds with food, and by now he definitely wanted to take the meds.

"So," Ty said when they'd finished eating and were cruising past San Bernardino on the 210, "What hornet's nest did you kick to cause this?"

"Mynogen."

"Nicole's company?"

"Yeah."

"How do they play into it?"

"There was a smaller company, ALJ Pharmaceutical Research, that supposedly had come up with a vaccine for the Marburg 2 virus. Mynogen bought them out, but they were having trouble confirming the trials. Nicky had been brought in to help analyze the data. But unbeknownst to the bigwigs at Mynogen, the guy they put in charge of the trials, Neil Carson, was a silent partner in ALJ. He made millions when the merger closed."

Ty's jaw dropped open. "How could they not know?"

Wynn shrugged. "We should ask them."

"So back up for me. How did you learn all this?"

"Nicky's old boss, Janelle Evans, was one of the folks I talked to yesterday. She told me that *her* boss, Neil Carson, had been fired and was rumored to have been having an affair."

Wynn paused to yawn. The meds were making him sleepy. "Anyway, Janelle also told me about the trouble Mynogen was having with the vaccine. I contacted Carson's ex-wife to follow up on the sex angle, but she squashed that and instead told me about the money. Thirty-six million."

Ty whistled.

"I don't know how it all fits, but that's a lot of motivation," Wynn said.

"So the ex-wife lives in Palm Springs?"

"No. She's in Thousand Oaks. Carson is in Palm Springs."

"Oh shit, Sean. Tell me you didn't go see him."

"I wanted to get a look. Ask him about Nicole."

"You see, that's the part Akins was talking about. When you get something like that, you need to bring it to us, let us handle it. You don't go confronting someone who might turn out to be a suspect."

Wynn stayed silent. He yawned again.

"Well, did you find anything?" Ty asked.

"Got quite an eyeful," Wynn said, images of Jasmine popping into his mind. "I've got no proof of anything, but I'm more convinced than ever this has something to do with that merger and the money, and not an affair."

"Sounds like we need to talk to Mynogen."

"Agreed. Tomorrow." Wynn found the button and leaned the seat back, then promptly fell asleep.

———

Four hours after speaking with Chan, Li and Huan walked into the warehouse office.

"Finally," said a thirty-something white guy sitting on a folding chair. He stood and put his hands on his hips. He was tall, close to six-foot-three, with an athletic build. "Maybe now you can tell us what's so important we had to sit here for two hours."

Next to him sat a balding, paunchy middle-aged man. He wore a short sleeve dress shirt, its underarms stained dark with perspiration. Three of Chan's men were seated around the room.

"Rick, Howard, I'm so sorry to keep you waiting," Li said, shaking the tall man's hand. "We noticed something odd about this latest shipment and thought it best for you both to take a look before we distributed it."

"What's wrong with it?" Rick asked.

"Why don't you come see for yourself?" Li opened the door to the warehouse and held it while Huan led the way. They passed through the large open space and down one of the aisles between rows of tall industrial shelving. "We've been getting reports that some users have found this last batch to be less effective. Has Neil changed the formula?"

"Of course not," Rick replied.

"And you both are familiar with how the product is made and would know if Neil did make any changes?"

"Yes. Of course. Neil couldn't make changes without us anyway."

Li smiled conspiratorially. "My guess is Neil couldn't do anything without the two of you, right?"

"You know it," Rick said.

"Howard? Do you agree?"

The balding, paunchy man nodded and mumbled in agreement.

"Well, maybe it's just my ignorance." Li pulled a matchbox-sized container out of his pocket, opened it, and pulled out a small white pill. "Can you explain to me how Jewel is made?"

"You know how it's made," Rick said. "We take the synthetic opioid and blend it with a neutral calcium base. Potency depends on the mix ratio."

"Yes, but where does the synthetic come from?" Li stopped at the end of the aisle.

"We make it. That's the secret formula. Only Neil and the two of us know that."

"But anyone with that knowledge, could make it, correct?"

"Well, yeah. Assuming they had a lab."

"I see." Li turned the corner into a twenty-foot-square open space. Clear plastic sheeting stretched across the floor. Chan, along with two more men, stood on the other side of the sheeting across the room. The man on Chan's left held a small wooden box.

"What is this?" Rick asked cautiously.

Chan spoke from across room. "My apologies for keeping you waiting. I wanted Li to be here for this."

"For what?"

"I understand the two of you have been putting in extra hours to get us caught up. We have a gift for each of you to show our appreciation."

Li hustled across the room and took the box from the man next to Chan. He strode to the center of the sheeting and held it out. "Well, don't just stand there. Come get it."

Rick and Howard stepped forward. Li opened the box to reveal two matching pistols. Smith and Wesson classic Model 27 revolvers. Polished silver barrels, wood-carved grips.

Rick reached in and took one.

Howard was more hesitant. "Are they loaded?"

Li held the box out to Howard, who gingerly reached in and took the remaining weapon.

"Wouldn't do you much good if they weren't," Li said as he backed away.

"Mr. Carson has become unreliable," Chan said. "And unnecessary. We believe it is time for one of you to take over the manufacturing of Jewel."

"What are you talking about?" Rick asked.

"Mr. Carson will be having an accident. We need to make sure the supply is not disrupted. One of you will need to take over for him."

"Hey, I know we were a pallet short," Rick said. "But we got it out the next day. It'll all be there on this week's shipment."

"This is not about one shipment. That was simply the final straw in a series of shortcomings by Mr. Carson."

"But he gets us the raw materials," Howard said. "Without that, we can't make anything."

"Doesn't Mr. Jameson arrange that?"

"Sometimes."

"There you go. Mr. Carson is unnecessary."

"So, what?" Rick said holding up the pistol. "You want us to kill Carson?"

"Oh, no. We'll make sure he has an accident."

"Then what?"

"You need to decide which one of you will take his place." Chan nodded, and seven guns appeared in the hands of his men, including Li and Huan, pointed directly at Rick and Howard.

"If you get rid of Carson, you can't kill us," Rick said.

"Not both of you," Chan said. "Consider this an interview. One of you will walk out of here with a job, manufacturing Jewel for me. And it will be a very secure job because you'll be the only one left who knows the formula and how to make it. The other, well..." He looked down at the plastic sheeting on the floor. "You each have the tools in your hands to ensure you get the job. Which of you will use it first?"

Rick and Howard stood frozen as comprehension dawned in their eyes.

"No," Howard whispered. "I won't do it."

"If you kill Carson and both of us, you'll have nobody," Rick said.

"True," Chan said. "But if neither of you passes the interview, then Carson will become necessary. Not the optimal candidate, but he'll do if no one else rises to the occasion."

Howard and Rick looked at each other, fear and uncertainty in their eyes.

Rick raised his pistol and pointed it at Howard.

"Rick, no," Howard said. "You can't do this."

"We've got no choice."

A gunshot blasted through the room and both men remained standing for a moment, then Rick's knees buckled as he fell to the floor.

Li handed his smoking gun to Huan, then stepped forward and took the pistol from Howard's hand. "Congratulations," he said. "I was rooting for you."

CHAPTER 25

By SIX-THIRTY THE next morning Ty was back in the station. He'd gotten Wynn home, placed his prescription and a glass of water next to the bed, then tucked him in, fully dressed.

Fuck it, Ty thought. *I'm not taking his clothes off. Friendship only goes so far.*

He'd gone home and quietly opened the doors to both Matty and Brie's rooms, checking to ensure they were both safe and sound before collapsing into bed next to Stacey. He brushed the hair away from her face and kissed her forehead, then sank into a deep sleep.

A little before six a.m. his phone startled him awake. The night duty commander. *Akins says get your ass in here. We've got somebody you might want to talk to.*

Now, as he walked past the lunchroom on his way to Akins' office, he grabbed a donut from a box on the counter. Taking a bite, he stepped into the open doorway and knocked on the frame. Gruebauer was already seated in front of the desk.

"Geez. You look like shit," Akins said by way of greeting.

"Sleep's been in short supply lately."

"Well, I'm hoping this might energize you. Come on." Akins got up and led Ty and Gruebauer down the hallway, eventually stopping at a door on the right where he motioned Ty inside. "Grueb will conduct the interview. You and I'll watch from in here."

The room was small, maybe eight feet by ten feet. And dark. A pair of recessed canister lights glowed dimly from the ceiling. Two folding chairs leaned against the wall, but the room was otherwise bare. A large window on the left looked into the room next door.

On the other side of the window, a kid of maybe nineteen or twenty sat slouched in one of four chairs at a table facing the glass. He was a little taller than Ty, at least six-one or six-two, and slender, with dark skin. His hands were out of sight beneath the table.

"Who is he?"

"His name's Michael Martin. He's an AD."

"They didn't cuff him?" Ty asked.

"He's here voluntarily."

Akins stepped up to the glass and pressed a button on a small console set into the wall. "Watch his hands."

"Roger that," Gruebauer's voice came back through a pair of speakers set in the ceiling.

They heard a knock on the door come through the speakers and watched as Gruebauer and another detective entered the room on the other side of glass. Grueb wore a small, white Bluetooth receiver in his ear that he used to communicate with Akins and Ty in the observation room. Akins pushed another button on the wall console and a red recording light came on.

From the other side of the glass, Gruebauer said, "Hello, Michael. You want to do me a favor and show me your hands?"

The kid raised his hands above the table, fingers spread. Empty.

"Thanks. You need anything? Water? Bathroom?"

"Nah, I'm good," Mikey replied.

Gruebauer and the other detective sat down around the table. "Okay. I apologize for making you wait but it took a little while to get organized. This is Detective Olsten, I'm Detective Gruebauer. I want to let you know that we are recording this conversation. Is that okay with you?"

"Yeah, sure."

"Great. Could you please state your full name."

"Michael Martin."

Gruebauer gave the date, time, and location for the recording, then said, "And Michael, you came here voluntarily, on your own this morning, correct?"

"Yeah."

"Why did you come in?"

"They killed Doc. And Jay-squared."

"I'm sorry Michael, so there's no confusion, please use their real names. Who was killed?"

Mikey exhaled heavily, frustrated. "DeAndre Renker and Jamaal Johnson. Doc and Jay-squared."

"And who killed them?"

"I don't know who pulled the trigger, but I know who gave 'em up. Devon Harris."

Ty muttered from behind the glass, "We know all this."

"What do you mean, gave them up?" Gruebauer asked.

"When that biker dude came around, he told Doc that Jay-squared was telling stories. Doc told Harris, and Harris called the suit. Next thing you know, Doc and Jay-squared are dead cause Harris gave 'em up."

"How do you know it was Harris? Did you hear him?"

"Shit, no man. I didn't hear him say it, but I know. Doc and I came back from talking with the biker and told Harris. Then Harris told us to leave the room and the next day Jay-squared gets whacked in the yard, and the day after that, Doc gets capped. Don't take no Sherlock to figure out what happened."

"Okay, okay," Gruebauer said calmly. "You were there when Doc told Devon?"

"Shit yeah, man. Right there."

"And you are a member of the Acid Dawn, correct?"

"Yeah. Four years."

"Then why are you telling us this?"

"Jay-squared and Trish, they my cousins. It ain't right."

"Who's Trish, Michael?"

"Trish Johnson. Jay-squared's sister. She and Doc were tight."

"Uh-huh. Who's the 'suit,' Michael?"

"Man, I don't know his name, but Harris knows him. A couple of years now."

"Well, then, how do you know him?"

"I seen him one time. I was with Harris when he went to meet him. He made me wait in the car while they talked, then when Harris came back, I asked who the suit was. He said that's our fairy fucking godfather and then I ain't never seen him again. But I know they still tight cause that's where Devon gets the Jewel."

"Let me make sure I understand. You're saying this suit, a guy you don't know, provides the Dawn with Jewel, and was also the person behind the murders of Jamaal Johnson and DeAndre Renker?"

"That's right."

"Did this suit also hire the ADs to kill that woman at Viacci's? The one Jay-squared was sent to prison for?"

"Yeah. I think so."

"You *think* so?"

"Man, I never talked to him, and Harris didn't say shit. But it all happened about the same time, so yeah, I think so."

"He doesn't truly know any of this," Ty whispered to Akins in the other room. "He's connecting the dots and drawing conclusions, but he doesn't actually know it. We need Harris."

Akins nodded, while Grueb continued questioning Martin in the next room.

"How long ago did you last see this suit?"

"I don't know man, a year. Maybe a little more."

"Would you recognize him if you saw him? Could you pick him out of a lineup?"

"I don't know. He was a skinny dude. I didn't get a good look at his face. I saw him from the back. A little from the side. It was dark."

Gruebauer shook his head disgustedly. "Michael, you've given us a lot of conjecture, but you haven't told us shit we don't already know. I thought you had something new for us. What *do* you know?"

Mikey paused and looked at Grueb like he was stupid. "I know where you can find Harris."

———

Wynn was awakened by his phone ringing on the bedside table. Reaching to answer it, a sharp pain shot from his left shoulder. He was suddenly aware of aches and pains all over his body.

"Hello?"

"Hi Sean, it's Lisa. Did I wake you?"

"Yeah, but that's okay," he said, rubbing his eyes. *Lisa Montgomery. I'd asked her to look at that list of names from Nicole's phone.* "Did you find anything?"

"I recognized about eighty percent of the names on that list and most of them were co-workers. Female. Of the few guys on there, I don't see anyone I would even remotely suspect Nicole might have been close with."

"Yeah, I'm beginning to think it was something else. Do you know anything about a drug you guys were working on called HCM?"

"Oh yeah. Our problem project."

"What do you mean?"

"Well, it's not unusual to have a drug that doesn't work out. I mean, as a company, you try things. Some of them work, some don't. That's why we have small-scale trials. Weed out the bad ones before they invest a ton of money. But not HCM. It was a bad one that got through. Mynogen invested a ton of money in that one and it never went anywhere."

"Did you work on it?"

"No. I don't think Nicole did, either."

"According to Janelle, she did. Janelle pulled her off another project less than two weeks before the shooting and had her start looking at it."

There was silence on the other end of the line.

"Lisa, you still there?"

"Yeah. Hold on."

Wynn waited a few moments.

"Shit," Lisa said.

"What?"

"Susan Braley. She was on that list of names you gave me."

"Yeah. So?"

"She was also working on HCM. Right at the very beginning."

"So?"

"She went missing. Just disappeared from work one day. They've got video of her in the halls, but they never saw her leave. Her car was still in the parking lot but it's like she just disappeared."

Wynn's chest went cold. "When?"

"About a year before Nicole was shot."

"You sure about that timeframe?"

"Maybe nine or ten months, but it was definitely before Nicole. We talked about it."

"Was Neil Carson overseeing the study at that time?"

"I think so, yeah. You don't think these are related, do you?"

"I don't know, but don't say anything to anybody. If they are, this is dangerous. Is there anything else?"

"No, I only wanted to let you know I didn't see any names that I'd consider suspicious for an affair."

Wynn thanked her and disconnected, then called Ty.

"Hey, good morning sleepyhead," Ty said when he picked up. "How are you feeling today?"

Wynn ignored the question. "We were right. It's Mynogen. HCM."

"Whoa. What do you mean?"

"I just got off the phone with Lisa Montgomery, one of Nicole's work friends. She told me there's a woman who went missing from Mynogen about a year before Nicole's shooting. She was also working on HCM."

"No way. What's her name?"

"Susan Braley."

"Good work, Sean. We'll check it out."

"Whoa! No fucking way I'm sitting this one out. I'm going over to Mynogen. You can either come with me or not, but I'm going."

"Okay, okay," Ty said quickly. "Come on down to the station and we'll get Akins' approval to have you come along, then we'll go talk to them together. You'll get a lot further with a badge behind you."

"No bullshit, Ty. If he locks me in a cell, you and I are going to have a problem."

"Understood. Get your ass down here but text me before you come in. I'll go talk to him and make sure it's all good. Besides, we may have a lead on Harris."

"How's that?"

"One of the ADs is giving him up. Johnson's cousin. Apparently, blood is thicker."

"Cool. I'll be there in thirty." Wynn disconnected, then hopped in the shower and downed a quick breakfast so he could take more of the pain meds. He ached all over, but this new information created an adrenaline rush that pushed the pain from his mind.

On his way out the door, he paused as he looked at the keys hanging from their hooks: The Lexus, the Sportster, and an empty hook where the Street Glide's keys used to hang.

Fuck it. Get back on the horse. He grabbed the Sportster's keys.

———

A sickening emptiness settled in the pit of Devon Harris' stomach. Sweat popped from his forehead despite the morning chill. He sat motionless in the dirt, not risking movement even to scratch the itches caused by the branches and twigs that assaulted his body.

Ever since he'd jumped off that balcony Saturday night, he hadn't spent more than six hours in any one place. He'd knocked on Mikey's door at two a.m. last night and had gotten a few hours of sleep on his couch. But when he woke up and found Mikey gone, it hadn't taken more than a minute to realize it was time to go.

Now, he watched from the shelter of a thick bush two blocks away as a pair of police officers, with guns drawn, passed within fifteen feet of him as they walked up the street toward Mikey's house. While he couldn't see any others, he imagined they were coming from all sides.

Sit tight, or run?

As hard as it was to sit, he knew it was the right move. They'd eventually get into Mikey's house, discover he wasn't there, and leave. Only then would it be safe to come out. To do so now risked running into other officers setting up a wider perimeter or catching the eye of a nosy neighbor wondering what all the fuss was about.

No, better to wait a few hours and let everyone clear out, then slip back onto the sidewalk and walk down the street like he didn't have a care in the world.

———

Ten minutes after leaving home, Wynn texted Ty from the police station parking lot: *I'm here. We good?*

Ty replied: *Akins wants to talk. Promises he won't lock you up.*

Wynn hesitated but went inside anyway. Ty met him in the lobby.

"I gave him the rundown; he wants a quick meet," Ty said. "Besides, we're still confirming the right person at Mynogen to talk to."

They walked down the hall to Akins' office, where Ty knocked on the doorframe before going in. "He's here."

Akins turned away from his computer screen and took off his reading glasses. "Sean, Ty told me about the accident. How are you feeling?"

"I'm good, Lieutenant. Thanks." Wynn remained standing. Sitting caused too much pain.

"Not to overstate the obvious, but that's two attempts on your life in what, the last four days? You sure you want to keep pushing this?"

Wynn nodded. "I'm good."

Akins stared back at him, then reached over and pushed the intercom button on his desk phone. "Jean, do you have a name at Mynogen yet?"

"Yes, sir," a female voice responded. "Stephen Oglesby. He's the CEO. I've confirmed he is in the office today."

"Okay, thanks." Turning back to Wynn, Akins said, "You want to catch these guys, make 'em pay, right?"

Wynn nodded.

"Then you need to understand that defense lawyers will have a field day if we let a civilian into the investigation. They'll scrutinize every step we take, and if there's even one miscue, they'll exploit it and more than likely win. Judges around here don't like it when we bend the rules. Now so far, *because* of the things you've done and *despite* some things you've done, Ty's got a pretty good foundation. We can independently account for each bit of vital information. I want to keep it that way. I'm going to let you go with him to visit Oglesby, but let me be very clear: you are there as an observer only. When Ty's talking to him, you don't say a word. Is that understood?"

"Yes, sir," Wynn replied.

Turning to Ty, Akins said, "If Oglesby asks, tell him Sean's a special consultant on the case. When Grueb gets back, take him with you so Oglesby doesn't assume Sean's your partner on this."

"Where's Grueb?" Wynn asked.

"Hopefully picking up Harris."

———

C'mon, Rick. Pick up, damn it. Carson held the phone to his ear as the call went to voice mail. He disconnected, having already left three messages. *Maybe Howard's heard from him.*

Carson got up from his desk and walked down the hall to the lab where Howard was sitting on a bench, suiting up for a shift inside the clean room. "Hey. Have you heard from Rick this morning?"

Howard startled. "Rick?" His voice came out as a croaky whisper. He cleared his throat and tried again. "Rick? No. I haven't heard from him. Why?"

"He hasn't come in and he's not picking up his phone."

"Hmm. Yesterday we finished those long shifts to get caught up. Maybe he tied one on last night and he's sleeping it off."

"Yeah, maybe," Carson said. A bead of sweat rolled down Howard's face. "You okay?"

"Yeah, I'm fine. How are you?"

Carson paused. "I'm fine," he said slowly. "You sure you don't know where Rick is?"

Howard looked down and started tying his shoe. "Nope. No idea."

"Let me know if you hear from him." Carson turned and walked back to his office. *That was weird. Even for Howard.*

Back at his desk, Carson picked up the phone and pulled up Stuart's number, then paused and put the phone down. He eyed the car keys on the edge of his desk.

It's probably nothing. Don't get carried away. Not yet.

CHAPTER 26

A HALF-HOUR AFTER Wynn and Ty left Akins' office, Grueb arrived back at the station, not in a good mood.

"That bastard's a damn Houdini," Grueb said when Ty asked how it went.

"Maybe we won't need him. Akins wants you to come with us to visit Mynogen."

"Sure. Why not? My own investigation into the ADs has gone to shit."

Mynogen's headquarters were located in Camarillo, not far from Lisa Montgomery's neighborhood. The complex consisted of four buildings, three single-story research facilities and a five-story administration high-rise. Even though he hadn't been there since Nicole's murder, Wynn recognized the tree-lined grounds as they pulled up in front of the main office.

"Did you know Oglesby from when Nicole worked here?" Gruebauer asked.

"Never met him," Wynn replied.

"Well," Ty said as he opened his door. "No time like the present."

They walked up the sidewalk and through the tinted glass doors into a broad lobby. A mahogany and granite reception counter tended by three young women sat immediately ahead.

A brunette on the right smiled. "May I help you?"

Wynn hung back while Ty and Grueb stepped forward. Ty flashed his badge. "Detectives Lenihan and Gruebauer. Here to see Mr. Oglesby.

"Is he expecting you?"

"I don't believe so, no. Can you take us to him?"

Ignoring Ty's question, she said, "In that case, let me see if he's available."

She picked up a phone and was about to punch a button when Ty reached over the counter and depressed the hook switch.

"If we wanted him to know we were coming, we would've called first. Now, do you know where we can find him?"

Stunned, the young woman lowered the phone from her ear and replaced it in the cradle. "I believe he's in his office."

"Great. Can you show us where that is?"

The young woman glanced at the other two receptionists as she rose from her seat and came around the end of the counter. "Right this way."

She walked over to a bank of elevators and hit the call button, then waited silently until the doors opened. Wynn glanced back at the counter before following the others onto the elevator. One of the remaining receptionists was already on the phone. The brunette held a keycard against a pad until the light turned green, then hit the button for the fifth floor.

When the doors slid open, a harsh-looking woman in a gray suit jacket and black skirt hurried out from behind a desk to meet them. Her dark hair was pulled back in a severe bun. A chain drooped in front of each ear from the temples of her horned-rim eyeglasses.

"I'm Madeline Smith, Dr. Oglesby's assistant. Can I help you?"

"We're here to see Mr. Oglesby," Ty said.

"*Doctor* Oglesby is in a meeting right now. Perhaps I can help you with something?"

"You can either tell him that he needs to cut his meeting short and come talk to us, or you can show us where he's at and we'll tell him." Ty flashed his badge again.

"Why don't you wait in here," Smith said, motioning to a door off the main hallway, "while I go get him."

She wants to get us out of sight, Wynn thought.

"No, thanks. We'll wait right here," Ty said.

When Smith hurried away, the brunette eased back toward the elevator. "If you're good here, I need to get back."

Ty nodded, and the three of them watched as she stepped back into the elevator.

When the doors closed, Wynn said to Ty, "You have a way with people."

"Sometimes it takes something stronger than honey."

Gruebauer smiled.

A couple of minutes later, Smith returned and escorted them down a richly paneled hallway. She knocked on a door at the end and held it open as they entered a large corner office. A tall, thin man wearing a dark suit, white shirt, and blue tie got up from behind a massive mahogany desk and came around to greet them.

"Hello, detectives. I'm Stephen Oglesby." He extended his hand.

Ty stepped forward and shook it. "It's nice to meet you, Dr. Oglesby. I'm Detective Lenihan. This is Detective Gruebauer. We're with the Ventura police department. This is Special Consultant Mr. Wynn."

"Special Consultant?" Oglesby said as he shook Wynn's hand, then motioned them to a group of four couches surrounding a glass coffee table. "How can I help you gentlemen today?"

"We're investigating a case that probably has nothing to do with you or Mynogen," Ty said as they all sat down, "but the name of one of your former employees came up and we'd like to ask you about him."

"Who's that?"

"Neil Carson. Do you know him?"

Oglesby stiffened when he heard the name, then took a deep breath before answering. "Yes, I know him."

Gruebauer jumped in. "We were wondering if you could tell us the circumstances regarding his departure from Mynogen."

"What do you mean?" Oglesby asked.

"We heard he was fired for a potential conflict of interest. He says he left voluntarily. We're wondering what the real story is."

Oglesby nodded, then reached over and pushed a button on a phone that sat on the coffee table. "Madeline, could you please have Marcia and Raymond come to my office? Immediately, please."

"Yes, doctor," Smith's voice came back over the speaker.

"If you're aware of all this," Oglesby said to the three of them, "you're likely also aware that Mynogen currently has active litigation against Mr. Carson. As such, I'd like to have our HR and legal counsel here when I answer your questions. Is that alright?"

"Of course," Ty said.

They waited in silence for a few moments before a gentle knock on the door was followed by a man and woman entering the room.

"Excellent," Oglesby said, standing. "Marcia, Raymond, these gentlemen are with the Ventura police department and have some questions regarding Neil Carson. Please join us." He motioned to an unoccupied couch. When they were all settled, he continued. "Now, detective, could you please repeat your question?"

"We're wondering if you could tell us the circumstances regarding Carson's departure from Mynogen," Gruebauer asked again.

"Yes, and you said that he's saying he left voluntarily, but you've heard he was terminated due to a conflict of interest."

"That's correct."

Oglesby looked at the woman, Marcia, who nodded. Oglesby said, "Our position is that he was terminated due to a conflict of interest that he failed to disclose."

"And did that conflict have to do with the acquisition of ALJ

Pharmaceutical and a study involving a drug called HCM?" Ty asked.

Oglesby smiled grimly. "You've done your research. Yes, it did."

"What price did Mynogen pay for ALJ?"

The attorney, Marcia, spoke up. "Forgive me, detectives, but I'm wondering why that's important. Perhaps if you could tell us why you're here, that would help us determine which of your questions we can answer. Otherwise, I'm afraid there's not much more we'll be able to say."

Ty sighed. "Mr. Carson's name has come up as part of a murder investigation. He is not, and I repeat, not, a suspect at this time. We're just trying to get some background on him to understand if or how he might be connected."

"That sounds an awful lot like a suspect," Marcia said.

"Let's call him a person of interest. Anything more than that depends on what you tell us," Ty replied.

Marcia looked at Oglesby and nodded.

"Four hundred million," Oglesby said. "That was the price we paid for ALJ. Plus, we sunk close to another hundred million into HCM. Worst decision we've ever made, largely due to Carson."

"Why is that?" Gruebauer asked.

"We hired Carson roughly five years ago. About a year after that, when the Marburg 2 virus started to make the news, he told us that ALJ had been working on it and was close to having a vaccine. Something called hydrexachloromine. HCM for short. Since he was already familiar with the people and the project, we put him in charge of validating their studies before we entered acquisition negotiations. He didn't tell us he owned nine percent of ALJ. And of course, he confirmed all their research. After we bought them, we could never get the same results. We suspect he falsified some of the reports, but so far, we've been unable to find exactly where."

Wynn's blood ran cold, but he stayed silent.

"And what would you have done if those studies hadn't been validated?"

"We wouldn't have bought them. It's that simple. We'll give a new drug three chances to pass a trial, which usually accounts for human error. If the drug can't pass in three, it's out. In this case that would have meant the acquisition of ALJ would have been called off."

Ty asked, "What about other people on the team? Surely you had multiple people looking at the results, right? Shouldn't they have been able to find it?"

The HR guy, Raymond, finally spoke up. "We had a lot of turnover on that project. Carson was not easy to work for. Everyone who was a part of it in the early days is gone."

"How many people would that be?"

"Seven or eight," Raymond said. "Carson fired four of them, two quit, and one... Oh my god. Is this about Susan Braley?"

"Miss Braley's disappearance is tangential, but not the main focus of our investigation. But that said, what can you tell us about her?"

"Only that she was last seen on a security camera here, but we don't have any record of her leaving. One of the security cameras was down that night, but that was for the delivery entrance. Very few employees ever leave through there."

"I assume you've already given that footage to the police as part of the initial investigation?"

"Of course."

"Can we also get a copy of the research on this HCM?" Grueb asked. "Maybe our folks can find something."

"That one's going to be tougher," Oglesby said. "We're happy to help any way we can, but without a warrant, we can't release proprietary research without the board's approval. Especially on a project that's already cost us three hundred million. They'd have my ass."

"Three hundred million?" said Ty. "I thought you said the total cost was closer to five hundred?"

"We'd only paid out half of it before we figured out what they were up to."

Ty paused. "Besides Carson, who's 'they'?"

"Alexander Leigh Jameson, the namesake behind ALJ Pharmaceutical Research, and his right hand, Stuart Legrea. Between the two of them, they pocketed over a hundred and twenty million."

CHAPTER 27

BEFORE LEAVING, OGLESBY told them that after selling ALJ to Mynogen, Jameson and Stuart opened a new start-up, J&L Enterprises, not far down the road in Thousand Oaks. Some kind of import-export business.

"J&L's only twenty minutes away. Let's go talk to them," Wynn said as they walked back to the car.

"Hold on, Sean," Ty said. "Wait 'til we're in the car."

When they were finally protected by the privacy of the car, Ty said, "Okay, Grueb, what's your take?"

Gruebauer measured his words slowly. "Carson's stake was thirty-six million. Jameson and Legrea potentially close to two hundred and forty, when it was all paid out. If Nicole or this Susan Braley were in a position to potentially discover the falsified reports and blow this deal up, yeah, I'd call that motive."

Ty nodded, "We're all seeing this the same way?"

Wynn nodded as if it were obvious. "So let's go!"

"Hold on," Ty said again. "We're still missing a couple of pieces. The falsified reports are just a theory. There's no proof of motive until we can actually find the fraud."

"Don't you have people who specialize in that stuff?" Wynn asked.

"Not that specifically. If their own people, who work on this stuff every day, can't find it, the odds of our people doing so are less than fifty-fifty. We'll get a warrant and give it a shot, but don't hold your breath."

"Okay. What else is missing?"

"A link. Something that ties them to Nicole's murder. Think about it. We've got killers with no motive, and people with motive but no killer. We need to find the thing that links them together."

"The suit," Gruebauer said.

"Who?" Wynn asked.

"Martin said Harris met with a 'suit.' Called him their fairy godfather. What do you bet he's the link?"

"Sounds reasonable," Ty said. "But Martin doesn't know who he is."

Wynn nodded. "We need to find Harris."

Gruebauer pulled out his phone and tapped a number.

"It's me. How's the canvas going? Any sign of Harris?" He listened a moment. "Stay on it. Let me know the minute you have something."

Grueb lowered the phone and looked at both Ty and Wynn, then shook his head.

———

The ADs are cracking, Devon Harris thought. He could understand, not forgive, but understand that bitch Lashika giving him up, but Mikey? *It's my own fault, really. I've been too soft on them. Ever since we started taking money from Mr. S, he's pressed us to keep a low profile, stay out of trouble. And what's that got us? Turned us into a bunch of pussies willing to give each other up at the first sign of trouble. Might be time to change teams. Join up with the suit's big-league team and re-make my rep, then come back and either own this place or burn it down.*

He pulled the burner phone out of his pocket and punched in the number from memory, surprised at how much his hands were shaking. The call was picked up right away.

"Well, well. Mr. Harris. We've been wondering if we'd hear from you." Stuart said.

"Pressure's been on, man. I've been laying low. Like you said."

"Yes, I did. Do you have any more names for me?"

"No, man. I already gave you Lashika. Besides Doc and Jay-squared, no one else knew."

"Are you sure about that?"

"Yeah, man, I'm sure. We're all good. But listen, the cops are getting close. I need some help."

"Okay. What do you have in mind?"

"Safety in numbers, man. I know you got another crew. Big time. Let me join up with them 'til this thing blows over."

"What about your crew?"

"We're scattering, man. Everyone's laying low. I'm thinking it's best to get out for a while."

"That doesn't show very good leadership, Devon. I thought you boys had a code?"

"We do. But there's a lot of pressure. I want to play it safe, like you said. Keep a low profile. Protect you."

"I appreciate that, but if you want to join another crew, you'll need to prove you're ready."

"Sure, whatever."

"Where are you now?"

"Ventura."

"Alright. You sit tight. I'll call you when we're ready. And Devon?"

"Yeah?"

"Make sure you pick up when I call."

———

Stuart hoped he'd played it right. He was anxious to get his hands on Harris, but the fact that he'd called, told him that Harris was getting desperate. *Don't want to spook him now. Need to find out where Li and Huan are and have them pick him up.*

———

Wynn was forced to wait patiently as he, Ty, and Gruebauer drove back to Ventura. *It's time for some old-fashioned police work,* Grueb had said, and while that might be fine for the two of them, Wynn had other ideas.

When they got back to the station, Wynn declined to go inside, figuring the less time he spent around Akins the better. Instead, he made an excuse about going home, then strolled casually to his bike, taking his time with his jacket, helmet, and gloves until Ty and Grueb went inside. He took out his phone and called Janelle Evans.

When she answered, he said, "Hi, Janelle. It's Sean. Do you have plans for lunch?"

"Today? No."

"Can you meet me in about a half-hour?"

"I guess so. Why? What's up?"

"I'll tell you when I see you."

They arranged to meet at a small deli, and once again Wynn arrived a few minutes early. The place was crowded, and the tables were tightly packed, making it less than an ideal location to have a discreet conversation. They slid into a table next to the window as another couple left.

"So, what's so urgent?" Janelle asked as they sat down.

"How familiar were you with those initial HCM studies?"

"At the time? As well as anybody."

"How about now? If you were to get a look at that data again, could you do anything with it?"

"Hmm, I don't know. If we couldn't find the discrepancies then, I doubt I could now."

Wynn winced as he shifted in his seat. The painkillers were wearing off.

"Are you okay?" Janelle asked. "You looked like you were walking a little stiff."

"Had a little accident yesterday. No big deal."

"What kind of accident? On your motorcycle?"

Geez. Not only does she look like Nicole, she sounds like her, too. "Yeah, but as you can see, I'm fine. Had my armor and helmet on, so it's all good."

"Alright. But I worry about you."

There it is again. "Thanks, I appreciate it, but I'm fine. So what about fraud?" he asked, refocusing the conversation. "You said the numbers didn't add up. Did you ever look to see if the numbers themselves were wrong?"

"Like somebody changed them?" she asked. "No. There are controls in place. They're checked and double-checked so by the time they get to us, we assume they're right. Why? Do you think somebody altered the data?"

"If they did, could you find it?"

"I don't know. Maybe. I'd need to look at the source data. We didn't normally get that."

"I thought you looked at all of it?"

She shook her head. "No. We looked for discrepancies within the data sets we were given. I can't remember an instance where the data set itself was wrong."

"If it was, would that cause the inconsistent results you had with HCM?"

"Maybe. Considering how thoroughly we looked at everything else, it's as likely as anything at this point. I'd have to see it."

"If we could get it, would you be willing to look?"

"Sure, I mean, I guess so."

Wynn picked up his phone and began texting Ty. "You said it's called source data?"

"Yeah."

"Anything else you would need?"

"I don't think so." Her brow furrowed. "Who are you texting?"

"A friend in high places," Wynn said. "Ty Lenihan. He's a detective in Ventura. He's gonna get a warrant to get the data from Mynogen. I want to make sure the warrant will cover everything you need. Can I give him your name to help his team review it?"

"When?"

"Later today. Tomorrow at the latest."

"I've got to get back to work."

"Ty will take care of that for you."

"Is it really that urgent?"

"I know this sounds crazy, but Nicky wasn't killed by accident. It was a hit. And I'm pretty sure it had something to do with HCM. We're getting close to finding out who and why, so yeah, it's urgent."

Janelle's jaw dropped. "You can't be serious."

"Unfortunately, I am. And you may be the only person who can help us prove it. Are you in?"

"Of course. Let me know when."

"Great." Wynn got up to leave. "Clear your calendar and keep your phone handy. Either Ty or I will be in touch."

———

Li watched from the passenger seat of a black Mercedes. It wasn't as comfortable as the Caddy, but that vehicle didn't exist anymore. Not just stripped for parts, but entirely disassembled following yesterday's chase outside of Palm Springs.

I can't believe this guy is still walking around, Li thought. He could see where the crash hadn't killed him, but he had to have suffered some broken bones at a minimum; spend at least a few days in the hospital. Li was even more amazed this morning when the tracker he'd placed on the Sportster started moving. Amazement turned to concern when he saw it stop at the Ventura Police Department, prompting Stuart to ask him and Huan to go back out on surveillance.

He lifted the camera to his eye and zoomed the telephoto lens through the glass to where Wynn and the woman were having lunch inside the deli. He snapped several pictures of the two of them, then zoomed in and took several more of the woman alone. By now they all knew Wynn's face, but she was an unknown. Must be important, though, considering Stuart wanted them to stay on Wynn instead of going to grab Harris right away.

He selected two of the pictures that best showed their faces and texted them to Stuart.

———

Wynn's phone buzzed in his hand as he walked from the deli out to his bike. It was Ty.

"Yeah?"

"So what's source data?" Ty asked.

"According to Janelle Evans, it's the most likely place fraud could be hidden in the study. Make sure your warrant includes it."

"Will my team know what to do with it?"

"Don't know, but Janelle will. She said she's willing to work with your guys to review it."

"Text me her contact info."

"Will do. You'll also need to smooth it over with her boss. Make sure she doesn't get dinged for helping us."

"No problem."

"Anything more on Harris?"

"Not yet. He's in the wind."

"What about Jameson and Legrea?"

"Stay away from them, Sean. If you want to help, put those computer skills of yours to use and get me some background, but by no means should you try to contact them. Remember what Akins said about the lawyers?"

"Understood," Wynn said. "Keep me posted."

He disconnected, then hopped on the Sportster and rumbled west to Ventura, back to his house, where he spent the next couple of hours researching Alexander Jameson, Stuart Legrea, and ALJ Pharmaceuticals.

Jameson, it appeared, had at one time been the darling of the pharmaceutical industry. Described as a bold pioneer with a vision for the future, he'd been featured in several professional magazines and websites. Even his personal life as one of L.A.'s most eligible bachelors had been chronicled in the society blogs. But his star seemed to disappear after the sale of ALJ. The most recent articles chronicled the failure of HCM and the legal battle with Mynogen that resulted. Including, as Amanda Carson had said, many of the financial details. Beyond that, there was little to find about his new company or his personal life.

Which was still more than he could find on Stuart Legrea. While photos of Jameson filled a Google image search, Wynn could find only one picture of Legrea, buried deep in the pdf pages of an old ALJ annual report, itself buried deep within Edgar, a website run by the Securities and Exchange Commission.

Wynn spent a minute examining Legrea's photo. It was an old professional headshot, black and white, at least ten years old. Legrea was thin, wearing the typical suit and tie, his light hair already receding high on his forehead, accentuating his sharp features. He looked familiar, but Wynn couldn't place from where.

About three-thirty in the afternoon, his cell rang.

"Hello, Mr. Wynn?"

"Yes?"

"This is Jean Fulton, with the Ventura PD."

Wynn recognized the voice. She was an assistant to Ty and Akins. "Yeah. I recall. What can I do for you?"

"I need to apologize that it's taken me a couple of days to get this to you, but Ty left me a message the other day to look in your wife's file to see if we have the name of the waitress who served the two of you the night of the shooting. Do you still want it?"

Wynn had completely forgotten. "Yes. Definitely."

"Do you have something to write with?"

"Yeah."

"Her name was Ingman. Marie Ingman."

———

Jasmine's head was in Carson's lap when his cell phone dinged with an incoming text message. He clicked on the picture, which immediately induced the human body's most primitive physiological response to danger: It drew blood away from his extremities and sent it racing back to his core.

"What's the matter, baby?" Jasmine asked. "I thought you liked that."

He pushed her out of the way and stood up, adjusting his swim trunks as he did so, then clicked on the next picture. His shaking hands made it hard to focus, but there was no doubt.

The phone rang in his palm, Stuart's name appearing on the screen. Carson slowly tapped the screen and put the phone to his ear.

"Do you know her?"

Carson swallowed, his mouth suddenly dry. "Yeah. Janelle Evans."

"Who is she?"

"She was the original target."

CHAPTER 28

TY FEARED HE had crossed a line with Judge Thompson and this latest warrant request. Even he had to admit the connection between Eunice Johnson, a deceased seventy-one-year-old woman, and a multi-billion-dollar pharmaceutical company was hard to explain. And though he sensed he was trying the judge's patience, Thompson once again listened attentively as Ty laid out the reasons for the warrant and granted his request.

Ninety minutes later, Janelle Evans arrived at the Ventura police department, and forty minutes after that, Ty, Janelle, and a team of forensic accountants descended on Mynogen. A few employees were already leaving for the day, and Ty knew that trickle would soon become a flood as the sun inched closer to the horizon. He stationed officers at all the exits and had them close the gates until the warrant was served. Oglesby had promised cooperation, but he wanted the place covered, just in case.

Ty strode across the lobby, pointed at the brunette receptionist and said, "Bring your key card." He didn't bother slowing until he got to the elevator.

Once upstairs, Madeline Smith hurried to catch up as Ty and his team marched down the hall to Oglesby's office.

"Please, Dr. Oglesby is in a meeting," Smith said.

Ty stopped. He wasn't completely insensitive to the optics. "You've got one minute. Get him out here."

Thirty seconds later, Oglesby came out of his office. "Detective Lenihan. I assume you have a warrant."

Ty held up the paper.

"May I?" Oglesby asked. He took the warrant from Ty and examined it while Marcia, the attorney, came down the hall. Oglesby handed it to her, and they all waited a few seconds while she looked it over, then nodded.

"What do you need?" Oglesby asked.

"Whatever she says," Ty said, nodding to Janelle.

An hour later, Janelle and her team had taken over a large conference room on the fifth floor. Outside the windows, long lines of cars backed up into the parking lots as employees were funneled to leave from a single exit. Officers searched each car, looking for any electronic media or physical papers that might have anything to do with HCM. Ty knew it was a long shot, but felt he had to make the effort.

"You might regret having driven your own car," Ty said, looking down into the parking lot. "That's going to take a while."

"Don't kid yourself," she said. "So is this."

"Well, if by chance we finish up in here first, we'll have a black and white take you home later. Avoid the line."

"I'd appreciate it."

Behind them, six workstations with dual monitors had been assembled by the Mynogen technology team on the large conference room table. Every e-file relating to HCM had been electronically cordoned off from everyone in the company except Oglesby, and access granted to Janelle's team. They were taking their seats as Janelle finished briefing them on file structure, then began divvying up the source files for them to review.

When she was done and they finally got to it, Janelle wandered over to where Ty stood.

"Do you have everything you need?" he asked.

"Almost. It's getting late and these folks are going to get tired and hungry. Can you get us a couple of urns of coffee and some sandwiches?"

He smiled. "You got it."

———

Across the campus in building four, Emil Tange returned to his desk after spending the last hour lugging workstations and monitors up to the bigwigs on the fifth floor. There were a lot of people in suits and even a few with badges clipped to their belts. *Surprise investigation. Cops are looking for something.*

Alarm bells went off in his head when he heard the lady he recognized as a former employee mention something that sounded an awful lot like "HCM." On the way back he asked his co-worker if he knew what was happening.

"Looks like the shit's about to hit the fan. Get your resume ready," he said.

"Why?"

"I'll give you one guess."

Emil stared back at him, blankly.

"The problem project, dummy. HCM."

Now back at his desk, Emil was confirming that guess as he tried to access the HCM file directory. He wasn't supposed to have access, but as the guy who built the security and determined who else could get to it, he could pretty much look at anything.

Including HCM.

But not today.

He was locked out, meaning someone way above his pay grade was paying attention. He hadn't specifically looked at HCM in several weeks, but this was the first time he was ever denied access.

Shit. He had hoped this day would never come.

And so had Neil Carson. Or so he'd said.

Emil had gotten along well with Carson during the time they'd worked together. Although the term 'together' might be stretching it. Carson had wanted Emil's help setting up the databases for that damn HCM study, so he'd treated Emil differently. The reality is he was a prick to almost everyone else, but he was always nice to Emil.

Because he needed me.

Carson didn't want Emil to just set up the databases, he wanted to understand them. Know how they worked. So he'd been extra nice as Emil patiently explained to him, line by line, how the database was constructed, where it would pull data from, what you could do with it, etc.

He'd also made it worth Emil's time.

While they'd worked together, but even more so the day he was fired. Carson had come to Emil's desk moments before being escorted out the door and handed him an envelope.

A thick envelope.

With cash.

HCM's my baby, Carson had said. *If anyone ever starts messing around with it or tries to corrupt those original files, you let me know, okay? There's more where that came from.*

Someone's messing with it now, Emil thought.

He tapped his finger on the keyboard. That last batch of cash had come in handy. Picked up some prime coke and a bitchin-hot hooker and still had more than half left over. But even that was long gone now. And he'd been feeling the need recently. *More where that came from,* Carson had said.

He picked up the phone and tapped a number.

"Who's this?" Carson's voice sounded stressed and bitchy, exactly like he'd remembered.

"Emil." He paused, waiting for Carson to respond. When he didn't, Emil said, "Neil. It's Emil Tange. At Mynogen. You told me to call you if someone ever started messing with the HCM files."

"Yeah, yeah, yeah," Carson said rapidly. "What's up?"

"A bunch of folks commandeered the fifth-floor conference room. I think they're cops. Had us set 'em up with the good stuff, so it looks like they're going to be here awhile. I don't know for sure, but I think they're looking at HCM."

"You don't know?"

"They didn't say anything around me. All I know is that I've had access to the HCM files ever since you left. All of sudden, now I don't."

"And you think they're cops?"

"I think so, but maybe not. I think you probably know one of them. It was that blonde lady that used to work for you."

"Janelle Evans?"

"Yeah, that's her."

"And when did this happen?"

"Maybe an hour ago."

"That's good, Emil. Thanks for letting me know."

"Last time you said you might help me out, if, you know, I kept an eye out."

"No worries, my man. I'll take care of you. Thanks for calling. I'll be in touch."

Carson disconnected before Emil could get in another word.

"Sure you will, asshole," he muttered.

———

Howard nearly jumped out of his chair when the new cell phone Li had given him began ringing in his briefcase. He lifted the case off the floor and set it on his desk, scattering pens and papers, and spilling what was left of his morning coffee. He thumbed the latches and pulled out the phone, turning away from the mess he'd created. "Hello?"

Li's unnervingly high voice came across the line. "Relax, Howard. You've already got the job, remember?"

Howard closed his eyes and felt the bile rise in his throat. "Oh, yeah. Sorry. What can I do for you?"

"Those production numbers you sent Mr. Chan earlier don't match with our shipments."

"What's wrong with them?"

"They're showing you're producing about ten percent more than we're receiving."

"Yes, that's correct."

"Why? Is that some kind of overrun?"

"Mr. Legrea has us hold ten percent back."

There was a pause on the line. Finally, Li asked, "Why?"

"I'm not sure. You'd have to ask him."

"Count on it."

The line went dead, leaving Howard to wonder who else was going to have an accident.

———

Stuart tapped his finger on the back of his cell phone. *This day's just getting better and better.* Not only was Wynn not dead from the accident yesterday, but now the cops were researching all the HCM data, led by none other than Carson's former lead analyst on the project. If anything good had come of this day, it was that Harris had reached out. *Let's see if he's as loyal as he says.*

Stuart pulled out his phone, found the number, and hit redial.

"Hello, sir," Harris said when he picked up.

"Hitterrrr," Stuart said. "Do they still call you that?"

"Sometimes."

"Alright. Are you ready to put that reputation to the test?"

CHAPTER 29

AFTER GETTING OFF the phone with Jean, Wynn did a basic search on Marie Ingman. When her picture came up, he couldn't believe his luck. She was the tired-looking blonde. The one who hadn't smiled at him when he first visited Viacci's in search of the hostess, Diana Williams, exactly a week ago. He called over to see if she was working tonight.

She was.

He hopped on the Sportster and rode down to the mall. The brunette hostess with the hair shaved close on one side, long on the other, greeted him as he approached the restaurant.

"Welcome to Viacci's. Will you be dining with us tonight?"

"No, thanks. Just meeting a friend in the bar."

"That's great. Please, go right in."

Wynn paused inside the front door and looked around. Though it wasn't yet six o'clock, the place was busy. Groups of all sizes sat around tables gently lit by candlelight while wait staff, all wearing black slacks and white shirts, hurried about.

He strolled around the far edge of the U-shaped bar and slid onto a stool with his back to the wall, giving him a good view of the kitchen entrance. He ordered an Amstel from the bartender, and had barely taken his first sip when he saw Marie emerge from the kitchen carrying a large tray of plates. Knowing it might be a while before she was free, he grabbed a napkin, scribbled a quick note, and caught the bartender's attention.

"What's up?" the bartender asked.

"Can you give this to Marie when you get a chance?"

"What is this, fifth grade?"

Wynn smiled. "I'm a friend of a friend. Just want to say hi."

The bartender took the note and read it. *Can we talk? About Diana.* He scrunched his eyebrows. "Looks like a fifth-grade note to me."

Wynn shrugged.

"I should warn you," the bartender said. "She's got a boyfriend. A UFC fighter. For your sake, I hope you're not stalking her. He'll kick your ass."

"I just want to say hi."

"Your funeral. But it'll be a while. She's busy. You want to order food?"

Wynn glanced through the windows near the entry. A small crowd was already waiting to be seated. It was going to be a long night.

"Sure," he said as he settled in to wait.

A short time later, Marie approached the bar to pick up an order. The bartender handed her the note. She looked at it, then looked a question at the bartender, who pointed a quick thumb in Wynn's direction. Marie looked across the bar and locked eyes with Wynn.

She froze for a moment, then picked up her drinks and walked away.

An hour later, long after Wynn had finished his meal and switched from Amstel to iced tea, Luke Creviston, the manager, wandered up beside him.

"Good evening, Mr. Wynn."

Wynn turned and wiped his hands with a napkin. "Mr. Crevis-ton. Good to see you."

"You too. Did you enjoy your meal?"

"It was great. First time I've eaten here since..."

"I understand. We're glad to have you back." Creviston paused. "I also understand you've asked to speak with one of our wait staff?"

"Yes."

"She... um... She's asked me to tell you she's not comfortable speaking with you."

Wynn paused. "I wonder why that is?"

"Truthfully, I don't care. When you came here last week we were, and still are, sympathetic to your situation. But whatever your need for closure, we can't have you disrupting our employees. I can only assume you found Diana's roommate and she somehow led you back here. For what purpose, I can't imagine. But now that you've finished and been informed she doesn't wish to speak with you, there's no reason for you to stay."

"You're asking me to leave?"

Creviston's look answered the question.

"And if I don't?"

"Calling the authorities is not in anyone's best interest."

The two men locked eyes.

Finally, Wynn turned back toward the bar. "Let me pay the tab."

"No need," Creviston said. He stepped back, clearing a way toward the door. "We're happy to take care of it for you."

Wynn paused again. "Okay. Thanks. I guess." Wynn slid off the barstool and walked to the exit. He'd been thrown out of his share of bars when he was in the Marines, but this was the most polite way it'd ever been done.

While Creviston may not care why Marie didn't want to talk to him, her reaction convinced him she knew something. He walked across the street to a coffee shop, bought a cup, and settled into a table next to the window that gave him a clear view of Viacci's front door.

———

This is either the break, or mistake, of a lifetime, Devon Harris thought as he peered through the curtains of a friend's apartment. Mr. S, a.k.a. "The Suit," said they had a job for him, taking out another blonde. *What is it with this guy and blondes?*

Mr. S had said someone would pick him up, part of the A-team. The big league. Harris wasn't sure if this was real or a setup, but he had no choice. The cops were getting close. And he'd been a good soldier, keeping his mouth shut and doing what Mr. S had asked.

Except for the last instructions.

Mr. S had told him to leave his hardware behind, that they'd provide whatever was needed.

Fuck that.

He kept his right hand inside his jacket pocket, wrapped around the butt of a Smith & Wesson .380. A black Mercedes SUV eased down the street, stopping at the curb out front, its occupants hidden behind tinted windows. Harris took a deep breath, then slipped out the front door.

The passenger window slid down as he approached, revealing a young Asian guy sitting shotgun.

"Hands."

Harris stopped. *This kid's A-Team?* He released his grip from the Smith & Wesson, then pulled his hands from his pockets and spread his fingers wide.

"Get in."

These guys aren't so smart. Harris opened the rear door and slid inside.

"What's your name?" the Asian guy asked as they pulled away from the curb.

"Hitter."

"Hitter, huh? Well, we don't have cool names like that. I'm Li. This is Huan," he said, indicating the driver.

You dumb shit, Harris scolded himself. *Trying to impress these guys with a stupid street name. Probably sound like I'm ten years old.* "I'm Devon. My friends call me D."

"I thought your friends called you Hitter?"

"You know how it is."

"Yeah, I know," Li said. "I also know Mr. Legrea told you to leave your hardware at home, yet here you are, packing."

"No, I'm not," Devon lied. *Legrea. So that's Mr. S's name...*

"You've got something awfully heavy in that right jacket pocket. I could tell when you showed me your hands. If you're not packing, what is it?"

You dumbass! Can't you say anything right? "Just a bit of insurance."

"Insurance, huh? That's cool. But we're all friends here, D, so there's no need for insurance. I don't need to see your hands, but if you want to be our friend, keep 'em out of your pockets."

Devon pulled his hands out of his pockets and laced his fingers between his knees. "So, what's the job?"

"Just some lady, working late tonight. Putting her nose where it doesn't belong."

"How are we going to do it?"

"I know you meant to ask, how are *you* going to do it? We're just here to point you in the right direction. Provide backup if needed. But Mr. Legrea was very specific. He wants you to do this."

"Where?"

"A parking lot. Quick in, quick out, nobody around. Should be easy."

They drove in silence for a few minutes before Li said to Huan, "How are you feeling?"

"Nerves, man. Like always."

Li turned back to Harris. "My man Huan here always gets a little nervous before a job. Usually, we've got a little something to calm him down, but we're all out tonight. You got anything?"

Here's my chance. "Yeah, man. I got just the thing." Harris reached into his pocket and pulled out a baggie with a dozen little white pills inside. "Try one of these."

"What is it?" Li took the baggie from him.

"It's called Jewel. I'm surprised Mr. S... I mean Mr. Legrea, doesn't hook you up."

"You get these from Legrea?"

"Yeah, man. About two hundred a week."

"No shit? You hear that, Huan? He must be holding out on us."

Huan nodded. "Must be."

"That son of a bitch," Li said. He handed the baggie back to Devon, turned around and faced forward, then whispered, "That son of a bitch."

———

Back on the fifth floor, the sandwiches were gone, the coffee urns empty, and the pace had slowed into a grinding drudgery. A half dozen people sat in front of computers around the large conference table, several more reading through stacks of paper between them. Ty eased into a chair next to Janelle.

"Anything?" he asked.

Janelle leaned back in her seat. "Not yet."

"You look beat."

She smiled. "I'm going to have to talk to your wife. Have her teach you some manners. You never say that to a woman."

He blushed. "Sorry. I know you've had a long day. You should go home and get a good night's sleep. Hit it fresh tomorrow."

"What if one of these guys finds something?"

"I've got your number. If it can't wait, I'll call you."

"Okay. I'm going to finish up what I'm working on, then I'll go. Is there still a line outside?"

"Nah, the lot cleared out a couple of hours ago. I've sent those guys home. The boss doesn't want to pay the OT. But I'm happy to have someone escort you if you like."

"No. I'm good. As long as I can get my car out."

"That should be no problem, it's wide open. Thanks for your help today."

"No worries. I'll see you in the morning."

"See you then." Ty got up and walked to the corner of the room.

He pulled out his phone and noticed he'd missed a call earlier from the Beaumont police department. There was a voice message. Something to do with Wynn's accident yesterday, he assumed. He tapped the phone and listened.

Detective Lenihan. This is Officer Muncie with the Beaumont police department. I was the responding officer to the Wynn motorcycle accident yesterday. I received a call from the tow company earlier today. It seems they found a tracking device on Mr. Wynn's motorcycle. I know some bikers install a LoJack in case the bike is stolen, but this was different. Anyway, it struck them as odd enough to call me, thought I'd pass it along to you. Call me back if you have any questions.

Ty disconnected from voicemail and called Wynn.

"Hey," Wynn said when he picked up.

"Back at you. Where have you been all day?" Ty asked.

"Doing what you told me. Researching Jameson and Legrea."

"Are you home now?"

"No."

"Where are you?"

"At a coffee shop across from Viacci's. I was hoping to talk to a waitress there."

"Not causing trouble, I hope."

"I've been good. What's up?"

"I got a voice message from the reporting officer in Beaumont about your accident yesterday. The tow company says they found a tracker on your bike. Did you know that?"

"A tracker? No, I didn't put it there."

"That's not good, Sean. I hate to jump to conclusions, but..."

"I hear you. Let me call you back."

———

Wynn hustled out of the coffee shop and down the block, finally crossing the street to the parking lot where his Sportster was parked. He opened the saddlebags and went through them, knowing exactly what he was looking for; he'd placed the same type of device on a vehicle in Wyoming a couple of months ago.

Finding nothing, he felt underneath the fenders and opened the battery cover. Still nothing. He used a washer he kept on his key ring to unscrew the seat bolt and lifted the seat.

There it was.

Less than half the size of his cell phone, wired directly to the battery, never to run out of juice.

He pulled out his phone and hit redial. Ty answered right away.

"Yeah, got one on the Sportster, too," Wynn said.

"And I'll bet you'll find one on your Lexus."

"Uh-huh."

"Think back. Where have you been over the past few days?"

"Janelle."

"What?"

"I had lunch with Janelle today. If they were tracking me, there's a good chance they saw me with her."

———

Ty wheeled around, looking across the room at the computer terminal where Janelle had been working.

It was empty.

"Gotta go," he blurted into the phone, then took off running down the hallway. There were two elevators. The digital readout above one indicated the car was on the first floor. Above the other, the readout switched from three to two. He scrambled around the corner and yanked open the door leading to the stairs, throwing himself down them four at a time.

Moments later, he burst through the stairwell door into the empty lobby. Outside, beyond the glass, Janelle was walking toward her car, lit by the orange sodium glow of an overhead streetlamp.

Ty sprinted across the lobby, out the doors, and along the sidewalk leading to the parking lot. Janelle was next to her car, reaching for the handle.

"Janelle!"

She turned. A muzzle flashed fifty feet to her right. The unmistakable pop of a handgun reached his ears an instant before the shattering glass.

"Get down!" Ty yelled as he pulled his Glock from his jacket and returned fire.

Janelle dropped to the ground and rolled under the car as more shots rang out. As he closed the distance, Ty recognized the shape in front of him. Devon Harris continued to fire toward Janelle until one of Ty's bullets whizzed past his head. Harris ducked down, then returned fire in Ty's direction.

Ty was completely exposed in the nearly empty lot. He dove behind the three-foot-tall, concrete base of a lamp post and crouched down, leaning against it, ducking his head. He was bathed like a spotlight in the same orange glow Janelle had walked through moments before, but outside that circle of light, all was dark. From somewhere in that darkness, an engine revved.

Reinforcements.

A sudden volley of bullets sent concrete chips flying around his head. He felt the sting of a bullet rip through his shoulder as a second volley came from his left, the direction of Janelle's car.

There are two of them.

Time slowed.

Adrenaline spiked through his veins, numbing the pain in his shoulder while making his senses hyper-aware.

He glanced to his left and saw Janelle, lying on her stomach beneath the car, her frightened eyes practically glowing in the dark. A man thirty feet to her left was beginning to crouch down, preparing to shoot under the car.

More shots, from Harris' direction, chipped the concrete behind him.

The revving engine was getting louder. In front of him. Coming closer.

Not a cop car. There are three of them.

With frightening certainty, Ty suddenly realized he was smack in the middle of a three-way attack, the center of a perfect triangle, each opponent separated by a hundred and twenty degrees. If he faced one, two would be at his sides. Face two, and the third would be directly behind him.

He had nine rounds remaining.

Protect Janelle.

The revving engine was now an unseen roar. He lifted his Glock toward the crouching man and squeezed off three rounds. Not waiting to see him fall, he spun around and caught a break. Harris was no longer hiding.

He was running toward him.

Shooting.

He's so close. How is he missing?

He wasn't.

Neither was Li, driving the Mercedes, coming from behind. The adrenaline couldn't fully mask the tiny pinpricks that stabbed through Ty's back, chest, and legs. He squeezed off three more shots and watched Harris drop to the ground before his legs gave way. He fell to the pavement, his head rolling to the side.

Toward Janelle. She was crawling out from beneath the car.

Thank God. She's safe.

A wave of warm relief rushed over his body.

Followed by a chilling cold.

He locked eyes with her again and was confused. Her lips were moving but her voice was muffled, as if far away. There were tears in her eyes.

What's wrong? It's okay. You're safe now.

The distant roar of the Mercedes faded as her tears dropped into darkness.

CHAPTER 30

THE NEXT MORNING, Wynn sat in the Ventura Police Department conference room, pictures of Devon Harris scattered on the table in front of him. It was hard to concentrate, the pain inside far more crippling than the bumps and bruises still healing from the accident. The last twelve hours had been a nightmare.

After hanging up with Ty the night before, Wynn raced east on the 101 to the Mynogen complex in Camarillo, only to be greeted by a police blockade at the entrance. Flashing red and blue lights from more than a dozen cop cars and ambulances lit the parking lot like a heavy metal rock concert.

"I'm working with Detective Lenihan!" he insisted at the cops blocking his way, but they were unsympathetic.

One of them took his name and said simply, "Someone will be out shortly."

Wynn parked the bike next to the curb and pulled out his phone, seeing he'd missed a call from Janelle, but she hadn't left a message. He called her back. No answer. He tapped Ty's number. It rang six times, then went to voicemail.

"It's me. I'm out front but these guys won't let me in. Call me back, or better yet, come get me. But call me."

He paced back and forth, finally noticing the news crews arriving on the scene, setting up their cameras, preparing for their live shots. As he wandered toward them, a brunette from channel four rushed over, her cameraman trailing two steps behind.

"Sir!" the reporter shouted. "Can you tell us what happened?"

"I just got here. I was going to ask you."

"All we heard is there was a shootout. Three people hit." She turned away, apparently not interested in talking if he wasn't a source.

A hand tugged on Wynn's arm. It was one of the cops from the blockade. "Detective Gruebauer is on his way," he whispered so the reporter wouldn't hear. "Come with me."

Wynn followed as the cop wove through the cruisers blocking the entrance. Across the parking lot, a row of police cars formed a wall, blocking his view of whatever carnage lay on the other side. A shape, silhouetted by the flashing lights, appeared from behind the vehicles and came toward him. A few moments later he could tell it was Grueb, walking slowly.

Wynn took a step forward, but the cop put a hand on his arm. "Let's wait here."

The spider-sense he'd been forcing to stay down, the one that warned him things were about to get bad, burst to the surface.

"How's Janelle?" Wynn asked when Grueb got closer. "Is she okay?"

"Janelle's fine."

"Thank God. The reporter said there were three down. Who are they?"

"We don't have an ID on the first one," Grueb said slowly. "But he's Asian. Considering what Ty was working on here, we assume he's Silent Mafia. The second is Devon Harris. He's dead."

Wynn's eyes went wide. "Fuck!"

"The third..." Grueb paused, then swallowed, as if trying to find his voice. "...is Ty."

"Fuck! Is he okay?"

Grueb looked him in the eye and almost imperceptibly shook his head.

The world tilted. "No. No, no, no, no. Can't be."

"He was hit almost a dozen times. Didn't stand a chance. Bled out before anyone got here."

"Is he still here? Is anyone working on him?"

"Sean. It's over. He's gone."

The world crashed.

Wynn spent the next hour at the scene where he spoke to Janelle, who told him what happened. Three guys. From all angles. They were coming after her, but Ty warned her, saved her life. He was a hero.

Wynn asked if she'd gotten a look at the driver of the SUV. Not much, she'd replied. The only thing she noticed was that his skin was fair. Not Black. Not Brown. Maybe Caucasian. Maybe Asian. She wasn't sure.

When the coroner took Ty's body to the hospital, Wynn followed, knowing Stacey would be there. Akins had sent someone to their house to pick her up, hoping to keep her away from the television.

Wynn sat in a waiting room down the hall from the emergency room, waiting for it. When it finally came, Stacey's cry was a long, mournful wail, echoing through the corridors, the weight of it settling firmly on his shoulders. It pushed him down, like a physical thing, forcing the air from his lungs, not allowing him to breathe. Darkness crept along the periphery as stars exploded across his vision. He welcomed the crushing darkness, relief from this agony.

Just a little more and it'll all be over.

But guilt is not merciful.

It allowed him to breathe; forced him to sit there. Conscious and aware that his actions had created this pain, had taken Stacey's husband, Brie and Matty's father. He pictured the finger paintings in Vanessa Carow's classroom, and how the Lenihan children's paintings would no longer be of blue skies and bright sunshine, but of dark clouds and stormy days. How Brie's daddy would never walk her down the aisle, how Matty's dad would never teach him to shave.

He knew pain.

This was something else entirely.

He sat until everyone went home. Akins and Grueb had come over, told him not to blame himself, told him they'd catch the guys who did this.

But the guys who pulled the triggers weren't necessarily the same as those responsible.

Jameson.

Legrea.

Carson.

And maybe even Ishan Chan.

Wynn had no proof, but his gut told him they were the ones responsible. Not only for Ty, but Nicole also.

He'd gone home and removed the tracker from the Sportster, then found and removed the one on the Lexus. Then he went inside and sat on the couch and stared at the blank TV. He took every nugget of information, those from two years ago and those from the past week, and turned it over in his mind, examining it like a puzzle piece, trying to figure out where it fit.

With each piece that came together, resolve hardened in the pit of his stomach. By the time dawn arrived, he had a picture. A few pieces were missing, and others were held together by assumptions instead of facts, but it was a coherent picture.

He put the guilt and the grief aside. Replaced them with purpose and intention. He knew what he needed to do.

Which led him back here, to the Ventura Police Department, and the photos of Devon Harris that Grueb had first shown him just a few days ago. Wynn shuffled through the pictures until he found the right one. The one they assumed was another drug deal, with the guy in the suit.

The image was dark and the angle was bad, but it was close.

Sunken cheeks, sharp nose. He zoomed in and took a picture of the photo with his phone.

Grueb appeared in the doorway. "What'd you find?"

"Hold on." Wynn pulled up the old ALJ annual report. "Take a look at this." He laid his phone with the picture of Legrea next to the picture of Harris and the guy in the suit. "Same guy?"

"Maybe," Grueb replied.

"If you had to make a bet?"

"If I had to? Yeah, same guy. Who is he?"

"Stuart Legrea."

"No shit? It makes sense. He had as much to lose as Carson."

"That he does. Mikey Martin's the one who told you about the suit, right?" Wynn asked.

"Yeah."

"You think he could pick Legrea out of a six-pack?"

"I don't know. He said he didn't get a good look at the guy, so it'd be sketchy at best. I'll do some digging this afternoon, but we'll need more."

"I might have something," Wynn said. "But it's pretty thin at the moment. I'll let you know if it turns into anything."

"Please do."

"If you're digging," Wynn said, "try to find some link between Legrea and the Silent Mafia. This thing has cost them two guys. There's got to be a connection."

Grueb nodded. "Will do."

They stood in silence for a few moments, each consumed with their thoughts. Finally, Grueb asked, "Are you going to see Stacey?"

"Maybe later."

"I'm sure she'd like to see you."

She needs an outlet to focus her blame and anger, Wynn thought. "Yeah, I'll try."

"That'd be good." Grueb took a couple of steps toward the door, then turned and looked back. He started to speak, then closed his mouth and exhaled heavily.

"What?" Wynn asked.

"Ty told me what you did in Wyoming over the summer. That cowboy shit."

"Yeah?"

"Looks like this has just turned into the wild west... I've always wanted to be a cowboy."

They locked eyes and Wynn felt the ice between them melt, the unspoken message becoming clear. *Whatever it takes to catch these guys.*

Grueb nodded, then walked away.

Wynn gave him thirty seconds, then strode through the maze of hallways to the crime analysis unit.

"Jason," he said as he stopped in front of the crime tech's cubicle. "Remember me? Sean Wynn. I was with Ty when he gave you that old envelope with the money in it last week."

"Yeah, I remember." His voice was low. "How are you doing?"

"Honestly? It doesn't get much worse. But we need to help Grueb catch these bastards. Did you ever come up with anything on that envelope?"

"Unfortunately, no. There was only one set of usable prints and they looked brand new. Probably from one of those names you gave me, but regardless, they weren't in the system."

"Did you check the individual bills?"

"Each one. There was a set on the bottom bill that matched the prints on the outside of the envelope. Whoever handled it probably took the money out of the envelope, took a few bills off the top, and put the rest back."

It made sense. Michelle Williams had said she used some for John's wake.

"What about opioid residue?"

"Strike two," Jason said. "Nothing. You were right about one thing, though. The serial numbers are sequential. They all came from the same place."

"And where's that?"

"They were issued from the Federal Reserve Bank in San Francisco and went to Wells Fargo."

"Do you know which branch?"

"No. Once it gets in the carrier's hands you can narrow it down, but you can't pinpoint it."

"Shit."

"Sorry. Wish I could be of more help."

"Maybe you can. Can you find an address for me?"

"Well," Jason said, suddenly cautious. "It'd be better if Grueb asked."

"Grueb's busy. And I can find my way around LexisNexis as well as anyone, but I don't have access to a computer here. You can save him a little time by helping me out or not. Up to you."

"Okay. What's the name?"

"Marie Ingman. Mid-twenties. Probably in Ventura but could be in the surrounding area also."

Jason found the address and gave it to him. "Hope it helps."

"Every little bit does."

———

That bitch has more lives than a cat! Neil Carson watched the morning news on television. The outcome couldn't have been worse. Janelle Evans was still alive, but one of Chan's men, an AD, and a cop were all dead. It wouldn't take a genius to start putting the pieces together now. And even though he hadn't ordered it, he *had* called Stuart and told him where Janelle was.

And worst of all, Emil Tange knew that he knew.

Can Tange be trusted? Probably not.

Carson remembered how he had taken care of Tange last time. It was clear he expected the same now. *Practically begged for a payoff. Maybe if I get something to him quickly, he'll keep his mouth shut.* The challenge would be getting to him before the cops.

Carson took a deep breath. Forced himself to calm down, to

think it through. *Maybe I should get out of town. Buy a couple of days. Call Tange and take care of him, then come back when the heat's died down.*

Carson slammed his coffee mug on the kitchen counter, harder than intended.

"What's the matter, baby?" Jasmine asked.

Carson ignored her as he walked to the bedroom, grabbed a bag, and stuffed a few clothes in it.

When he came out, Jasmine saw the bag. "Where are you going?"

"Something's come up at work. I gotta go."

"Again?"

"Don't start, Jaz. You know how my job is."

"Yeah. It's a pain in the ass. How long will you be gone?"

"A few days. I'll call you later when I know more."

He didn't bother kissing her as he rushed out the door.

———

Li watched as Carson's garage door rose and the Acura SUV backed out onto the street.

After the shooting at Mynogen, Li had gone straight to Chan, who was surprisingly calm about losing another man. Li was also struck by Chan's lack of reaction to the news that Stuart was holding back ten percent of the Jewel supply, and distributing it through the ADs.

Almost like confirmation of something he already knew.

Chan had asked only a couple of questions, then sent Li to Palm Springs.

He let the Acura get about a block ahead before following in a new Range Rover. It was his third car in as many days, as the Mercedes he had driven yesterday was now undergoing the same fate as the Caddy. He hoped he wouldn't have to do the same with the Rover. He kind of liked it.

Staying a block behind, Li followed as Carson drove north out of town, then picked up Highway 62 as it curved to the northeast, toward Joshua Tree National Park. He silently cursed himself as he glanced at the gas gauge. Less than half a tank. There was very little northeast of Palm Springs until you reached Las Vegas, over two hundred miles away. He doubted the Rover had that kind of range.

Twenty minutes later, as they entered the small town of Yucca Valley, Li was relieved to see Carson turn into a self-service gas station. He pulled into a strip mall a block away, then reached into the center console and pulled out a GPS tracker. Like the burner phones, he kept several on hand in the warehouse and had grabbed two before heading to Palm Springs. He flipped the switch to turn it on and quickly pulled up the app on his phone to connect.

As Carson filled his tank, Li searched his phone's browser for the gas station's number, then called the station.

A young male voice answered. "Hello?"

"Hi. Is this the Star Mart on Twentynine Palms?"

"Yes."

"Do you have a guy there in a black Acura SUV? I don't know his name, but he left his phone at the restaurant."

"Let me check." There was a slight pause. "Yeah, he's here."

"Can you page him to come to the phone?" Li got out of the Range Rover and tucked his Ruger into the back of his pants. He stayed out of sight while making his way closer to the gas station.

"Sure. Hold on."

Li heard the page on the overhead speakers above the gas pumps, as well as on his phone. "Will the gentleman in the black Acura please come inside."

He ducked behind a parked car when he saw Carson look around. *This is going to be close.* He felt the Ruger in the back of his waistband. *Fuck it. There's always option two if he sees me.*

Li peeked around the rear of the car as Carson walked across the parking lot. He disconnected the call and stuffed his phone into his pocket. When Carson entered the store, Li hustled from his hiding spot over to Carson's Acura, stopping just long enough to shove the tracker into the wheel well. Knowing he wouldn't have time to run back to his car, Li stood up and calmly walked over to where another customer was filling his tank.

"Hey, I'm sorry to bug you, but I was wondering if you know the way to Joshua Tree?" Li kept his back to the store on the opposite side of the pump beside Carson's car.

"Straight ahead. About eight miles."

Li heard Carson come around the back of his car and open the door. "This way?" he said, making his voice unnaturally low.

"Yeah. Just keep going. Can't miss it."

"Hmm. Okay." Carson's engine sprang to life. Li pulled out his phone and looked down. He turned his body and stepped behind the pump as Carson pulled away.

"Okay, man. Thanks," Li said as he walked back to his car.

———

It was shortly after nine-thirty in the morning when Wynn pulled up in front of the Lenihan house. Several cars were already parked in the street out front. It was the last place he wanted to be, but knew it was part of his penance. With any luck, they'd tell him Stacey was sleeping and he could come back later.

He walked up the sidewalk, an image of himself approaching the gallows springing to mind. An older gentleman, with gray hair and eyes red from tears, answered the bell.

"Hi. I'm Sean. I know it's not a good time, but is Stacey available?"

"Sean Wynn?" the man asked.

"Yeah."

"Come on in. I'm Bill. Stacey's dad. She's been asking about you."

Imaginary hands seemed to grab him and pull him into the house.

Bill led the way past a formal sitting area down a short hallway to a living room where a half-dozen people sat. Open photo albums were strewn about on the floor and coffee table. Stacey sat in the middle of the couch with what appeared to be her mother and a sister on either side. Her eyes were red, her cheeks stained by tears.

Wynn felt the tingling of a noose tighten around his neck.

Bill said, "Stacey, you have a visitor."

Stacey looked up from the photo album on her lap, her face expressionless. She slid the album to her mother, got up and walked over to him, like an executioner approaching the lever. He waited for her outburst, for the floor to drop away, to leave him dangling in the wind.

Instead, she wrapped her arms around him in a tight embrace and began to cry. Wynn folded his arms around her as his own tears dripped into her hair.

After a long moment, she pulled herself away. "Ty told me a story about you."

He waited for her to continue.

"He said you almost single-handedly took down a ring of sex traffickers this past summer."

Wynn shrugged a little.

"Grueb told me they think the guys who killed Ty were the same ones who killed Nicole. He said they'd get justice for both of us now."

He nodded.

Her face turned hard. "I don't want justice. I want you to kill them."

CHAPTER 31

WYNN RODE ACROSS town to the address Jason had given him for Marie Ingman. He was pushing his luck, but he had a hunch. Stuart Legrea was already associated with ALJ and therefore also with Mynogen, and the photo with Devon Harris connected him to the ADs. If Marie could ID Legrea as the man who paid off Diana Williams, it would all fit.

He pulled to the curb a block away from Ingman's apartment. According to the address, she lived on the third floor of an eight-story complex located just north of the 101. He took an outdoor stairwell on the end of the building and found her apartment about halfway down the hall. Hip-hop music came from inside.

He knocked on the door, loud enough to be heard over the music but not so loud as to be threatening, then stepped to the side and turned his back. When the door opened, he turned around and stepped forward.

"Oh, fuck no," Marie said when she saw who it was. Wynn stuck his foot in the door as she tried to push it closed.

"Relax. I'm not here to hurt you. I just want to talk."

"I've got nothing to say to you."

"I think maybe you do."

"I'm gonna call the cops." She pushed the door harder against his foot.

"Please do. If you've seen the news this morning, you know a cop was killed last night. He was a friend of mine. And I think you've got information that can help us find who murdered him. I'm sure they'll want to talk to you."

"What are you talking about?"

"Diana Williams, the shooting at Viacci's, and the killing of that cop last night are all related. If you'd relax, I want to show you a picture and ask a few questions. That's it. I'll stay right here in the hall."

Marie let up the pressure on the door. "What picture?"

Wynn took out his phone and opened the picture he'd snapped of the photo of Harris and Legrea. "Before I show you this, you should know I talked to Diana's roommate. She told me that the night before the shooting some guy came in and gave Diana five thousand dollars to make sure my wife and I were seated at a particular table there on the patio of Viacci's. She also said you knew about it. That Diana gave you a thousand dollars to help her out. Is that true?"

Marie opened the door wider and leaned out, turning her head to look each way down the hall. "Come in."

Wynn stepped inside and Marie closed the door behind him. The apartment was small. And dirty. Dishes were piled high in the sink and clothes scattered about the living room.

"I don't know anything," she said.

"For a thousand bucks, you must've known something."

"I was standing next to Diana when the guy came in. He asked if either of us would be hosting the next night. When Diana said she would, he got all secretive. Pulled her aside and talked for a minute or two, then he handed her an envelope and left. She came back over and started making fun of the guy, saying, 'Oooh, big spender. Let's see what he thinks it'll take to reserve a prime table at the hottest restaurant in town.' When she opened it, we couldn't believe our eyes. That was more money than either of us had ever seen."

"So you saw the guy?"

"Yeah."

"What'd he look like?"

"I don't know. An average middle-aged white guy."

"Is this him?" Wynn handed her his phone with the picture of Legrea zoomed in on his face.

"I don't know. Could be."

"Come on. Take a good look. It's important."

She looked again but shook her head. "It's not a great photo."

Wynn took the phone back, pulled up a browser, and found the old ALJ annual report that had Legrea's photo. "How about this one?" he asked as he handed her the phone.

She studied the picture carefully. "I don't know. It's been two years and I see more than a hundred people a night. It could be, but I couldn't swear to it."

Damn! Wynn took the phone back and had an idea. He pulled up a search engine and typed in a name. Several photos appeared. He picked the best one and showed it to her. "What about this guy? Could this have been him?"

"Wow, yeah. That looks a lot more like him."

"Are you sure?"

"Like I said, it's been two years, but yeah, that's more likely."

Neil Carson.

"Why didn't you go to the cops at the time of the shooting?" Wynn asked.

"They said it was a random gang thing."

"Five thousand dollars didn't raise your suspicion?"

"You've gotta understand. The night of the shooting it looked like a coincidence. Then Diana dies and the next day they arrest that gangbanger. It looked like it was over. Problem solved. If I'd gone to the cops, they would've asked for the money. And for what? More evidence? I needed that money, and it wasn't going to do them any good, so why turn it in?"

Wynn shook his head. He hated it, but he understood where she was coming from. "Alright. Thanks." He stepped toward the door.

"What does this have to do with the detective that was killed last night?"

"It means we're getting close."

———

Wynn rode home and parked the Sportster in the garage, then hustled upstairs to grab his Glock from the bedside dresser. He stepped into the large walk-in closet that at one time had been a second bedroom. His clothes hung neatly across less than half of one wall.

The entire opposite wall was covered by a massive steel vault, twelve feet wide, eight feet tall, and two feet deep. Its wood-veneered cabinets and drawers protected by an electronic lock. He punched a code into the keypad and waited as the deadbolts slid back and a small, LED light turned green, then opened the heavy steel doors to reveal his personal arsenal.

An assortment of semi-automatic rifles, shotguns, and pistols hung on the wall in front of him. He pulled a Smith & Wesson M&P15 from the wall and then filled a backpack with spare magazines for both the Glock and the M&P. He closed and locked the cabinet, slipped on a shoulder holster for the Glock, then grabbed a loose-fitting, button-down shirt to wear over the holster. Gathering it all up, he took the weaponry out to the garage and placed it in the Lexus. As much as he preferred riding the Sportster, four wheels were needed for what he had planned today.

Three hours later, he once again took the Bob Hope exit into Palm Springs and drove along streets named for famous Hollywood celebrities. It was a mild curiosity the first time he'd seen them. He paid no attention today.

He parked a block away from Neil Carson's home, checked his Glock, then got out and strolled casually up the sidewalk. A golf course fairway ran behind the houses, but the yards were enclosed by a six-foot, stucco privacy wall, preventing him from accessing Carson's property directly. He walked up the street until he came to a cart path, then took it between two houses, coming out on the golf course behind the houses.

Turning left, he made his way between the wall and the tree-lined fairway until he reached Carson's backyard, where rap music drifted over the wall. He worked his way along until he came to a gate, also solid for privacy, but with small gaps on either side. Peering through, he realized he was directly behind Carson, who was sitting exactly where he had been when Wynn visited a few days ago. The back of his head leaned against the top of a chair as if sleeping. Jasmine was nowhere to be seen.

Wynn checked the hinges and latch mechanism on the gate. Definitely rusted. Potentially loud. He eased his way a few feet further along and grabbed the top of the wall, then hoisted himself up and over, the sound of his jeans scraping along the top of the wall covered by the music. He dropped into a crouching position on the other side and pulled out his Glock, waiting for any reaction. Carson's head moved side to side, but he didn't turn around.

Staying low, with the Glock extended, Wynn crept forward. As he came up behind Carson, Wynn was able to see over his shoulder. Jasmine was on her knees between his legs.

He placed the barrel of the Glock against the back of Carson's head. "I hate to interrupt, but we need to talk."

Jasmine looked up and her eyes went wide. She leaned back.

"Shit, man. She said she wasn't married." The voice came from the guy, but it wasn't Carson's.

Wynn eased to the side so he could see the guy's face. Not Neil Carson.

"Where's Neil?"

"Fuck, dude! I don't even know who that is."

"Shut up. I'm talking to Jasmine. Where's Neil?"

"He's not here," she said.

"Where is he?"

"I don't know. He left in a hurry this morning. Said he'd be gone a few days."

"Where'd he go?"

"I told you I don't know!"

The guy in the chair whimpered.

"You said he left in a hurry. I take it this trip wasn't planned?"

"No. He was watching TV and started freaking out. Stuffed a few things in a bag and said he'd be gone a few days, then took off."

"Has he done this before?"

"Yeah. From time to time, but never like this."

"Where does he go?"

"He's got a little house up in the desert. I think he sometimes goes there."

"Where is this place?"

"I don't know. I've never been there. But when he comes back, his car and clothes are all dusty. He says it's from being in the desert."

"But you don't know where this place is?"

"Hell no. We're far enough away from L.A. right here."

Shit. Dead end. Wynn paused as he considered what to do next.

"You're not going to tell him about this, are you?" Jasmine asked.

"On two conditions. First, I was never here, no matter who asks. Got it?"

"Yeah. Got it."

"And second, if you see him, you call me and tell me where he is."

"Sure. Okay."

Wynn gave her his phone number and made her repeat it back. Twice.

"Why are you looking for him?" Jasmine asked.

"He's not a nice guy, Jasmine. He's messed up in some bad shit."

"What are you going to do to him?"

Wynn nodded toward the guy, still sitting in the chair. "Do you really care?"

Jasmine paused. "No. I guess not."

Wynn re-holstered the Glock and walked out through the house.

Back at the Lexus, Wynn pulled out his phone. If Carson's current, likely soon-to-be-ex-girlfriend didn't know where this house in the desert was, maybe his ex-wife did. He dialed Amanda Carson's number.

"Hello?"

"Amanda. It's Sean Wynn. I need your help."

"What's up?"

"Neil's in danger and he's taken off. His girlfriend in Palm Springs says he's got a place in the desert. Do you know anything about it?"

"Well, yeah. It's up near Johnson Valley. What do you mean he's in danger?"

"I can't go into it now, but it was enough to make him take off without telling anyone where he was going."

"Are you the danger?"

"No. I just want to talk to him, like the other day. I think it might be some of his old business associates."

"They can have him, as far as I'm concerned."

"Agreed. But I've got to talk to him first. Can you tell me where this place is?"

"Maybe I can do one better. Hold on."

Wynn waited. Muffled noises came through the phone line.

"Got him," Amanda said.

"You know where he is?"

"Assuming he's got his phone on him, yeah. He's not too smart. Never changed his phone number. I can still track it."

"Great. Where is he?"

"He's at the cabin. Twenty miles east of Johnson Valley."

"Can you send me the address?"

"Hold on."

Wynn waited again until his phone pinged with an incoming text message.

"Got it. Thanks, Amanda. I'll be in touch."

CHAPTER 32

WITH THE TRACKER in place, Li allowed Carson to get several miles ahead while he filled his tank. Carson had taken Highway 247 north, leaving Li wondering where the hell he was going. Forty minutes later, Li watched the red dot on the tracker app leave the main highway and head off to the east. He had to zoom in as far as the app would go before what he assumed was a dirt road finally appeared on the map.

A few minutes later, Li's assumptions were confirmed as he came upon a dirt turnoff to the right, protected by a cattle guard and barbed wire fence. He stayed at least two miles behind as the dusty road meandered through an ocean of sand accentuated by a sparse bed of scrub brush, pinyon pines, and gray, granite outcroppings. It rose over rolling hills that provided a 360-degree view for miles around, then dipped into low valleys where the world closed in. Tributary paths spurred off the main road every mile or so, which according to the map led to houses or other structures several miles away.

Eventually, the red dot separated from the dirt road, indicating Carson had turned into a driveway. Li pulled to the side and waited while he watched the dot curve through a series of S-turns, eventually taking a sharp hairpin curve and stopping.

Li eased off the brake and followed until he found the driveway at the base of a rocky hillside. Low, gnarled trees sprang up from among the cactus plants and thorny bushes. He was still a mile from where Carson had stopped, so he pulled in and drove until the road passed beneath the shadow of a large boulder. With no real options to hide the car, Li left it parked next to the boulder and set off on foot through the prickly brush.

Thorny branches tore at his clothes and scratched his arms as he climbed, the air heavy and still in the afternoon heat. Within minutes he was cursing himself and Carson. *Should've taken him out at the damn gas station.*

Eventually, he saw the roofline of a two-story house at the top of the ridge. Staying hidden, he hiked up the hill and scoped out the front of the house. Two single-car garage doors were closed at the far end of the house where the driveway entered the property, while a wooden staircase led up to a deck on the second floor where the front door was located.

Hoping the back might provide a more discreet entry, Li circled around. A faded redwood deck extended from the rear of the house, supported by large posts as the ground sloped away. A small set of stairs on the left provided access to the deck from outside, while a single door, next to a set of large plate-glass windows, provided access from inside the house. Further along to the left of the stairs, another door looked like it might provide access to the garage.

Staying low, Li continued to circle to the left until he got to the far end of the house, out of view of the large windows, then darted forward to the corner of the garage. Getting a better look, he now saw that the garage door was approximately ten feet from the stairs that led up to the deck.

As Li was about to ease his way over to the garage door, Carson emerged from the house and stepped out onto the deck. He walked to the railing and placed a pair of binoculars to his eyes. Seeing an opportunity, Li pulled out his Ruger and rushed forward, taking the stairs in two giant steps onto the deck.

"Hello, Neil," he said as he pointed the Ruger at him.

————

Wynn topped off the Lexus' gas tank before leaving town, a habit he'd developed on the Harleys. He then drove more than an hour north of Palm Springs before his navigation map directed him onto a dirt road that led east into the desert. The road meandered through a barren, desolate landscape, heading generally east as it rose to the top of rocky bluffs before falling away into sandy valleys.

He stopped at the top of a hill, noticing a rooster-tail of dust rising from behind a fast-moving vehicle maybe two miles away. Heading in the opposite direction. On a different road. He pulled a pair of binoculars from the glove box. Zeroing in, he saw it was a dark-colored SUV with tinted windows, too far away to tell the make of the vehicle or see who was driving.

He tapped the 'zoom out' feature on his navigation and found the road the SUV was on. He traced it backward. Eventually it met up with his own, about a mile before the turnoff to Carson's cabin.

His spider sense tingled.

Easing his foot off the brake and onto the gas, he rolled gently down the other side of the hill. He waited until the SUV was directly opposite him across the wide valley, then pushed down on the gas and took off down the road, fishtailing on loose dirt and spitting up a high rooster-tail of his own.

Seven minutes later, he slid to a stop where the two roads met, then jumped out and hustled over to the intersection. Deep, imperfect tracks in the loose dirt indicated a recent, fast-moving vehicle had slid around the turn.

Might have been the SUV. Might not.

He followed the tracks further along until he could see where the tires finally caught hold and gripped the road, leaving perfect tread impressions in the loose dirt. He snapped a quick picture with his phone, then jogged back to the Lexus.

A mile later he once again pulled to the side and hopped out at the intersection leading to Carson's cabin. He scoured the area for tire tracks, but the road here was rocky and rough, nothing soft to preserve a print.

Back in the car, Wynn drove slowly up the mile-long driveway. The path turned and twisted around large rocks and through wash beds as it rose steadily. He couldn't see the property, but the general incline of the road told him the house was set higher on the hill, likely giving Carson a good view of anyone who approached.

Rounding a hairpin turn, Wynn finally saw the house a hundred yards away, sitting at the top of the ridge, silhouetted against the late afternoon sky. For a moment he considered stopping and trying to sneak up, but quickly dismissed the idea.

If he's watching, he's already seen me.

Wynn eased the Lexus upward, finally stopping on a sandy-dirt area flattened for parking below the house. Getting out, he scanned the ground for fresh tracks. One set led into the garage. He took out his phone and pulled up the picture he'd snapped moments ago.

Not the same. Two vehicles. Carson's is one...

The house itself was a modest two-story built on top of the ridge-line that sloped up past the far end of the house to the north, and down and away from the garage end to the south. It was fairly plain, rectangular shaped with dark wood siding bleached tan by the sun. Two, single-car garage doors were closed on the near end. A set of wooden stairs led up to a deck and the front door on the second level.

The living space must be upstairs. Maximize the view.

Wynn walked over to the garage door and peered in a window. An Acura SUV sat on one side. The other was empty. He paused at the bottom of the stairs.

"Neil?" He called out. "It's Sean Wynn. Are you here?"

The air was silent.

And hot. Not even a breeze.

Looking up the stairs at the front door, he noticed a couple of birds flying high above, dark specs silhouetted against the bright blue sky.

"Neil? I'm coming up."

He slowly walked up the stairs, alternating his gaze between the front door and a large, plate glass window next to it. The window was like a mirror, reflecting nothing but sky.

Reaching the top, he crossed the twenty-foot wood deck and knocked on the screen door.

"Neil! Are you home?"

There was no response. Heat from the sun's rays reflected off the screen door. He checked for a doorbell, but not finding one, opened the screen and knocked on the main door.

No answer.

Wynn drew his Glock and turned the knob, pushed the door open, and stepped inside.

"Neil? It's Sean Wynn. Are you here?"

Glancing around, Wynn saw nothing out of place. The door opened to a spacious living room that stretched the full width of the house, with large windows on either side. As Wynn had suspected, the house sat at the very top of the ridge, giving views of the sunrise to the east and sunsets to the west. A dining area and kitchen sat at the far end of the living room where a set of stairs led down. Behind him and to his left, a hallway led to several doors, presumably bedrooms and bathrooms.

Wynn crept cautiously through the living room, back to the kitchen and dining, and finally over to the large windows on the opposite side of the front door. A large wood deck extended away from the lower level at the back of the house.

Neil Carson sat slumped in a chair at the far end of the deck, a dark stain on the wood beneath him.

Wynn raced through the kitchen, grabbed a towel on his way,

then vaulted down the stairs and out through a ground-floor doorway, onto the back deck where Carson sat.

"You're a loud son-of-a-bitch," Carson wheezed, "but your hearing isn't worth shit."

Wynn felt momentary relief at hearing Carson speak, but then looked closer at his stomach. Two gunshot wounds to the abdomen. He'd seen this before. In the Marines. Afghanistan.

Not good.

Without immediate attention, it was a slow and painful way to die. Wynn bunched up the towel and pushed it against the wounds.

"Who did this?"

"You mean who pulled the trigger..." Carson gasped for breath, "or who gave the order?"

"Either. Both."

"Chan's boy, Li, pulled the trigger. But as far as who ordered it..." Carson coughed and groaned. "I'm guessing the same people that killed your wife."

"Who was that?"

"Alexander Jameson. Stuart Legrea. Either one. Take your pick."

"Why?"

"Get me a fucking doctor and I'll tell you."

Wynn pulled out his phone. No signal.

"Go out front," Carson wheezed. "The signal's better out there."

Wynn ran back into the house, and up the stairs to the deck out front. One weak bar flashed on his screen. He punched 911.

A woman's voice came on the line. "Nine-one-one. Who am I speaking with?"

"I've got a gunshot victim. I need flight-for-life."

"Okay, sir. Who am I speaking with?"

"Never fucking mind! I need a medevac!"

"You said a gunshot victim, sir?"

"Yes!"

"Is the victim breathing?"

"Yes. He was a minute ago."

"Sir. Is the shooter still there? Are you or anyone else still in any danger?"

"No. The shooter's gone."

"Okay, sir. What's the address?"

"We're in the desert, east of Johnson Valley. The address is..." Wynn pulled up the address from Amanda Carson's text and gave it to her.

"Just a moment, sir." There was a pause on the line, then, "Okay, sir, flight-for-life is on its way. Can you stay—"

Wynn hung up the phone and went back out to Carson. His head was slumped forward, his face pale and his lips blue. The dark puddle beneath him had grown. The towel had fallen away and was sitting on the deck. Wynn picked it up and pushed it back against Carson's stomach.

"Stay with me, Neil. Help is on the way. You said Jameson and Legrea killed Nicole. Why?"

Carson lifted his eyes. "Wasn't supposed to be her. Evans was supposed to be sitting there."

"But you gave the hostess five thousand dollars to seat Nicole and me at that table."

"Not you, you stupid shit... Evans... Your wife... wasn't supposed to be there. Evans was getting close to realizing the numbers we gave her were bullshit... She was the one supposed to be killed so she wouldn't fuck up the deal."

Nicole's murder was a case of mistaken identity?

Carson coughed and wheezed.

"C'mon, Neil. Stay with me. Was this about HCM?"

The corners of Carson's mouth turned up in a painful smile. "HCM was play money."

"What do you mean?"

He lifted his head. "HCM was a front for what ALJ really produced. Black market, synthetic opioids. Now they call it Jewel... For their new thing, J&L Enterprises. Get it? J&L? Jewel?"

"Yeah, Neil. I got that part. How'd the rest work?"

"I ran a small unit manufacturing it. Three guys. Hid them under research and development. We produced more than the rest of the company combined. But when Chan got involved, it grew too much, too fast. He could sell more than we could make. We had to hire more people. It became harder and harder to hide what we were doing behind the legitimate drugs. Alex thought if we were bought out by a larger company, we could increase production and still hide in the bureaucracy."

"Chan? As in Ishan Chan?"

Carson nodded. "Yeah." He wheezed again. His voice was slowing, losing strength.

"And the ADs are part of this?"

"No..." There was a long pause. Wynn was afraid Carson might not speak again. Telling the story was taking all his strength. "Stuart's... idea. They were patsies. Have them make the hit... then take the fall." His chin slumped to his chest.

"Neil. Stay with me." Wynn tapped his cheeks. Tried to get him to come around. "We need proof. How can we prove any of this?"

"My attorney... She has papers."

"Who's your attorney, Neil?"

"Hmm..."

"Neil! Who killed Detective Lenihan last night?"

Carson moved his lips, but no sound came out.

"Who killed the cop last night?"

But the question remained unanswered as Carson stared emptily at the floor.

CHAPTER 33

"WHAT DO YOU mean, you can't reach Carson?" Alexander Jameson sat behind his desk while Stuart slumped in a chair in front. "Where is he?"

"If I knew, that would imply I could reach him," Stuart replied. "But as I just told you, he hasn't answered his phone all day. Either his office or cell."

"What about Rick or Howard? Did you ask them?"

Stuart sighed. "I spoke with Howard. He hasn't seen either of them all day."

"Rick's missing, too?" Jameson finally looked up from his computer.

"Howard said they were pulling all-nighters to get caught up." Stuart sat up. "Thinks Rick went on a bender and is sleeping it off."

"Has he done that before?"

Stuart sighed. "The man likes to party, but no, he's never missed work before."

"Shit. This thing has gotten way out of hand."

Stuart nodded quietly.

"Is it paranoid to think the worst?" Jameson asked.

"Under the circumstances, I'd call it prudent."

"What do we do?"

"Close ranks," Stuart said. "We protect ourselves and Howard, at all costs. We can always find another distributor, but finding someone who can make it is not so easily solved."

"Agreed. So how do we protect him?"

"I've already taken steps," Stuart said. "I talked to him an hour ago and told him you wanted to see him. He's on his way here. Once we have him, I'll put him in a hotel somewhere 'til this thing cools down."

———

As soon as he was back on the main road, Li checked again for cell reception.

Finally.

He dialed Chan, who picked up on the second ring. "Yes?"

"It's done. Carson's off the board."

"And Wynn?"

"Not yet, but I've got a plan," Li said.

"Good. I'm going to send a couple of guys to invite Jameson and Legrea over for a little conversation. How long before you'll be back?"

"Three hours."

"Go straight to the warehouse."

———

Wynn sat on the shaded deck next to Carson's body, the house blocking the late afternoon sun as it sunk toward the western horizon. The picture he'd pieced together this morning was now clearly in focus. A few details were still missing, but there was no longer any doubt as to what had happened to Nicole, why, or who was responsible. The third killer involved in Ty's ambush was still a mystery, but the list of suspects was small, no doubt someone related to either Stuart Legrea, Alexander Jameson, or Ishan Chan.

Overhead, the two birds he'd seen soaring above the house earlier had been joined by a half dozen others. Lower.

He looked at Carson's body. *Nature knows.*

With nothing more to do for, or learn from Carson, he walked around the garage to his Lexus, still parked out front. He didn't want to be here when flight-for-life or the cops showed up. He made his way down the rocky driveway, onto the main dirt road, and headed back toward Ventura. When he finally picked up cell reception, his phone pinged like a winning slot machine with a flurry of incoming text messages.

All from Grueb. All asking, *Where the hell are you? Call me.*

He punched the number.

"It's about damn time." Grueb's voice came over the cabin speakers. "Where are you?"

"In the desert, north of Palm Springs."

"What the hell you doing out there?"

"Neil Carson had a cabin. Looks like he was trying to hide out."

"Had?" Grueb said.

"He's dead. And no, not by me. By the time I got there, one of Chan's men, a guy named Li, had already been there and put a couple in his gut. Left him to die slowly. I got there before he passed, even called flight-for-life, but he died before they got there."

"Did he say anything?"

"Not about Ty, but a lot about Nicole. The short version is that she was a case of mistaken identity. They were intending to hit Janelle Evans. She was getting close to realizing HCM was bogus, but they needed the merger to cover a larger operation. They're producing Jewel on the side. The whole thing is run by Jameson and Legrea, with Carson doing the manufacturing and Chan providing distribution."

"Jewel, huh?"

"Named after Jameson and Legrea themselves. J and L."

"Cute." Grueb paused. "You said one of Chan's men killed Carson?"

"That's what he said."

"If they're all working together, why would they do that?"

"Dissension in the ranks?"

"I'm betting an internal coup," Grueb said. "No distributor is going to kill their manufacturer without a way to replace them."

"Makes sense."

"And the smart money says one of them had a hand in killing Ty."

"One, or all of them," Wynn said.

"Agreed," Grueb said. "Are you carrying?"

"Yeah."

"Enough?"

Wynn thought of the M&P in the back seat. "A Glock and an MP15. I'd hate to think I'll need more."

"Good. Then you'll like what I found today."

"What's that?"

"Another location for J&L Enterprises. We knew about the office in Thousand Oaks. They've also got a warehouse in Torrance," Grueb said.

"I'm still a couple of hours out."

"Tell you what. I'll go check the office. If I find anything or need you to come there, I'll call you. Otherwise, head toward Torrance. We'll meet up down there and go check out the warehouse together."

"Is Akins good with that?" Wynn asked.

"He said you weren't part of the official investigation, right?"

"Yeah."

"Well, neither is this."

——————

"That was Howard," Stuart said as he disconnected the call. "Said he'll be here in about fifteen minutes."

"Good," Jameson replied. "I'll have Ralph let him in."

"Ralph?"

"The security guy out front."

Stuart raised his eyebrows. He'd never bothered to learn the man's name. With nothing better to do, he dialed Carson's cell for the twentieth time today. Still no answer. He leaned back against the wall, too nervous to sit.

"Chan's supposed to get a shipment tonight," Jameson said.

"So?"

"He's going to be pissed if it doesn't show up."

"We should hope to hell he is."

"Why's that?"

Stuart pushed off the wall and resumed his slow pacing. "That would mean he doesn't know about Neil or Rick. He'd be expecting his usual shipment with no reason to know it's been delayed. If he's calm, we have to assume he not only knows why, but had a hand in it."

Jameson nodded as the two men exchanged a look. The sound of a door closing came from down the hall.

"That's Howard," Stuart said. "Let's get out of here."

They stepped into the hallway where two men with raised guns walked toward them. When they were a few feet away, one of the men said, "Mr. Chan would like to see you."

———

Dusk had nearly turned to dark as Howard pulled into the parking lot of J&L Enterprises. A few cars still littered the lot, including Mr. Jameson's Tesla, parked right outside the entrance. He pulled into a spot and hustled toward the front door, the light from inside illuminating the lobby.

Howard stopped short as he reached for the door handle. Inside, peeking out from behind the counter, the top of a man's head was visible as he lay face-down in a pool of blood. Across the lobby, a door opened, and Jameson and Stuart were pushed through it, followed by two men with guns.

Howard leaped away from the door and sprinted down the side of the building, finally hiding behind a bush forty feet away. The four men pushed through the glass door and crossed the parking lot where Jameson and Stuart were forced into a dark SUV and driven away.

———

Grueb was leaning against his unmarked Crown Vic when Wynn pulled into a short-term parking lot just off the 405 near LAX.

Wynn buzzed down the passenger window. "Hop in."

When they were back on the street, heading for the freeway, Wynn asked, "What have we got?"

"A dead security guard at the J&L office in Thousand Oaks. Shot in the head. No one else around. Jameson and Legrea's cars were still in the lot. I've had about an hour to figure out what it means."

"And?"

"A coup is the only thing that makes sense. Chan must have gotten fed up with losing men while protecting these guys. Taking 'em out eliminates that avenue of investigation and allows him to control the entire Jewel operation."

"Less potential for blowback if they're dead."

"Agreed."

"I need them first," Wynn said.

"Understood. And if one of them had a hand in killing Ty, I want 'em."

"Any reason to believe they're at the warehouse?"

"No, but it's as good a place to start as any."

Twenty minutes later, they exited the freeway and took an arterial boulevard south for a couple of miles. They turned onto smaller side streets before eventually rolling past an old, three-story warehouse surrounded by a concertina-topped chain link fence.

"They don't want visitors," Wynn said.

"Kind of makes you wonder why."

Midway down the block, floodlights and cameras covered a single, gated entrance.

"Keep going," Grueb said.

Wynn cruised past the gate and turned onto a side street, pulling to a stop a block away.

"You said you were armed?" Grueb asked.

"A Glock and an MP15."

"Bring 'em."

Wynn put on his shoulder holster and loaded it with the Glock, then grabbed the M&P and placed extra magazines into his pockets. Grueb grabbed the floor mats out of the Lexus. Wynn gave him a questioning look.

"It's our way in," Grueb explained.

With Grueb carrying the floor mats and Wynn the M&P, they stayed a block away from the warehouse as they circled to the farthest corner, opposite the entry gate.

"Do you see any cameras?" Grueb asked.

Sodium streetlamps cast intermittent pools of pale orange light down either side of the chain-link fence, the light sparkling off the razor-sharp concertina that angled inward from the top. Wynn peered into the darkness between the lights. "I don't see any, but I can't make any promises."

"Me neither. Come on."

They continued to make their way around the outskirts of the warehouse until they spotted a junction in the fence, where two posts stood a few inches apart. Grueb rushed forward into the dark patch between two streetlamps and dropped one of the floor mats, then hefted himself up and threw the other mat onto the concertina wire between the two posts above. Wynn handed him the remaining mat and watched as Grueb positioned it beside the first, then gently climbed over the fence, the mats protecting him from the razor-sharp wire.

"You've done this before," Wynn said.

"No, but I've seen it at other crime scenes. Be careful."

Wynn nodded and climbed the fence, handing the M&P to Grueb when he got to the top and eased himself down the other side.

A double lane of asphalt separated the fence from the back side of the three-story building. It stretched a hundred feet in either direction. Forty feet to their right, four concrete steps led up to a steel door, providing the only break in the otherwise solid wall.

"Left or right?" Grueb asked, handing Wynn the M&P.

"Left."

Crouching low, they jogged down the side of the building. Stopping at the corner, Grueb peered around the other side to where a dozen freight trucks were parked, several backed up to more than twenty loading bays that lined this side of the building.

"First one?" Grueb asked.

Wynn nodded.

"Cover me."

Wynn slipped around the corner holding the M&P to his shoulder, sighting down the barrel, looking for targets among the trucks scattered throughout the lot. Grueb followed close behind as they made their way down the side of the building to the first door.

When closed, the roll-up doors of the loading bays sat more than three feet above the outside asphalt, indicating the floor of the warehouse was elevated to allow for easier loading and unloading of the trucks. When they reached the first bay, Grueb grabbed the door handle and pushed up, but to no avail. The door didn't move.

"No good. Let's try the next."

They tried three more doors, all with the same result, until they came to the fifth door, which had a truck backed up to it. Wynn squatted low to see under the truck while Grueb squeezed himself between the truck's bumper and the concrete wall. Grabbing the handle, Grueb heaved the door up a mere two inches. It squealed in protest.

"It's open," he whispered. "But loud."

Grueb peered under the door into the dark warehouse. Seeing nothing, he held his breath and pushed the door up another fifteen inches. It squealed the first few inches, then rolled up quietly the remainder of the way. Grueb used the truck's bumper as a step to lift himself up to sit on the warehouse floor, then, drawing his gun, he laid back and rolled beneath the door. Wynn followed a moment later, then pulled the door closed behind him, plunging them into darkness.

They waited a full minute, allowing their eyes to adjust. Slowly, Wynn became aware of a large open space next to the loading doors. Further in, tall rows of industrial shelving stacked with crates and boxes created a neat maze of aisles that extended off into the darkness.

Far to their left, a faint light leaked down three of the aisles. Wynn crawled forward on his belly until he was even with Grueb, who nodded in the direction of the light. Wynn returned the nod, and they slowly got to their feet and made their way across the open floor to the end of a row. Pausing to glance up each aisle before they crossed it, they quickly made their way deeper into the warehouse. When they got closer to the light, Grueb held up a closed fist.

Stop.

Listening intently, Wynn heard it, too. Voices. Coming from the direction of the light.

Moving slowly, they made their way across several aisles until they were just one aisle away from the voices. Their view through a tall row of shelving stacked with crates was obstructed by a large sheet of cloudy plastic that hung from a giant roll on the other side. Working their way left, they were finally able to see eight men in an open space, roughly twenty feet square.

Seven of the men stood in a circle around the eighth.

Who was on his knees.

On a wide sheet of plastic.

CHAPTER 34

THE MAN KNEELING on the plastic was bloody and bruised, his lips puffy and cracked. His sharp nose was bent to one side, his left eye almost completely swollen shut. Wynn had never seen him before, but with Alexander Jameson standing between two Asian men, one older and one younger, he knew the man on the plastic had to be Stuart Legrea. Three other men held guns pointed at Legrea, while the fourth stood beside him, his fists covered in blood.

Wynn glanced at Grueb and silently mouthed the question, *Ishan Chan?*

Grueb nodded.

Using hand signals, Wynn indicated Grueb should stay where he was, then slipped back to the end of the row, and worked his way three aisles to the left to get a better view. All the while, Jameson and Chan's voices drifted through the room.

"That's enough, Chan. Let him up. You've made your point," Jameson said.

"The fact that you think you can still tell me what to do proves that I have not," Chan replied. "Apparently you don't realize the difficulty of your position. While Mr. Legrea may deny he was breaking our agreement by selling Jewel through the ADs, we know this to be true. Li has confirmed it."

"How so?" Jameson asked.

Chan nodded to the younger man, who said, "That gangbanger, Harris, offered me some. Said he got it from Stuart."

So that's Li, Wynn thought. He slipped between two boxes beneath a four-foot-high shelf and settled into position behind a large crate. The space created the perfect bunker. The opening between the top of the crate and the bottom of the shelf above created a textbook porthole to watch what was happening on the other side.

Wynn brought the M&P to his shoulder and sighted in on Li. *I've seen this guy before. The diner. And the freeway.*

"He could've gotten it from anywhere," Jameson said. "Probably made that up to impress you."

"I've also seen the production records from the lab in Palm Springs," Li said. "I know they were producing more than they delivered. Howard confirmed it."

After a slight pause, Chan said, "So, Mr. Jameson, I hope you see the position that puts you in. Either you are unfit to lead because you don't know what your employees are up to, or you knowingly looked the other way, thereby making yourself complicit in his deception."

"I trust Stuart. If he says there's a misunderstanding, we need to give him a chance to explain."

"By all means," Chan said. "Stuart, please tell us, is Mr. Jameson unfit to lead, or did he know what you were doing?"

Jameson was about to protest when Stuart mumbled a weak, "Fuck off."

Chan shook his head. "I was hoping for better." Turning to Jameson, he said, "Have you ever killed a man, Mr. Jameson?"

"What?"

"Have you ever killed a man? Not ordered a man to be killed, and stood aloofly to the side while your orders were carried out, but actually pulled the trigger? Drove a knife into someone's heart?"

"No. Of course not," Jameson said.

"Then you have one last chance. Now that Mr. Carson is dead, Howard has told me he needs you to get the raw materials to make Jewel, so I may still have a use for you. But I must know that I can trust you. A test, if you will."

Li pulled his Ruger from behind his back and pointed it at Jameson's face.

"I... I don't understand," Jameson stammered.

Chan pulled a Sig Sauer from inside his jacket and held it out, butt-first, to Jameson. Two of the other men shifted their aim, away from Stuart and toward Jameson.

"You've already proven that you're not fit to lead this operation. I'm now in charge of Jewel. The only question that remains is: can you be a soldier? Can you follow orders and do the actual work?" He nodded toward Stuart.

"What? You want me to kill him?"

"He's cheated me. What kind of leader would I be if I allowed him to live?"

A weak voice called from the shadows on the other side of the group. "Stop! That's enough."

Everyone in the room turned toward the voice. Wynn couldn't believe his eyes as a short, paunchy, middle-aged man with a receding hairline stepped into the light, pointing a gun at Chan. "I can't let you do this."

Chan slowly turned toward the voice. "Hello, Howard."

"I can't let you do this, Mr. Chan," Howard said.

Li and the four gunmen slowly spread out around the clearing.

Knowing Grueb was sighting in on targets from his hiding spot three aisles over, Wynn tracked Li with the M&P as they moved around the space.

"Do what, Howard?" Chan asked.

"I can't let you kill them."

"You misunderstand, Howard. This is simply a bit of negotia—"

Sudden movement in the periphery was followed by a hollow

pop. A bright red spray of blood flew from Li's hand, causing him to drop the Ruger. Looking up from his sights, Wynn saw Stuart on his feet, turning to the man who'd been beating him. He fired a small pistol point-blank at the man's head. He went down in a heap.

Chaos erupted as gunshots blasted everywhere. Howard flew backward when

a barrage of bullets pummeled his body. Wynn scanned the room, searching for Li, but he had slipped away. Instead, he focused on the next closest target and squeezed the trigger, dropping one of the gunmen, then turned his aim toward Chan, who had flipped the Sig Sauer in his hand and was pointing it toward Jameson.

No! Wynn squeezed the trigger, but it was too late. Chan's pistol spat once, causing the back of Jameson's head to explode just as Wynn's bullet punched through Chan's chest.

Wynn swung the M&P through a full arc, searching for more targets, but in a span of less than ten seconds, there was no one left standing. Chan, Howard, and Jameson were all down, along with the four gunmen. Stuart and Li were nowhere to be seen.

———

Stuart Legrea sat behind a crate, trying to figure out how many others were in the warehouse. Howard, bless the little twerp's soul, had appeared out of nowhere and provided the perfect distraction for Stuart to reach the Kimber Micro handgun he had strapped to his ankle.

But there were others. Cops, probably. People who'd spent a lot of time on the shooting range, for sure. After he'd shot Li and the first gunmen, Stuart had turned just in time to see the second of Chan's henchmen drawing down on him. He'd thought he was dead; knew he'd never be able to pull his gun around fast enough to get a shot off before the guy fired. But out of nowhere, two bright red circles appeared on the guy's chest. Precision shooting. From someone who was trained.

Not waiting to see more, Stuart dove to the floor and rolled down one of the aisles. He crawled to a hiding spot between two crates inside a row of shelves until the shooting stopped.

———

Wynn scanned the bodies sprawled throughout the space in front of him. As best he could tell, all were dead. If not, they soon would be. Jameson, Howard, and one of the gunmen all had severe head wounds, while large pools of blood were already seeping from around Chan and the three others. No one was moving.

But that still left Stuart and Li. *They know we're here, but they can't be sure how many*. It was a conundrum. *Move, and I give away my position. Wait, and they'll get away if they decide to run.*

Looking across the aisles, he scanned the general area where he'd left Grueb, his view blocked by the three rows of stacked shelves that stood between them. Knowing the safest way to search the place was together, Wynn turned and scanned the aisle behind him. He eased out of his hiding spot and crept down the aisle. When he reached the end of the row, he glanced both ways, then slowly started making his way across the aisles toward Grueb.

———

Stuart couldn't believe his luck, or what he was seeing. Still hidden between a pair of crates inside the large row of shelves, that bastard Sean Wynn had dashed across the aisle to his right and was now creeping past the end of the row a mere four feet in front of him. Stuart transferred the Kimber from his right hand to his left, then wiped his hand on his pants and transferred the gun back. Adjusting his position slightly, he raised the gun toward the back of Wynn's head.

———

Wynn paused at the end of each row, catching his breath and glancing up the aisle before darting across. Two down, one to go. Grueb should be up the next aisle. He peeked around the corner and saw nothing.

A faint smell wafted through his nose.

Sweat. Body odor.

Close.

Wynn buckled his knees and dropped into a seated position, jamming his back against the last crate at the end of the row. He shoved backward with his legs. The crate slid back six inches before Wynn heard a grunt from behind. A gunshot cracked the air. He dropped the M&P, then spun around the corner and took a single step up the aisle.

Stuart Legrea was boxed between two crates, hiding in the same way Wynn had moments ago. Stuart's right hand held a small pistol, and was pushed over his head against the bottom of the shelf above. Wynn reached between the crates and grabbed Stuart by the shirt and yanked him out, using his left hand to grab Legrea's right wrist as he tumbled from beneath the shelves.

Stuart kicked his legs as Wynn swung him across the aisle, crossing their feet and tangling their legs. Wynn felt himself falling, his momentum spinning his body beneath Stuart. He landed hard on his back, his head barely missed the sharp steel post supporting the shelves on the opposite side. Stuart smashed down on top of Wynn, expelling the air from his lungs.

Wynn's grip slipped from Stuart's sweaty wrist as he saw the Kimber being swung toward his face. He surged upward, flinging his forehead into Stuart's already broken nose. Blood spurted into Wynn's face and gushed down like rain as he tossed the thinner man to the side, then crawled after him, desperately clawing for the gun still in Stuart's hand.

Stuart moved slowly, dazed. He rolled onto his back, his arms flopping away from his sides. Wynn clamped his hand down on

Stuart's right wrist, pinning it against the concrete floor, but the arm, slick with blood, slid beneath his grip.

Stuart twisted his wrist and pulled the trigger, sending a nine-millimeter slug whizzing past Wynn's ear. Wynn scrambled forward and grabbed the wrist with both hands, then pulled his knees up, placing his right shin into Stuart's armpit. He rolled onto his back and slipped the other foot underneath Stuart's shoulder and pressed it hard against his neck.

"Drop it!" Wynn used both arms and legs to hold Stuart's bloody wrist immobile in a two-handed armbar.

Stuart's face turned away. His left hand reached out and found the grip of Wynn's discarded M&P15. He now had a gun in each hand.

Wynn pulled harder on Stuart's arm. "Drop it!"

He had neutralized the Kimber, but the M&P kept coming, rising off the floor.

Memories flooded Wynn's mind. Nicole. Her smile. Her touch. Her voice.

And Ty. His laugh. His family. Stacey.

According to Carson, Legrea was the last survivor of those ultimately responsible for all of it.

Stacey's words popped in his mind. *I want you to kill them.*

The M&P turned in Wynn's direction. Stuart's finger found the trigger.

Wynn pushed his foot down, putting more pressure on Stuart's neck. "Don't do it!"

The opening at the tip of the barrel widened as the rifle turned toward him.

Wynn kicked hard with his left foot. The cracking sound of Stuart's neck snapping bounced off the concrete. His arm went limp. The M&P clattered to the floor.

Wynn lay still for a moment, then removed the Kimber from Stuart's lifeless hand and pushed the arm away. He rolled onto his knees and placed two fingers on Stuart's contorted neck, feeling for a pulse.

There was none. He slumped back against a crate.

Grueb raced around the corner, panting and out of breath. "You okay?"

"Yeah," Wynn replied. "Where were you?"

"Going after the kid." He paused and sucked in a lungful of air, then took in the blood covering Wynn's arms, face, and shirt. "You sure you're okay?"

"Yeah, not mine." Wynn paused. "I was hoping to take him alive."

Grueb knelt and put a finger on Stuart's neck. "Not gonna happen." He turned and swept the dim warehouse around them. "We got one more out there."

Somewhere off in the distance came the echo of running feet followed by the slam of a closing door.

CHAPTER 35

UNBELIEVABLE, LI THOUGHT. He raced down the entry ramp onto the 405 South, his injured right hand stuffed beneath his left armpit. They had been minutes away from controlling the entire Jewel market, and then in thirty seconds, it all went to shit.

When the fuck did Howard grow the balls to confront us?

He had other questions, but they didn't matter. Right now he had two concerns. The first was how to keep the Silent Mafia alive. *Other players are gonna try to steal our turf.* But without Jewel, or any way to make it, the economics would be tough to buy the loyalty of those he needed.

He pulled his hand from under his armpit. The bullet had gone all the way through, creating holes in both the front and back. *Straight through. Just like Jesus. The Savior. Maybe that's what I can become. Rise from the ashes and create a new enterprise. If not with Jewel, then something else.*

His mind shifted to the second concern. *No one will follow me if I allow Mr. Chan to go unavenged.*

He reached his injured right hand to the glove box and flipped the release lever. Pain shot up his arm. Reaching in, he pulled out a spare Ruger to replace the one he'd dropped when Stuart shot him.

Placing the pistol on the seat beside him, he dug around until he found the RollJam. The small LED flashed green. He smiled. He'd planned on taking the 91 East toward the lab in Palm Springs, but instead turned north onto the 110. He tapped the navigation screen with his right index finger, leaving bloody smears. It became stickier and messier as he typed the six letters of his new destination.

Seventy-three miles. An hour and ten minutes.

Oxnard.

———

Cops from the Torrance Police Department were the first to show up when Grueb called it in. Wynn had offered him the keys to the Lexus and told Grueb to take off, that he'd stick around and take the heat for the eight bodies inside the warehouse, but Grueb was having none of it. *We're in this together,* Grueb had said.

They found their way to the office at the front of the warehouse, and a bathroom where Wynn washed Stuart's blood from his arms, hands, and face. It was still on his shirt. Nothing he could do about that.

They met the first black-and-white as it arrived, then waited until a SWAT team showed up and cleared the warehouse, ensuring there were no more hostiles inside. With Li in the wind, and Carson, Jameson, and Legrea all dead, Wynn was beginning to feel the familiar post-operation letdown. He sat quietly as media trucks gathered on the street outside and set up their cameras for their live broadcasts.

Shortly thereafter, a detective from the Torrance PD pulled them aside. They gave the short version without adding much detail. When pressed for specifics, Grueb said he preferred to wait until Akins got there, so he only had to tell the story once.

"You'll be going through this way more than once," the detective said.

Grueb just shrugged and Wynn went along. With all the bullets that flew, it was going to be a puzzle to figure out which guns had killed which people. They knew they had each taken out a pair, not including Stuart, but there was no need to elaborate. The evidence was all right there.

Standing next to one of the cop cars, Wynn felt his phone vibrate in his pocket. Pulling it out, he saw Vanessa Carow's name on the screen. *Probably saw it on the news again, checking to see if I'm okay.*

He shot her a quick text: *Can't pick up, but I'm fine. You ok?*

The reply was immediate: *Pick up the phone asshole.*

A few seconds later a photo popped onto the screen. A selfie, taken in the mirror of a frightened Vanessa. Li's bloody hand grasped her neck, his other held a gun to her head. The phone rang in Wynn's hand.

He stepped away from the cop car and put the phone to his ear. "Okay. You've got my attention."

"Good," Li's high-pitched voice came over the line. "If you want to see her again, you'll get your ass home and into that tin can you call a boat. You've got sixty minutes."

"How do I know she's alive?" Wynn caught Grueb's eye and motioned him over.

There was a slight pause, then a muffled scream came over the line, followed by Li's voice. "Sixty minutes."

———

One hour didn't give Li much time to do what he needed, but he didn't want to give Wynn time to coordinate any countermoves.

"On the floor," Li demanded.

"Why?" Vanessa asked, her voice shaking.

"Shut up and get on the floor!" Li held the gun to her head and forced her down, then knelt on top of her. He set his gun on a coffee table and used a zip tie to bind her hands behind her back.

"Stay put." He got up and went into Vanessa's kitchen.

Pulling a baggie of little white pills from his pocket, he took one out, then used a knife from a butcher block on the counter to cut it in half. He got a glass of water and went back into the living room. "Roll over."

Vanessa shifted her weight and rolled onto her back, her arms still bound behind her. Li reached down with his left hand and grabbed Vanessa by the hair, then pulled her into a sitting position and dragged her backward until she leaned against a couch.

"Open your mouth."

Vanessa's eyes went wide. "Is that what you used to kill Diana?"

Li ignored the question. He had no idea who Diana was. "Open up!"

Vanessa screamed and bucked and tried to wriggle away. Li jumped on her and pulled her into a sitting position, then slapped her twice across the face. She clamped her lips tightly and turned her head to the side, but Li pushed her into the couch and squeezed her nose shut. Thirty seconds later, Vanessa gasped for breath and Li shoved the pill into her mouth. He held her head back and poured the water down her throat, causing her to swallow, then cough and sputter as the water splashed over her face.

"Good girl. Now sit still for ten minutes and we'll get out of here."

While waiting for the Jewel to take effect, Li washed his bloody hand in the sink and wrapped it in a kitchen towel. He pulled out a chair and sat down to watch the girl.

He had to give Carson credit. The problem with most opioids is that they either caused immediate highs and crushing lows, like heroin; or gradual, lesser highs that lasted for hours and then slowly faded, like oxycodone. Carson had somehow created a relatively fast-acting drug where the height and duration were directly proportional to the amount taken. Li hoped that a half tablet would make the girl complacent, relaxed enough to follow instructions, but still able to walk and function.

Ten minutes later, Li cut the zip tie from her wrists and led her out the front door of the small house and into the back seat of his

Range Rover. He buckled her in and re-tied her hands in front of her.

He drove north on Harbor Boulevard, then took side streets until he parked a block away from Wynn's house. He stuffed one of the burner phones into his pocket and grabbed the RollJam before pulling Vanessa from the back seat. She mumbled sleepily but stood on her own as he closed the car door.

Taking her by the arm, he led her up the street to Wynn's driveway, where he held his breath before pushing the button on the RollJam.

Let's hope this works.

The door immediately slid upward. He steered Vanessa inside and tapped the button on the wall to close the door, then ushered her through the back of the garage and around the side of the house to the patio. Wynn's dinghy was tethered to the dock, and more importantly, the neighbor's cabin cruiser was still moored to the dock next door.

He pushed Vanessa down the plankway and examined the space between the two docks. It wasn't more than five feet. He could easily make the jump, but the girl was already swaying. No way she was going to make the leap.

Instead, he grabbed the tether rope and positioned Wynn's dinghy between the two docks. Using it as a bridge, he guided Vanessa into the small boat. He then climbed onto the neighbor's dock and held his hand out. "C'mon."

"Where are we going?" she mumbled.

"Taking a little ride. Give me your hands."

Vanessa stood and reached her bound wrists out to Li, then swayed as the boat shifted beneath her. Losing what little balance remained, she fell, plunging into the cold, dark water.

"Shit!" Li dropped to his stomach and reached with his good hand as Vanessa struggled to keep her head above water. He finally grabbed her by the arm and dragged her onto the dock. He sat for a moment, catching his breath, then got to his knees and pulled the burner phone from his pocket and tossed it onto the wooden bench seat of Wynn's dinghy. He climbed to his feet and pulled Vanessa up, then hurried her onto the cruiser.

Li hadn't done a lot of boating, but he knew enough. The boat was a late model Sea Ray Sundancer, with a main control panel containing dual ignition keys in the cabin below deck. He considered Vanessa. She'd be more secure in the cabin, but he wanted to keep an eye on her. Besides, who knew if the owner might keep a weapon down there.

He pushed the shivering and still dripping Vanessa through the cockpit and small walkway that led forward, then tossed her onto a cushioned recliner built into the bow. Turning, he untied the forward mooring line, then checked the cabin door that led below deck. It was locked.

Raising his foot, he smashed his heel down on the handle, feeling the door give a little. He raised his foot again and kicked at the door over and over until it loosened from its hinges. He glanced up at the row of houses, making sure no new lights came on. Seeing none, he pulled the broken door aside, then scrambled down the stairs. He found the main control panel and turned the two ignition keys, then hustled back up the stairs to the cockpit.

Ideally, he'd run the blowers for a few minutes before starting the twin engines, but there was no time. He pushed the ignition buttons and the engines purred to life. Hustling aft, he untied the rear mooring line, then resumed his position at the helm. He slowly eased the boat away from the dock, through the harbor, and out into the blackness of the ocean.

CHAPTER 36

"WHY'S HE WANT me in the dinghy?" Wynn asked as he pushed the Lexus over a hundred miles per hour west on the 101.

Grueb had seen Wynn's reaction to Li's phone call back at the warehouse and come over to find out what was going on. When he saw the photo of Li and Vanessa, he grabbed Wynn by the arm and hustled him away from the cops and over to Wynn's Lexus. They were gone before anyone could stop them.

"Could be several reasons," Grueb replied, his knuckles white, gripping the armrest as Wynn swerved between two slower vehicles. "Could be an ambush. Could be he wants you to take it somewhere. Could be a wild goose chase."

He didn't say the last possibility, the one Wynn feared most. *Could be he left something, or someone, for me to find.*

A road sign indicated twenty miles to his exit, while the clock on the dash read 2:12 a.m. *Fifteen minutes. It's gonna be close.*

"Can you swim?" Wynn asked.

———

Vanessa's teeth chattered as she huddled in a fetal position at the front of the boat, her cheek pressed against the vinyl seat. The boat hurled across the waves, creating a cold wind and constant spray that added to the misery of her already soaked clothes. The one good thing, whether it be due to the low dosage the Asian guy had forced her to take, or her little dip in the harbor, is that her Jewel-induced haze was already beginning to lift.

Occasionally, she would raise her head to see where they were going. At first, she was hopeful, as the guy seemed to stay within a mile of the shoreline, but then he turned out to sea, and any hope of swimming for it, even if her hands weren't tied, disappeared.

Eventually, the boat slowed and came to a stop, rolling gently in the waves. Vanessa sat up and looked toward the shore, the only recognizable landmark being the Ventura Pier jutting out into the ocean, its lights now barely tiny pinpricks in the distance.

———

Wynn squealed to a stop in front of his garage just as the sixty minutes were expiring. He raced out the back door and down the dock where a ringing was coming from the dinghy. It had been moved and was drifting five feet away from the dock. Reaching down, he grabbed the rope and pulled the boat in, then picked up and flipped open the phone. "Hello?"

"Close," Li said. "I almost thought you hadn't made it."

"Where's Vanessa?"

"She's right here, with me."

"Is she okay?"

"She's fine. A little woozy, but nothing that won't wear off in time. If you want to see her, take that little boat of yours and get out of the harbor, then head north toward the pier. Leave your own phone at home. You won't need it. Keep this one on you. I'll call you in thirty minutes."

"This thing isn't built for the ocean. It'll take forever."

"Then you'd better hurry," Li said. "You've got thirty minutes. And come alone."

The line went dead.

Shit. Wynn raced back to the garage, where he grabbed a spare can of gas. "How's it coming?" he asked.

"Tight," Grueb replied. He pulled up the front zipper of Wynn's neoprene wetsuit he was now wearing. "Apparently, I need to try that kata thing you do. Were you right?"

"Unfortunately. He left a burner in the dinghy. He wants me to take it, alone, to the Ventura Pier, then he'll call again. We've got thirty minutes."

Grueb held up his gun. "You got more nine mil?"

Wynn reached beneath the workbench to a hidden shelf and pulled out a box of ammo, handed it to Grueb.

"Waterproof?" Grueb asked.

"No more than usual." They both well knew the problem with regular ammunition. Depending on how well it was manufactured, it might stay dry if submerged. Maybe it would. Maybe it wouldn't. There was no way to know until it was fired.

Wynn went to a cabinet where he stored his wet suits. "Put it in here." He tossed Grueb a waterproof bag with a long strap.

Grueb placed his gun and the ammo in the bag. "You set?"

Wynn grabbed a jacket and put it on, covering the Glock, still in his shoulder holster. "Yeah."

"Then let's go," Grueb said. "I can put these on in the boat." Grueb handed Wynn the neoprene booties, gloves, and head bib, then grabbed a bodyboard and rope from the wall.

Taking their load down the dock, they stashed the neoprene gear and gas in the boat, then Wynn used a carabiner to attach the rope to a pair of cleats along the back transom of the dinghy. He then tied it to the bodyboard. He knotted the rope so the board would float a few feet behind the dinghy and tossed the rest of the coil onto the floor next to the outboard motor.

While Wynn pulled the cable to start the engine, Grueb untied the mooring tether, and they were underway.

It took five minutes to get out of the harbor, but once beyond the protection of the breakwater, even gentle waves buffeted the tiny boat.

At first, Wynn stayed parallel to the shore but soon found the occasional swells to be too much. Hidden by the inky blackness of the night, large breakers would appear out of nowhere, threatening to overturn the small vessel. He corrected by alternately turning forty-five degrees out to sea to meet the waves at an angle, then zigzagging back toward shore as they made their way north.

Exactly thirty minutes after the last call, the phone in Wynn's pocket rang again. "Yeah?"

"You're behind schedule."

"Tell that to the current."

"Your friend is lucky I'm in a forgiving mood. Go to the end of the pier, then head straight out. Use the lights on the pier to set your bearing and just keep going. We'll find you."

"Is she okay?"

"She's fine. And as long as I don't see any other boats or helicopters, she will be. But if I see anyone besides you, she's shark bait. Got it?"

"Yeah, yeah. I'm alone."

"Good. We'll see you soon."

The line disconnected.

Wynn looked at Grueb. "Time to get wet." He cut the engine back to idle, then hauled on the rope, bringing the bodyboard alongside the dinghy. While he unknotted the rope, Grueb slid over the side and onto the board. Wynn handed him the bag with the Glock.

"How long's the rope?" Grueb asked.

"Seventy-five feet. Ready?"

Grueb nodded and pushed away from the dinghy. Wynn squeezed the throttle and watched as the rope fed into the water, Grueb and the bodyboard soon lost to sight.

Within minutes, Wynn arrived at the far end of the Ventura Pier and turned the dinghy straight into the approaching waves. The further he went, the larger the swells became, smashing against the small bow and throwing a constant spray of salt water into his face. Wynn scanned the ocean looking for another boat, but the only things visible were the fading lights along the shore as they receded into the distance.

Looking back to check his bearings, Wynn saw the distinctive red and green glow of marine sidelights approaching from his five o'clock position. He cut the little outboard engine, hoping the boat would shoot past Grueb before Li noticed him trailing in the water.

As Wynn rose and fell in the rolling seas, the fatal flaw in his plan became apparent. There was no way Grueb was going to be able to get off an accurate shot, with a handgun no less, while both the shooter and the target were rolling on the ocean. He'd have to get close. Real close.

Soon, the glowing lights grew near enough for Wynn to make out the familiar lines of his neighbor's boat as it drew even. Li's high-pitched voice came from the cockpit.

"You know, Wynn," Li said as he slowed his engine so his voice would carry across the water. "For a simple tail, you've become a real pain in the ass."

Wynn said nothing.

"The thing I don't get," Li said, "is why Stuart had us following you in the first place. What do you have on them?"

"They killed my wife." Wynn shifted in his seat while the cabin cruiser began a slow circle around the smaller vessel.

"That's rough. I can see why you're pissed."

Wynn stayed silent. The crescent moon faded behind a cloud bank, leaving only the faint glow from the larger boat's running lights.

"But Mr. Chan and I had nothing to do with that," Li continued. "And yet, in your rush for vengeance, you've killed two of my partners, and my boss."

"In self-defense. And only one partner."

"That may be true. But your cop friend, working on your behalf I assume, killed the other last night."

"What do you know about that?"

"I know those stupid gangbangers Stuart hired can't do shit without help."

"So?" Wynn asked.

"So I helped," Li replied.

Wynn's fist clenched as the cruiser circled toward the back of his dinghy. *C'mon, Grueb. Now's your chance.* He could finally make out Vanessa sitting in the bow. "You were the third gunman?"

"An eye for an eye," Li admitted. "But you're still up."

"How do you figure?"

"Your wife and the cop are only two. Versus Xiang, Huan, and Mr. Chan. It seems I still owe you. Hence, your friend here."

"If you touch her, I will hunt you to the ends of the earth."

"Look around, Wynn. We're already there." He paused. "And honestly, whether you bleed out, or drown, I don't care." With that, Li raised the Ruger with his left hand and fired five quick shots.

Wynn heard the bullets whistle past and punch into the water. He rolled backward, pitching himself into the ocean and kicked off his shoes, then swam hard beneath the waves until he was ten yards away. Breaking the surface, he watched as Li shot three more rounds into the dinghy. The tiny boat began to sink.

Gotta unclip the board! He stroked silently back to the half-submerged dinghy and unclipped the carabiner from the cleat, then clipped it to his belt loop and glanced back at the cruiser. A small dark shape appeared on the edge of the swim platform at the rear of the boat.

"Stuart told me you were a Marine," Li shouted across the water. "Too bad you weren't a Navy Seal. At least then maybe you'd stand a chance."

The dark shape grew into an arm, stretching across the small platform, reaching for a handle.

C'mon, Grueb!

Suddenly, Vanessa's voice screamed from the bow. "Sean! Use this!" She tossed a life jacket over the side of the cruiser, splashing into the water thirty feet to Wynn's left.

"You bitch!" Li rushed to the forward seating area and pushed her down, then knelt on top of her and placed the gun to her head.

Any time, Grueb! Wynn watched as Grueb, with a gun in his right hand, pulled his torso onto the swim deck, his legs still trailing in the ocean. *A few more seconds...*

"I can swim all night, Li," Wynn called out, attempting to draw Li's attention. "You won't stop me that easily."

There was a slight pause, then Li shouted, "Let's see how well *she* swims!" He grabbed Vanessa by the shirt and flung her over the bow, her scream cut short as she splashed into the ocean.

Wynn watched helplessly as the loss of weight at the front of the boat coupled with the rolling sea sent a heavy wave over the rear swim deck. The sudden swell rolled Grueb onto his back and washed the gun from his hand as Li raced to the cockpit. Wynn reached into his jacket and pulled out his Glock, praying his ammo had somehow stayed dry.

Just as Li registered Grueb's presence, Wynn sent a shot blasting through the fiberglass canopy above Li's head. Wynn kept shooting, emptying his magazine and giving Grueb time to regain his feet as Li ducked low.

When the shots ended, Grueb rushed into the cockpit, lowered his shoulder, and charged headfirst into Li like an NFL linebacker. A sharp crack from Li's Ruger split the air as Grueb slammed into Li, sending the smaller man flying over the side and splashing into the water.

Wynn dove beneath the surface and stroked hard to where Li bobbed in the waves. He came up beneath him and ripped the Ruger from Li's hand. The kid thrashed wildly and tried to push Wynn down, kicking and punching while trying to keep his head above the surface.

Wynn smacked the kid in the face, then felt the tow rope tug on his belt. He grabbed the rope and looped it around Li's neck, then spun him around. Taking a deep breath, Wynn put his knee in the middle of the smaller man's back, pulled tight on the rope and rolled beneath the waves.

Li thrashed and kicked, initially at Wynn, then at the water in a desperate attempt to reach the surface. Wynn held him back, allowing his weight to drag them both down, his lungs beginning to protest as they sank further into the murky depths. A huge bubble escaped Li's mouth, followed by a few frantic movements of his arms and legs, and then he was still. Wynn held on to the rope until his lungs were ready to burst, then pushed the body away and kicked hard for the surface.

Breaking through, he heard Vanessa screaming his name.

He gasped for breath. "I'm here!"

"Sean! Where are you?"

He spun around in the water, finally spotting her holding onto the life jacket twenty feet away. "I'm here." He swam toward her as she did the same.

"Oh, thank God! Where is he?"

"He's gone, Vanessa. He's gone." Wynn hauled on the rope, drawing the bodyboard closer.

"What are we gonna do?"

Wynn glanced around, suddenly realizing Grueb and the cruiser were nowhere in sight. He continued to draw on the rope until the board came up behind him. He slid it between them as they each grabbed on. "Where's the boat?"

"It took off right after the guy fell in."

"Was there anyone on it?"

"What? No, I didn't see anyone."

He paused a moment, picking up the faint rumble of the boat's engines fading in the distance.

"Grueb!" Wynn called out.

Vanessa looked at him, confused. "What are you—"

Wynn held up a hand. "Shh. Grueb! You out there?"

The only sound besides Vanessa's heavy breathing were the waves lapping against the board.

CHAPTER 37

FIVE DAYS LATER, on the Tuesday following Ty's death, a memorial service with full police honors was held at the Resting Acres cemetery. More than a hundred police cars, all with their lights flashing, escorted the hearse through the city from the church to the cemetery. Hundreds of Ventura County residents lined the freeway and overpasses as the procession passed by.

Stacey, wearing a black dress, a black, broad-brimmed hat, and large sunglasses, held Matty on her lap, while Stacey's father, Bill, held Brie. Stacey's mother and Ty's parents filled out the first row of white, wooden folding chairs. The rest of the family was seated in two rows behind them, while the almost three-hundred-person congregation stood in a large circle around the flag-draped casket.

Following the invocation, the pastor from Ty and Stacey's church said a prayer and blessed the casket with incense. A bell was rung twenty-one times, each note allowed to ring a full five seconds. Eulogies from the Mayor, Chief of Police, and several others, including Lieutenant Akins, had been given at the church. Bagpipes played a mournful rendition of "Amazing Grace" as the flag was ceremoniously removed from the casket, folded, and presented to Stacey.

When the final notes faded away, a female dispatch voice broadcast from a single speaker.

"Bravo three, please respond."

Fifteen seconds of silence passed. A slight breeze rustled through the trees.

"Bravo three, please respond."

Wynn reached up and wiped a tear from his eye. He stood in the front row directly opposite Stacey. Standing next to him, Vanessa squeezed his other hand in both of hers.

"Bravo three, your watch has ended. Rest in peace."

After a brief moment of silence, the pastor gave a final, silent blessing, then turned and walked away, signaling the end of the service. Wynn, Vanessa, and Grueb stood back while Akins, the Mayor, and several others formed an informal line to give Stacey and the family their condolences.

"Thanks to you, we're only doing this once," Vanessa said to Grueb.

"One is plenty," Grueb replied, his left leg in a brace, crutches beneath both arms. Across the casket, Akins was hugging Ty's mother.

Janelle Evans and her husband, Alan, approached. "Hi, Sean. How are you?" She gave him a tight hug.

"All things considered, as well as can be expected," Wynn said.

"I know. Me too." Then turning to Grueb, she said, "It's good to see you again, Detective. How's the recovery coming?"

Grueb nodded, "Slow, but a little better each day."

"And who's this?" Janelle asked, turning to Vanessa.

"Vanessa Carow. A friend," she replied as she shook Janelle's hand.

"I see. Well, we can all certainly use more friends." Janelle winked at Wynn.

Vanessa smiled and looked down.

Alan nudged Janelle. "Tell him."

Wynn creased his eyebrows. "Tell me what?"

"After Lieutenant Akins had us come in and told us the full story of how I was supposed to be Jamaal Johnson's original target, Alan asked me a question I don't think we'd ever considered before."

"What was that?"

She took a deep breath. "He asked if I'd ever told anyone at Viacci's that we were celebrating our anniversary that night. I'm not sure you want to hear this, but while I obviously told Neil Carson and some other folks around the office where we were going, we never told the staff at Viacci's that it was our anniversary. We don't like anyone making a fuss or drawing attention. They had no idea we were supposed to be the ones at that table."

Wynn wasn't sure what to do with that information. He was still struggling to fully process how he felt about what Neil Carson had told him. That yes, it was in fact a hit, but carried out on the wrong target. It all had the familiar feeling of a post-operation letdown, after the adrenaline had faded and he was left to ponder how tiny decisions or seemingly random events could mean the difference between life and death.

Gonna dream about that one tonight.

He was saved from responding when Stacey joined their group. She had left Matty and Brie with her parents on the other side of the grave. When Janelle saw her, pain flashed across her face.

"Mrs. Lenihan," Janelle said. "I can't tell you how sorry I am."

Stacey's eyes were hidden behind large sunglasses, preventing Wynn from reading her face.

"You're Janelle Evans, right?"

Janelle nodded.

"You're the one Ty was trying to reach when he got shot."

Janelle nodded again. A tear ran down her cheek.

"I'm so glad you're alright." Stacey reached out and embraced Janelle. "Thank you so much for coming."

Tears that Wynn imagined were equal parts relief, guilt, and sorrow flooded down Janelle's face as she returned the embrace, whispering, "I'm so sorry. So sorry."

"It's okay," Stacey said. "Ty was doing what he loved. It's not your fault."

The others in the group stepped back to give the two women their moment. When they finally separated, Janelle whispered something Wynn couldn't hear, then she and Alan walked away.

Stacey gathered herself and turned toward Wynn. "Grueb told me what happened."

When Grueb had rushed Li on the boat, Li had gotten a shot off, hitting Grueb in the left thigh. Thankfully, the bullet missed the femoral artery, but it was still enough to knock Grueb off his feet. When he fell, he accidentally pushed the throttle, sending the boat cruising straight out to sea. It had taken a few minutes for Grueb to climb back up to the controls, turn it around, and start searching.

Grueb finally found them, almost two hours later, floating on the bodyboard as dawn broke over the ocean. He'd lost more than a pint of blood, and was close to passing out, but refused to go in without Wynn and Vanessa.

"Was that everyone?" Stacey asked.

"Yeah," Wynn said. "That was everyone."

She nodded. "Good." She paused for a moment. "If you ever figure out how to move on from this, let me know. I thought getting revenge would help, but so far, not yet."

Wynn glanced at Matty and Brie, then back to Stacey. "Give it time. You need to be strong for those kids. It'll never go away, but it will get easier."

Stacey leaned forward and gave him a big hug. "Thank you," she whispered. She broke off the embrace, then hugged and thanked Grueb, then went back to her family.

The three of them stood for a moment in silence. Wynn glanced at the casket. *Gonna miss you, Lenny.* He inhaled deeply, then turned away with Vanessa's hand still in his.

"Wynn!"

He turned back to see Lieutenant Akins approaching.

"I'm glad I caught you," Akins said. "We have a meeting with

Carson's attorney this afternoon at the station. She asked specifically for you to be there. Three o'clock. Can you make it?"

Wynn looked at Grueb, who shrugged in an *I have no idea* kind of way.

"Three o'clock? Sure."

"Great. We'll see you then. You too, Grueb."

CHAPTER 38

WYNN ARRIVED A little before three and was escorted to a large conference room. Instead of the faux-leather chairs in the small room, the chairs here were real leather, a dozen of which surrounded a large walnut conference table.

The Chief of Police sat at the head of the table, while Akins and another man in a suit sat along the left side. Next to them sat Stephen Oglesby, CEO of Mynogen, along with his attorney Marcia, and yet another man Wynn didn't recognize. Along the right, sitting across from Oglesby, Wynn was surprised to see Linda Trilby, Jamaal Johnson's attorney. A woman and two other men, all in suits that appeared considerably more expensive, sat next to Trilby.

"Sean, thanks for coming in." Akins rose from his chair and escorted Wynn to the head of the table. "This is Chief Harmon," he said as Wynn shook the Chief's hand, "and I believe you know Dr. Oglesby and Ms. Trilby."

Trilby didn't bother to rise or shake Wynn's hand; she just nodded and looked back down at her papers. Oglesby rose and shook Wynn's hand, then Akins escorted him to the empty seat at the foot of the table next to Grueb. "The rest of these folks are attorneys,

either from Mynogen or McDermott and Schmidt," Akins continued. "Ms. Trilby asked that you be here, but only as an observer."

Wynn sat, thinking, *What the hell...*

"Before we start," Trilby said, handing a piece of paper to the
woman on her left, who then passed it down until it reached Wynn,
"I'd like to ask Mr. Wynn to sign this Non-Disclosure Agreement. As
the only non-attorney or non-law-enforcement-official in the room, I
think it's only prudent that we get some legal assurance that he will
not repeat any of what is discussed here today."

"Hey, you asked me to be here," Wynn said. "I'm not signing
anything 'til I know what the hell's going on."

Akins looked down from his seat at the far end of the table.
"Sean, trust me. Sign it. You're going to want to hear this."

The suit to his right offered a pen. Wynn took it and signed the
form, pausing as he noticed the weight and texture of the McDermott and Schmidt letterhead. He handed the form to the guy, who
passed it back to Trilby.

"Now that that's taken care of," Trilby said, "let's begin. We're
here today to discuss the contents of a package that one Mr. Neil
Carson left in my firm's possession with instructions that the
package be opened only upon Mr. Carson's death. As that trig-
gering event has been confirmed by the county coroner last week, I,
as Mr. Carson's rightfully engaged attorney and per Mr. Carson's
written instructions, opened and read the contents of said
package."

She paused to take a breath. "On a personal note, I must say I
was highly disturbed by what I read, as I assume many of you who
have had the chance to review these documents were also."

There was a slight mumble of agreement and several nods from
around the room. Trilby continued. "While the admission of fraud
regarding the drug HCM perpetrated against Mynogen by my client
and his accomplices, Alexander Jameson and Stuart Legrea, was bad
enough, I don't think any of us were prepared to read about the
establishment and ongoing operation of a major drug ring, including

the murder of three innocent women, Susan Braley, Diana Williams, and Nicole Wynn."

Wynn's stomach dropped when he heard his wife's name.

Trilby continued without acknowledging Wynn in any way. "In these documents, Mr. Carson admits to falsifying HCM-related research in an effort to entice the board and management of Mynogen to pursue a buyout of ALJ Pharmaceutical Research, which is now under litigation. These documents have been provided to Mynogen's legal counsel for their litigation against the estates of Messrs. Carson, Jameson, and Legrea."

Trilby paused to take a sip of water, then pressed on. "In these documents, Mr. Carson also mentions a laboratory located in Thousand Oaks, owned by J&L Enterprises, at which the street drug Jewel was manufactured. It is my understanding that when police searched the facility, no such laboratory was found. It is believed that Mr. Carson moved the lab to Palm Springs but did not update the documents in our firm's possession. Lieutenant Akins, do you have any update?"

Akins cleared his throat. "Palm Springs police are investigating. They believe they've found the location, but so far, all the employees they've interviewed seem to know nothing about Jewel. We know that one of the supervisors at the lab was killed in the shootout at the warehouse in Torrance last week, but the other supervisor is missing. PSPD is continuing to look for him."

Akins nodded to Trilby, indicating he was finished, then she continued. "Further, in these documents, Mr. Carson admits to strangling Ms. Susan Braley approximately three years ago on the Mynogen premises, calling Mr. Jameson for assistance, who then sent Mr. Legrea to dispose of the body. Mr. Carson indicates he was unaware of where or how Mr. Legrea disposed of the body, and because Mr. Legrea is now also deceased..."

Several eyes turned toward Wynn.

"...we will likely never know the location of Ms. Braley's body. The Camarillo Police Department as well as the Ventura County

Sheriff's department have been given copies of these documents and will either continue or wrap up that investigation as appropriate."

Trilby paused again to take another sip of water and catch her breath. "Regarding Ms. Williams, Mr. Carson alleges that on the night of August 16th, Mr. Legrea broke into Ms. Williams' apartment and forcibly injected her with a liquid version of the synthetically produced opioid known as Jewel. It should be further noted that Mr. Carson admits to providing Mr. Legrea with the opioid, which Mr. Carson and his team, including Mr. Jameson and Mr. Legrea, were producing. Again, these documents have been provided to Detective Gruebauer of the Ventura Police Department, who informs me that the investigation into Ms. Williams' death has been re-opened."

Grueb looked at Wynn and nodded.

"Finally, in these documents, Mr. Carson alleges that Mr. Legrea, with Mr. Jameson's full knowledge and consent, hired members of the Acid Dawn street gang to murder one Janelle Evans, an employee of Mynogen. Mr. Carson alleges that a mistake was made in identifying the target, causing the death of one Mrs. Nicole Wynn instead. An investigation into the death of Mrs. Wynn has been re-opened by the Ventura Police Department."

Grueb leaned over to Wynn and whispered, "It's a formality. We need to do the paperwork to put a bow on it, but it's all wrapped up."

Wynn nodded.

Trilby continued to drone on for another twenty minutes, primarily about legal precedents, the rights of the deceased, and the status of the ongoing litigation. The Mynogen attorneys interrupted a few times, but by then, Wynn was no longer listening. He'd drifted off into himself, completing once and for all the picture he'd put together the morning after Ty's death. He now had to decide what to do with that picture. It would always be a part of him, but would it hang in the front of his mind? Or would he put it away, in the dark recesses, never to be forgotten, but maybe no longer allowed to steer the direction of his life?

Wynn had one last question he wanted to ask Trilby in private, away from the cops and lawyers. But when the meeting broke up, Wynn was approached by several of the McDermott and Schmidt attorneys who offered both their condolences and congratulations. By the time he could break away, Trilby was gone.

CHAPTER 39

THAT EVENING, WYNN told Vanessa what had happened to Diana while they had dinner on his patio. Considering what she'd been through, Vanessa had taken a leave of absence from the school and had been spending most of her days, and nights, at Wynn's house. While she was indeed sleeping in Wynn's bed, he had spent the nights on the couch, still not quite ready to go there.

Vanessa fell asleep while they watched TV, so Wynn carried her up the stairs and tucked her into bed. She woke as he was stepping out the bedroom door.

"Thanks for letting me stay here," she said. "It makes me feel safe. But I feel bad kicking you out of your bed."

Wynn smiled. "It's alright. I have to go out for a little while. Shouldn't be more than an hour."

"Now? This late?"

"This is when the people I need to see are out," he explained.

"Okay. Be careful."

"Will do. Get some sleep."

Wynn closed the door, then went downstairs and out to the garage where he hopped on the Sportster and rumbled away. Ten minutes later, he pulled into the parking lot outside of Lucky's, the all-night diner. He was glad to see it was busier than it had been the last two times he'd been there. The glass on the broken windows had been replaced, but the front door was still boarded over with plywood.

He stepped inside and made his way to the counter where he settled onto a stool. The waitress, Karen, came out of the kitchen, saw him, and immediately turned around and disappeared back into the kitchen. Moments later, the big, burly cook came out.

"I'm a little surprised to see you here, Marine," he said. "Are you expecting any of your friends?"

"Definitely not," Wynn said. "I just wanted to come back, get a cup of coffee, and apologize. I'm very sorry for the trouble I caused."

The cook looked at him for a moment, then turned around and grabbed a pot from the coffee station behind him and poured a cup. "Apology accepted. As far as I'm concerned anyway. Karen might be another story. She's a tough one. But all that shooting, and two guys dead? That freaked her out."

"Let her know I'm sorry. It won't happen again."

"Will do." He paused, then said, "That cop that was killed last week, Detective Lenihan. He was one of the responding officers here, wasn't he?"

"Yeah."

"That's too bad. He seemed like a good guy."

"One of the best." Wynn's eyes were suddenly wet.

"Did they catch the guys who shot him?"

"Yeah. They got 'em."

"That's good."

Wynn paused a moment. "Hey, can I get one of those donuts to go?"

"Sure." The cook walked over to a tray where a few leftover, day-old donuts sat beneath a glass cover. He took one out, put it in a bag, and walked over to the cash register.

"Ring it up separate from the coffee." Wynn handed him his credit card.

The cook rolled his eyes. "Just take it."

"No. I insist. But separate tickets."

The cook sighed and rang up two separate tickets. One for a single cup of coffee, the other for a donut. Wynn took a pen from a cup next to the register and wrote a note on each.

Navy, thanks for your help.

On the second one, he wrote, *Karen, Sorry for the trouble.*

He added a thousand-dollar tip to each ticket, turned them over, and slid them back to the cook. He turned and walked toward the entry, leaving the bag on the counter.

"Hey, Marine!" the cook called out as Wynn reached the door and looked back. "You're welcome here anytime."

Wynn nodded, then pushed through the door.

———

The next morning, Wynn was out on his patio finishing his morning kata when Vanessa came out with a cup of coffee, still in her pajamas. Her long black hair hung loose and disheveled around her shoulders. She sat in one of the large chairs and pulled her feet up beneath her, then drew a pillow to her chest and wrapped her hands around the warm mug to ward off the morning chill.

"Do you do this every morning?" she asked.

"As often as I can." He did one final sun salutation, then grabbed a towel off the back of a chair and a bottle of water. "Have you got any plans for today?"

"Not really."

"Want to take a ride?"

"Sure. Where to?"

"Santa Clarita. Diana's mom. I told her I'd let her know if we learned anything."

"Won't the police do that?"

"I told her I would. Besides, I think she'd love to see you."

Vanessa nodded her agreement, so they called to make sure Mrs.

Williams would be home, then had breakfast and cleaned up before hopping on the Sportster for the hour ride.

When they arrived, Mrs. Williams greeted them at the front door and held Vanessa in a long embrace as tears streamed down her face.

Grueb had already informed her that they were re-opening the investigation as a murder. Wynn tactfully answered as many of her questions as he could without revealing any of the overly gruesome details. The important thing was that her baby didn't die of a self-inflicted drug overdose, and wasn't involved in anything illegal or immoral. She was a good girl.

When Wynn finished answering her questions, Mrs. Williams—*Call me Michelle, please*—pulled out an old photo album, and she and Vanessa spent the next half-hour looking at old photos and reminiscing. Vanessa glanced up and mouthed, *Sorry*, but it was clear she was enjoying it as much as Mrs. Williams.

"Listen," Wynn said. "I have someone I need to go see. Vanessa, why don't you stay here, maybe take Michelle out to a nice lunch, and I'll come back and pick you up this afternoon." With that, he slipped out the door and was soon cruising his way back to Ventura.

———

Two hours later, after waiting in the lobby of McDermott and Schmidt for twenty minutes, Wynn was escorted back to Linda Trilby's office.

When Wynn had settled into a chair in front of Trilby's desk, and the receptionist left them alone, Trilby asked, "Did Rebecca give you a copy of the Non-Disclosure Agreement?"

"She did."

"And have you read it? Do you have any questions?"

"Yeah, I read it," Wynn said. "And no, I don't have any questions."

"Then what can I do for you, Mr. Wynn?"

"I'd like to see the original that I signed."

"Why do you want to see that? I assure you the copy is one hundred percent accurate."

"I'm sure it is. I'd still like to see the original."

Trilby looked at him suspiciously, then turned her chair around and pulled a file from the credenza behind her. Turning back, she opened the file, found the form, and handed it to Wynn.

He laid the form on the edge of her desk, then reached into his jacket and pulled out the letter he'd received from Jamaal Johnson, the one with the three words, *It wasn't stray,* that started it all. He opened it and laid it on the desk next to the NDA.

The paper was the same.

"How long did you know?" Wynn asked.

"Know what?"

"That Jameson and Legrea had Nicole killed."

"As I said the other day, when Mr. Carson's death was confirmed, I followed his instructions and opened the package."

"I don't think so."

Trilby sat back and crossed her arms. "Please, I'd love to hear it. Tell me what you do think, Mr. Wynn."

"I think you opened it a month or more ago. I think you saw what was in there and felt like you had to do something, but you couldn't just turn it over to the cops. You'd be disbarred. So instead, you went up to see Johnson in the pen and not only encouraged him to write this letter to me, but also gave him the paper to write it on. I think this was your way of getting the investigation re-opened."

"And you're basing all that on a piece of paper?"

Wynn shrugged. "What are the odds?"

Now it was Trilby's turn to shrug. "Long, but not impossible." She paused. "So what are you going to do with this little theory?"

"Stacey Lenihan is going to have a tough time. Ty hadn't been a cop long enough to earn a full pension. And the kids are going to need to go to college."

"That's an unfortunate situation."

"It is. Do you still represent Neil Carson's estate?"

"I do."

"I imagine it could be tough to track down all of his accounts. Who knows where he might've hidden some of that Mynogen money? Or even some of what he made from Jewel? He could've put it in a trust fund somewhere. Maybe an anonymous donation. Hell, you're the lawyer. You must deal with that stuff all the time."

"Yes, I do."

Wynn shrugged. "Well, there you go."

They locked eyes across the desk for a long moment until Trilby nodded ever so slightly.

"Thank you for letting me look at that NDA." Wynn took the letter from Johnson and put it back in his pocket. He slid the NDA across the desk to Trilby. "My lawyer says I should read everything before I sign it, but you know how it is."

"Your lawyer is smart."

"He is," Wynn said. "But I've been finding myself in situations lately where I might need someone more... flexible."

Trilby paused. "From what Lieutenant Akins has told me about you, I can see why that might be important."

Wynn raised his eyebrows.

"If there's ever anything I can do," Trilby said, "give me a call."

Wynn rose from his seat and stepped to the door, pausing as he opened it. "Thanks," he said as he turned to leave. "I think I will."

--- THE END ---

For more Sean Wynn thrillers, including a free short story, visit
www.keithjweber.com.

Dear Reader,

If you enjoyed *Intentional*, please let your fellow action/adventure/thriller readers know by telling your friends about it and/or leaving a review at Amazon.com or wherever you downloaded the book. Your review will help other readers discover Sean Wynn and allow me, a grateful author, to continue to tell his story. Select reviewers may also be part of the Sean Wynn "Advance Team," with early access to unreleased novels as well as special content and events. As always, I too, would love to hear from you. If you have comments, ideas, or would just like to talk about books, writing, or motorcycles, feel free to reach out. You can reach me at my website at:

www.keithjweber.com

With Gratitude,

Keith

ALSO CURRENTLY AVAILABLE

Night Rules, Volume 1 of the Sean Wynn series: Former Marine Sean Wynn would prefer to mind his own business. Prefer he didn't see two men stalking a woman at a remote Wyoming rest area. But the last time he ignored something that didn't look right, his wife wound up dead.

The Interviews, a Sean Wynn short story. Special Agent Mark Ruiz needs help with a case—a bad one. Is Sean Wynn the right guy to help? Maybe talking with the people who know him best will shed some light on just who is Sean Wynn.

Sean Wynn returns in late 2024!

A woman's been murdered, a man's been kidnapped, and pieces of him are being mailed to his parents. But the kidnappers don't want money; they want a boy. The problem? The boy's been dead for seven years. Can Sean Wynn find the man while there's still something left to save?

ACKNOWLEDGMENTS

Writing is a solitary activity, but creating a book cannot be done without the help of countless others. In this case, that includes Lynne Bulmer, Veronica Falk, Josie Grey, Laura Ingle, Bette Kosmolak, Carrie Lange, William Nuessle, Dave Pasquantonio, Juan Rangel, James Snell, Carly Stephens, and Stacey Sweeney. Many, many thanks to all of you.

ABOUT THE AUTHOR

Keith J. Weber is a long-time writer, short-time author. After spending decades writing everything from advertising copy to magazine articles and financial education, his debut fiction novel *Night Rules,* along with its sequel, *Intentional,* were both released in 2024. An avid motorcyclist, Keith enjoys riding the majestic mountains of Colorado as well as the magical Black Hills of South Dakota. On a Friday or Saturday night, you may even find him strumming a guitar with his band at a local brewery.